The
Hunter

The
Hunter

Jennifer Herrera

G. P. Putnam's Sons

New York

PUTNAM
— EST. 1838 —

G. P. PUTNAM'S SONS
Publishers Since 1838
An imprint of Penguin Random House LLC
penguinrandomhouse.com

Library of Congress Cataloging-in-Publication Data

Names: Herrera, Jennifer, author.
Title: The hunter / Jennifer Herrera.
Description: New York : G. P. Putnam's Sons, [2023] | Summary: "A riveting atmospheric suspense debut that explores the dark side of a small town and asks: How can we uncover the truth when we are lying to ourselves?"—Provided by publisher.
Identifiers: LCCN 2022027581 (print) | LCCN 2022027582 (ebook) |
ISBN 9780593540213 (hardcover) | ISBN 9780593540220 (ebook)
Subjects: LCGFT: Thrillers (Fiction). | Novels.
Classification: LCC PS3608.E7716 H86 2023 (print) | LCC PS3608.E7716 (ebook) |
DDC 813/.6—dc23/eng/20220613
LC record available at https://lccn.loc.gov/2022027581
LC ebook record available at https://lccn.loc.gov/2022027582

Printed in the United States of America
1st Printing

Book design by Nancy Resnick

For David

The
Hunter

But what if I should discover that the least among them all, the poorest of all the beggars, the most impudent of all the offenders, the very enemy himself—that these are within me, and that I myself stand in need of the alms of my own kindness—that I myself am the enemy who must be loved—what then?

—C. G. Jung, *Memories, Dreams, Reflections*

He who wants to be a sickle must bend himself betimes.

—Jacob and Wilhelm Grimm, *Grimm's Fairy Tales*

1

Thursday, November 2

I WOULD NOT HAVE PULLED THE TRIGGER.

It was just after ten when I tuned the boxy police scanners to their stations. I set the Bearcat to cover Precincts 1, 5, and 7. The HomePatrol would hit Precincts 20 and 24. I tuned the Whistler to listen in on Precincts 19 and 23.

I lined them up on the marble coffee table next to the picture of Simone on Eric's shoulders at the Bronx Zoo. The photo of me in dress blues, shaking the police commissioner's hand. My leather holster, empty now, yet clinging to the shape of its old duty, its new regrets.

On the windowpane, I watched the same scene that played out a thousand times each day, like the jumbled pieces of a puzzle I was sure would never fit. A hand that was my hand reaching for my sidearm. My Glock aimed at my partner's head. A thumb that was my thumb cranking back the hammer. My voice, a command: Don't move.

I would not have pulled the trigger.

I knew this like I knew my own name. What I didn't know was why I had done it, why I had blown up my life for the sake of a perp who was caught hours after I helped him get away. This was three, maybe four, minutes of my life. Yet, like an explosion, it had devastated everything.

I turned up the volumes on the scanners until they hurt my ears. I closed my eyes. I waited for the static to drown out my noise.

On the north block of Seventy-Ninth at Columbus, an officer called in a Level 1. Shots fired. Dispatch sent an Emergency Service Unit for an evidence search.

At the Port Authority, a man was struck by a northbound A Train. A robbery. A traffic accident. A suspicious vehicle on Fifty-Seventh and Lex. But no homicides. I sat on the sofa that still carried Eric's musk and wool scent. I sipped water like I had a reason to be sober. But there were no homicides.

On other nights, when a Signal 7 had come through, I would piece together enough of the scene to interrupt my regularly scheduled spiraling. A woman killed in her apartment was usually a domestic. A man killed in the park was a mugging gone awry. Shot in a vehicle meant gang violence. Sometimes drugs. After a while, these images would blot out the memory of how I'd ruined everything. Finally, I could sleep.

But not tonight.

It was close to midnight when my cell buzzed. It was my little brother. He'd already tried me three times this week. Each time

I felt a little guiltier for not answering. If he really needed me, I told myself, he'd text.

As I waited for voicemail to pick up yet again, outside my window, the video-arcade lights of the Empire State Building shifted from blue to red. I used to love their predictability, the way they could surprise me. Now as they blurred against the rain, all I felt was an overwhelming sense of the city's indifference to me, even after all I'd done to keep it safe.

I swiped to answer the call.

"Leigh? It's me, Ronan."

"I know who it is," I said, my voice a little hoarse. "Your name comes up on my phone."

"I know, but it's polite. Hey, sorry to call so late. I've been trying to reach you. Did you get my messages?"

I assured my brother that, yes, I'd gotten his voicemails, which had all said, unhelpfully, *Call me back*. Yes, I was fine. I was Busy Evaluating My Options. I was Reassessing and Regrouping. I was Planning Next Steps. I was the same as every other time he'd called over the past six months, still trying to imagine the future, still stuck trying to decode the past.

"I'm sorry, Leigh." Over the line, a pause like an axe swinging. "And Eric? Are you guys still separated?"

"I knew it was coming," I replied. By which I meant, I hadn't seen it coming at all.

I stood up too fast, stumbling. I strode past the uncluttered living room, cavernous now with Eric's things gone, and into the galley kitchen, where it was always dark, always wet smelling. I started opening a bottle of wine with the corkscrew I'd left out after I'd put my four-year-old to bed. I never started drinking until after she was down. I pretended this made me virtuous.

"You know, Leigh," Ronan said, "*we* would hire you."

The cork popped, loud like a safety disengaging. It jolted my gut. *We,* as in the Copper Falls Police Department. *We* as in the tiny police force housed in the stone building just off the main street. In winter, they hung Christmas lights. On the Fourth of July, they had a booth for twisting balloons into hats. I said, "I can't ask you to do that."

"You don't have to. That's why I've been calling. It's already done."

"What do you mean it's already done?" I pulled the screw from the cork. "You're just asking me now."

"I cleared it with the chief. Leigh, you're hired."

"Ronan." The corkscrew clattered against the bowl of the sink. "I didn't ask for this."

"Hey, calm down. It's no big deal. You're my sister, right? It's my job to help." As Ronan spoke, I pulled a glass from the open shelving. I filled it to its brim. The glug was loud, like a drain emptying into a sewer. But if Ronan heard, he didn't say. In my family, alcohol was believed to disinfect even psychological wounds. In this, we were all devout.

I stood at the counter. I held the glass to my lips. "Does your chief even know why I was suspended?"

"He didn't ask so I figure he doesn't care."

I went back to the living room. I shook my head. I swallowed another mouthful of wine.

"I'm telling you, Leigh, he loves the idea. A big-city cop? On his squad? Plus, we don't have any women."

"So I'd be a quota hire?"

"Is that any worse than being hired because you're my sister?"

I eased onto the sofa in front of the window. I placed my glass on the arm.

"Come on," Ronan said. There was a smile in his voice that begged me to reciprocate. "Don't you miss it? Even a little?"

It'd been fourteen years since I'd stepped foot in the place I'd grown up. Yet I could conjure its image as effortlessly as if I'd just left: sunset oaks that arched over the drive leading up to the old house. Knobby balustrades like turrets surrounding the porch. Wide, wooden stairs that bent with every step. In the distance, the waterfall, the creek. Everywhere, the scent of water.

I pictured the rooms—all those rooms—cathedral height and embellished with decorative woodwork. Ceilings stamped in tin. The house was beautiful from a distance. Yet even in my memory, even after all these years, I could still sense it. That residue that could never be washed away, like stains after a flood. The water recedes and you paint over its marks. Yet still the mold grows. It will always grow. You will always be sick from it if you stay inside that house.

"That's a generous offer." I rubbed the warmth back into my skin. "Please, extend my thanks."

Ronan made a sound like a tire deflating. In the background, the floor groaned. "You didn't even think about it."

"I did think about it. But I'm not going to uproot my life."

"Your roots are here, Leigh. We're here. Me. The uncles. The town. Everybody. Would it be so bad? Coming back?"

Before me, raindrops raced. Behind them, new ones wove

down their tracks. I wished for lightning, for the bray of thunder. Outside, there were only sirens. Their urgency. Their rush. They faded as they sped away.

"Look," Ronan said.

I took a drink.

"I know you're some big-time detective. I know small-town policing isn't, like, on your vision board or anything."

"I don't have a vision board."

"But before you turn us down, please just remember one thing."

I stared at the callus on my trigger finger. It had turned yellow, the way leaves change color before they fall.

"Here, at least, we look after our own."

The slap was not subtle. But it was also deserved. I had, after all, abandoned my family to become a soldier in a faceless city. I had put my trust in people who weren't my own. *Really Leigh,* I could hear him thinking, *in a city like that, what did you expect?*

I looked away from the police scanners, toward the tunnel of my kitchen, gray scale now, cast in darkness. "What would I even do there?" I was just humoring him. I needed him to see for himself this wouldn't work. "I'm a detective," I said, "not a beat cop. There's no major crime."

A tinge of hope spread through Ronan's voice. It made me feel sorry for him. "I can think of lots of major crimes. There was that family reunion. The one where everyone got burned alive? The FD says that was arson."

I knew what he was talking about. It was Copper Falls lore. "That was more than sixty years ago."

"Okay. Well. How about those guys who tried to cook up meth? Out in the Sticks?"

"I'm homicide," I said. "Dead bodies only."

Ronan was quiet for a long moment, so long in fact that I thought I'd finally ended the conversation. I expected him to say something too earnest, to add a *You can't blame a guy for trying*. Then the calls would stop. "Leigh," Ronan said. "There's something else."

"Unless it's a dead body, I don't care."

"It's not a dead body."

"Then I don't—"

"It's not one dead body." Ronan's voice sounded strange, reluctant. "It's three of them."

2

AS SIMONE AND I STEPPED THROUGH THE GOLD, REVOLVING doors of the entrance to Eric's building, the chill of autumn gave way to the sterile breath of indoor space. We reached the doormat, and my daughter stilled. She watched me with concern. That's when I realized I was holding my breath.

I worked to smile. I said, "Did you know armadillos have hair on their bellies?" I touched the stuffed armadillo in her hand. His name was Arnie, and she took him everywhere.

Simone brightened. "And did you know they eat worms?"

"That's funny. Because I heard they eat spiders." I used my fingers to imitate legs crawling up her shoulder. Simone giggled. I held her tiny hand in mine. I exhaled as we stepped across the parquet floor, toward the tall desk in the lobby.

The doorman wore a suit that was too big for his frame. He smelled of pepper and cologne. He said, "Your name?"

"Leigh O'Donnell. This is Simone Walker. We're here to see Eric Walker."

I always said this when I dropped off Simone. Yet the door-man, whichever one it was, always looked at me with conde-scending amusement, as if I were a tourist who'd asked for directions to Central Park. Eric had noticed this, too. Not just with doormen, but with witnesses, suspects, prosecutors, other cops. It was something about the way I spoke or how I dressed, or that my teeth were a little crooked in front. Yet even when I was new to police work, Eric had never underestimated me. Not ever. Not once.

The doorman replaced the receiver on the hook. "Mr. Walker is coming down."

"No," I said. "We go up."

"Mr. Walker was very clear. He asked that you wait."

"But this is his daughter. I'm his wife."

There it was again, that look. I felt the impending explana-tion of how lobbies worked, the invitation to sit on the sofa and enjoy the people watching of Madison Square Park.

I picked up my daughter. I started us toward the bank of elevators.

"It won't do you any good," the doorman said to my back. "I have to unlock them."

I posted us in front of a wide beveled mirror with a scroll-work frame. I was breathing deep now, trying to make myself calm. Simone wrapped her arms tighter around my neck. She held Arnie in the crook of her elbow. She said, "Say again. About the ball?"

I met my daughter's eyes. We were the spitting image of each other, Simone and I, just painted with different palettes. Whereas my skin was pale and pink, hers was dark and brown. My hair was light and wavy. Hers was brown and textured. I had green eyes and hers were the color of cherrywood. But I couldn't look at her and not see myself. I couldn't look at her and not see Eric. I said, "When armadillos get scared, they curl up into a ball. Their armor seals them shut. That way, no one can hurt them."

Simone cuddled Arnie as she hugged me tighter. I inhaled her shea butter scent. I felt sealed up. Yet I knew this particular armor had a chink.

Behind us, the elevator pinged. We turned, and the doors swept open. Then there he was. My husband.

Eric was six foot two, sturdy, with ropy muscles. He had the same dark skin as his daughter. The same cherrywood eyes. But whereas Simone's face was expressive and open, his was cool and guarded.

He came toward us wearing the smile he reserved for press conferences and people he didn't like. He said, "Hey there, baby." He wasn't speaking to me.

Simone reached for him. I let her weight release into his arms until mine were empty and his were full. I clasped my hands just to have something to do with them.

"I'll have her back Sunday night." Eric pressed the elevator button.

"I need her back tomorrow," I said.

The elevator chimed. He stepped into it. "Sunday. It's what we agreed."

I took a breath. Was I really doing this? "Tomorrow is when we leave for Ohio."

It was only then that Eric turned. Only then that his eyes met mine. A fire lit inside of me, out from my chest, up to my throat. Eric stepped out of the elevator. The door closed behind him. He worked his jaw. He said, "You didn't tell me you were taking a trip."

"It was just decided." I was electric under his gaze. "I want Simone to meet my family."

"You don't have any family."

"I don't have any parents." My father had died from a heart attack freshman year of high school. My mother had died less than a year later, from grief. "But I have family." The way I said it felt like a plea.

"Right." He evaluated my face. "And now it's important that you see them, even though you've never visited?"

"I've been busy," I said. "It doesn't mean I don't care."

In his eyes there was this flicker. Like I was a witness with inconsistencies he needed to bring to light. He did this sometimes, went from being my husband to being a captain with the NYPD. He did it with the shift of cadences, with the tone of his voice. He did it and my pulse fired. I wanted to run my fingers underneath his clothes until that tension between us bucked and released.

"I'll have her to you tomorrow morning." Eric looked away. "When will she be back?"

"Two weeks. Maybe three."

His eyebrows lifted. "Three weeks?"

Eric asked Simone to play on the couch. After a beat, she scrambled away, Arnie in hand, book bag bouncing. When she reached the lemon-yellow sofa in the corner of the lobby, Eric pinned me with his eyes.

"Why are you going to Ohio?"

"You said it yourself. I never visit."

"Why now?"

"I have time."

"Why else?"

I shrugged.

A sharp intake of breath. A voice like an explosion: "Leigh, please. Just tell me the truth." Eric held me with his eyes. Color was rising in his cheeks. It rose in mine. I didn't take my eyes off him. He didn't look away.

Push me. Keep pushing. Don't ever stop.

At last, I said, "I am telling you the truth." What I meant was *I need to do this.* What I meant was *This is how I right our course.* What I meant was *Trust me. Please.*

Eric inched closer. His skin had a chemical scent I didn't recognize. I ignored it. He said, "Leigh, it's backwater out there."

"You're worried she won't be safe?"

"Yes," he said. "I am."

We both looked at Simone. She was bouncing on the couch, preparing to stand. Eric was right to be concerned. The people in Copper Falls were all white. But it was also true that they didn't care about anything but their own town and their own petty squabbles. They believed they weren't racist because, in a place so white, race was irrelevant. I knew that wasn't true. Race was always relevant. But I could shield Simone for three weeks. I said, "I grew her inside of me."

Eric brought his eyes to meet mine.

"I'd never let anything happen to her. Whatever else you think about me, you have to believe that."

The thing that passed between us was like that moment after sex, that moment when wanting gives way to relief. You know it's only temporary, but at least for now the throb of it is gone. A line split across Eric's forehead. I wanted to skate my finger across it, to show him that I still knew him, that I still loved him, that I wasn't done with our family yet.

His eyes broke away. It was like a string between us had been cut. "I'll wash her hair before I drop her off." He pressed the button for the elevator. I staggered. He called Simone back.

I stood disbelieving that he would just let us go, hundreds of miles from where he'd be.

Where was the Eric who'd lifted a man by the collar for grabbing my breast? Where was the Eric who'd dressed down a sergeant for questioning my judgment when it was clear I was right? Where was the Eric who'd fought for me? Fought for our family? How could he stop fighting? Just like that?

"Keep her safe," he said. "Don't be thoughtless."

"I'm not thoughtless."

"You have my daughter."

"I'm not thoughtless."

Simone and Eric stepped into the elevator. Simone waved. The doors shut. Then my family lifted to a higher level, one where my voice couldn't reach them.

3

THE HOUR-LONG DRIVE FROM THE DETROIT AIRPORT TO Copper Falls, Ohio, is unremarkable. Congested factories give way to shorn fields with patches of forest mixed in. It's a drive you can't turn on the radio for because the Michigan stations fade as soon as you cross the border, and the Ohio ones fade as soon as you get into the country. This is what it is to live in between.

In Ronan's minivan, with my brother in the passenger seat and Simone in her car seat in the captain's chair, I merged onto the highway. I did this automatically, as if traveling by instinct, the way a bird knows to fly south when its home no longer sustains it. Amid the hum of diesel engines and the rush of heavy wind that blasts across the Midwest in sheets, Ronan asked about the flight. He asked about Simone's stuffed armadillo, about what they liked to do together, about the weather in New

York. He apologized that his wife, Cathy, and their boys couldn't be there to greet us. They were camping. They'd be gone all week.

After Simone fell asleep, I said, "Tell me about these bodies."

Ronan frowned. "Still as sentimental as ever."

"Just to the point."

"As I said before, they could be straightforward suicides."

"Then this will be a short trip."

Ronan sighed with his whole body, letting the meat of his shoulders fall back against his seat. The sketch of wrinkles around his eyes didn't release. Drawn back like that, he looked like our father. I focused my gaze outside.

The edges of the city wheeled by, giving way to patches of amber and flax. The yolk-yellow sun was low in the sky. It made me think of wart-covered pumpkins on stoops for Halloween. Of teapots exhaling cloudy breaths. Of foggy windows. Of crackling fires. Of the quiet that only visits the city early in the morning but that lives here every day.

"You know that journalist?" Ronan said. "The one who wrote that thing on us some years back?"

"Yes," I said. Of course I knew Mason Vogel. He was this lanky kid from high school who'd worn a pewter ankh and a leather trench and said things like *futile* and *significant dexterity*. He'd always seemed comically out of place. We'd been friends, in the way of flotsam finding flotsam. Then more than friends, for a time.

"He's back," Ronan said. "He's working on another story about us. It's got people worked up."

"Because he's writing about the dead bodies?"

"They are people you know. William Houser was one of those super-nice guys who would do anything for anybody. Neil Mayer was just this awesome trumpet player. Everybody said he had talent. Duncan Schott? Okay, so I don't know a ton about him. But he was very good-looking. He once modeled for a Sears catalogue."

"William Houser, Neil Mayer, Duncan Schott," I repeated. "Those are their names?"

"Yeah," Ronan said, not looking at me. "Those are their names." My brother flexed his fingers over his thighs. It was clear he wished he were driving. But I'd insisted, and he'd backed down. That's how things always went with us. He said, "People don't trust Mason. Not after what he wrote about us before."

"You mean the *Rolling Stone* thing?"

"Yeah," Ronan said. "That."

Seven years ago, I'd been at the dentist's office, leafing through a random magazine, when I'd flipped the page and there she was, Mason Vogel's mom. She'd been wearing a Sunday dress with a Peter Pan collar and an apron stitched over with lace. She held out a platter of cookies. It looked like an advertisement for the sort of product that didn't exist anymore, like steel vacuum cleaners or one of those playpens for the back seats of cars. Behind her stood Copper Waterfall, surging upward like fireworks made of glass. Block letters read WELCOME TO COPPER FALLS: THE IDYLLIC TOWN THAT NO ONE LEAVES ALIVE.

The story chronicled the lives of the three high school seniors who'd killed themselves on the same night. I hadn't actually read the piece in full. But I'd gleaned enough to know the basics. Three boys were planning to leave Copper Falls after they graduated. Only, the night before graduation, all three had hurled themselves over the falls and died.

In the story, Mason had made it seem like there was a conspiracy to keep them in Copper Falls, an intentional insularity that'd made them unable to imagine a life outside their hometown. The obvious hole in this theory was that both Mason and I had left, among many others over the years. We'd survived. But then again, journalists were in the habit of choosing their facts.

I said, "Mason sees a connection between the two sets of deaths?"

"It's not like last time. Nothing like last time actually."

"But they were all men?"

"Yes."

"They were all found in the plunge pool of the falls? Drowned?"

"But they were adults this time, Leigh. Not kids. These guys were twenty-five."

"The same age the high schoolers would've been had they lived?"

Ronan set his jaw. He looked out the window.

I nodded. "Right."

I pulled off the highway, swinging around a cluster of gas stations, twenty-four-hour diners, and a musty bar that pretended it served food. The road was so narrow that traffic could only go one way. I'd forgotten how large the ditches were out here. You could fit a whole car inside them and still have room to open your door. I rolled down my window and let the autumn air rush in to meet me. I rested my arm on the sill. I said, "And the people in town? What do they say?"

"It was such a shitshow after his last story ran. You have no idea. We had all these reporters coming to town looking for *fresh angles*. Goth kids came to commune with the Class of the Dead. This one guy put a hex on my kid."

I said, "A hex?" I examined my brother.

In so many ways, Ronan and I looked alike. We had the same light hair and the same sturdy frames. Both of us had green eyes. But whereas mine were dark and mossy, his were the color of sea glass. They were rare, I'd once read, green eyes. Yet our whole family had them. "Shit, Leigh."

"I'm just surprised," I said. "You didn't used to be superstitious."

Ronan pointed out his window. "No, Leigh, you're missing the turn."

That's when I saw it. Sugar Ridge Road, skinny and black, ditches like gutters. As it rolled out the corner of my eye, my breath spilled over my lips. I felt my neurons, like bells ringing. Instinctively, I adjusted my hand on the wheel.

The space between heartbeats grew wide. The sole of my boot slid from the gas pedal to the brake. My arm wrapped over the sill to hug the door as we turned.

The thrum of the engine pulsed against my wrist like a second heartbeat. The minivan nosed onto Sugar Ridge Road just as the tires lifted up on my side. We all slid to the right.

Simone let out a cry. Ronan held on to the dash. We careened onto the meager stretch of grass separating the road from the ditch.

I felt each bump, each growl of the engine in my head as a rush of blood.

The tires screeched. Simone cried louder. Ronan bellowed.

I wanted to assure them they had nothing to worry about. But there wasn't time. These were only seconds. Yet from those seconds, my skin, my blood, my bones knew we'd made it onto Sugar Ridge. We hadn't missed a thing.

I eased the wheel left to straighten the car. The horizon shifted back to parallel. The tires pounded against the asphalt. Wisps of hair fluttered away from my face. Ronan let out a breath. Simone drew hers in.

"They teach you stunt driving in New York City?" Ronan said. His voice was half laugh, half condemnation. "And in a minivan? Hell, I didn't think the old girl had it in her."

I knew what Eric would have said. I was impulsive. Reckless. I should have taken the long way and just admitted I'd made a mistake. Yet I also knew he was wrong. I'd acted on instinct. But sometimes instincts keep you safe.

I looked back at Simone. Her chest was rising and falling in deep, intentional breaths. She was, by some miracle, still holding on to Arnie. But there were tears in her eyes. I felt a pang in my chest. I hated that I'd hurt her. "Did you know," I said, searching for a line from the animal fact book we read together, "that armadillos are very fast runners?"

Simone met my eyes in the mirror. She didn't smile.

"They're faster than humans. Faster than most cats. And most dogs."

Her chest rose and fell.

"Hey," I said. I reached behind me to grab hold of her hand. "You okay?"

She extended her fingers. We were too far away to touch.

"I'm—"

"Look," Ronan said.

Up ahead, a hand-lettered sign came into view.

A blink, maybe two. Then both of my hands returned to the wheel. Then a quake cracked open my ribs.

Suddenly, there were two of me: the adult detective and the teenage girl. The one with power and the one with none. The sterile sutures, sewn tight, and the wound that could never heal, only avoid infection.

Both versions were real now. Only, I'd never meant for them to meet.

The slab of oak was held up by twin posts.

WELCOME TO COPPER FALLS.

4

THE ROAD SHIFTED FROM ASPHALT TO BRICK, FORCING US TO slow. In the mirror, my child's eyes were wide. Her mouth was open. Her tears were drying.

"Isn't it pretty?" Ronan said. He was looking at Simone.

Simone's face showed the same wonder I'd felt when we'd moved here from Cleveland when I was a kid. Until then, all I'd known were the shadows of high-rises and the smell of burnt rubber. I'd thought all streets stank of soured milk and rotten scraps. I hadn't known they could smell like cut grass and honeysuckle. I hadn't known they came in brick.

Up ahead, Queen Anne houses spread out over the horizon in hazy amber and blush rose and robin's-egg blue. They had wraparound porches and angled bay windows and steeply pitched towers topped with finials that caught the sun. Bushy oaks with gnarled trunks and copper leaves shaded their driveways. They were lined with boxwood or gas lanterns or flowers that managed to cling to life even though it was the season for dying.

On our right, the antiques shop with the spinning wheel stood next to the ice cream parlor, where the jerks wore paper hats. On our left sat the tiny grocery store with transom windows. The specials were chalked in white. A gallon of milk for two bucks. A dozen eggs for a dollar. Just the same as when I'd left.

Nestled off from the road, past a grassy knoll, stood the library, tall and octagonal, with climbing ivy that ran all the way to the gazebo. Marigolds, orange and yellow, bloomed around it. The scent of clover. The burn of woodsmoke. I hated that it was all so beautiful.

"Out of all the houses," Ronan said. He was still facing Simone, whose eyes were trained on the little girls playing with Hula-Hoops, "your mom's is the prettiest."

"Don't say that," I said. "It's not mine."

"It's half yours. You still pay the taxes, don't you? Besides, in a minute she'll see for herself."

"No, she won't," I said. "We're going to the B and B."

"Come on," Ronan said. "The uncles are waiting to see you. They want to meet Simone. Uncle Bear left a car for you. Uncle Eamon put out food. Uncle Frankie is probably halfway through eating it, but still." Then, softly, as if he were embarrassed for me, "It's been fourteen years. They don't blame you. For not coming back. They loved her, too."

The tires hummed against the brick. The breeze paged through the leaves. I set my mouth.

That's when I glanced at the rearview mirror. Simone was looking out the window at the bright flowers, at the children playing. Her eyes were wistful, the way you view a threshold you're sure you'll never cross.

"Okay," I said. "But only for a minute."

I didn't look away from Simone until her chin lifted up from her chest, until her eyes widened again. I swallowed and turned us down the long drive leading to the old house.

The sun rippled over the cobblestones, giving the impression we were traveling down a very old, very bumpy river, leading to the sort of mythical place you couldn't get to by foot. We passed the purling creek and mossy rocks. We passed raised flower beds bursting with thick-leaved plants. A dozen ornate birdhouses nestled into the crooks of the trees, like a tiny village you could only see if you looked up. As Ronan pointed these out, Simone followed the line of his finger. She smiled as if she were witnessing magic.

And it *was* magic, that I could have been gone for so long and that the leaves would still bruise purple in places and shine goldenrod in others, that the sunlight would still filter through them like stained glass. It was so different from New York, which oscillated between monochrome and neon, where there were patches that could pretend at beauty until the blare of sirens cut short the dream. As we dipped under the arch of foliage, as the light speckled the car, twinkling and shadowed, the driveway widened like the mouth of a river. Its source finally swallowed us up.

There it was.

The house.

It was exactly as I remembered it, down to the arched doorway and the old-fashioned weather vane spinning on top. It was white and cinnamon. There were valance grids and a long chimney that pumped out smoke. It was a family house, built by a family that had no relation to ours. My father had won it in a game of poker from a man who'd thought he was running hot.

When I was a kid, Dad used to say, half-serious, that it was a gift from the faeries. Then he'd add that any favor the *aos sí* grant always comes at a price. I remembered being a girl looking out my bedroom window, wondering what that price could be. I remembered being a teenager, looking out that same window, wishing I still didn't know.

I pulled up to the curve of cobblestones leading to the porch. The heavy wooden door swung open. Uncle Eamon and Uncle Frankie filed out. They were gray-haired now, dressed in Copper Falls Formal, as we used to call it, with button-down shirts and stiff trousers. Shoes that winked at the sun.

Frankie bounced between his feet. He was tall and lanky, with arms too long for his frame. Whereas Frankie was cartoonish and floppy, Eamon was stiff and nondescript. Medium build. Medium features. He was the sort of man who'd have been the perfect criminal because no one would remember his face. Eamon stood like he'd accepted Communion. As we drove toward them, the sunlight shifted across their faces, casting them in bronze.

"Where's Bear?" I asked. Bear was the middle of my mother's three brothers. His real name was Ryan. But no one called him that.

"I'm sure he's around somewhere," Ronan said. "You know him. Not one to stand on ceremony."

"So they all really still live here?" I asked this even though I knew they did. They'd moved into my parents' house freshman year of high school, after Dad's heart attack, to help out my mom. They'd stayed after sophomore year, once Mom's body gave out, too.

"They like it here," Ronan said. "Objectively speaking, it's charming."

"You'd think they'd get tired of each other."

"No," Ronan said. "I wouldn't think that."

Ronan's words came back to me, that *they loved her, too.* I wondered if he was right. If the uncles really did understand why I couldn't stay. Maybe it was the same reason they couldn't leave.

A beat. Then Eamon smiled demurely. Then Frankie's long arm stretched as he waved.

Ronan threw his arm over my seat. He grinned at Simone. He said, "Did you know, your mom had the biggest room in the whole house? It's at the top, right up there. See? That balcony? She thought she was so lucky, having that room all to herself. But nobody else wanted to climb all those stairs."

Simone's eyes traced the house. The smile dropped out of her. "I don't like tall things."

Ronan shot me a *Please translate* look.

"She doesn't like heights," I said. "Rooftops scare her."

"Well, they don't scare your mom," Ronan said. "She used to sit up there and pretend to look at the stars. But really she'd be spying on everybody. She always wanted to know everyone's secrets." Ronan turned to me. "You remember? The telescope you had?"

I did. I remembered how, with it, I could see all the way to the falls. I said, "What did the uncles do with it? The telescope?"

"It's up there. My boys were messing around with it at one point, searching for aliens, I think. But you know Eamon. He never throws out anything."

I made the decision in an instant, as if it were a turn I'd miss if I didn't react fast. I cranked the handle of the door. I stepped one foot onto the cobblestone. It was like ripping off a Band-Aid, the kind that uproots hairs. I said, "The B and B won't miss us for a couple of days."

As soon as I stepped onto the porch, Frankie caught me in an octopus hug. He kissed me on both my cheeks because, in his words, that's what classy people did.

Eamon straightened his glasses and offered me a gentle hand. Simone clung to my side.

"Come on," Eamon said. "Let's get you settled."

We passed through the oversized wooden door with its whimsical woodland carvings and into the vestibule streamed with colored light. Simone's gaze traced the shape of the stained-glass windows on either side of us. She watched the motes that floated in the filtered blues and oranges and reds. "It's like a church," she said.

"Yes," I said. *This place was once holy to me, too.*

With Simone holding my hand, we followed my uncles through the double-hung door. We came into the room that smelled like candle wax and water dried by the sun. White wainscoting trimmed its edges. Porcelain sconces lined its walls. A baby grand piano sat in the center. Yet no one had tucked in the bench.

In an instant, I saw my mother there. Her body bent into a question mark as her long fingers climbed across the keys. The floral kick of her perfume slipped between my ribs, in that cavity that was supposed to be protected. The pain was sharp.

I turned and walked us faster through the house, past the Tiffany-style lights. Past the spindled banisters that traced the periphery. I swallowed something hard. My mouth tasted of rust. Simone whispered, "Mommy, you didn't tell me."

"What didn't I tell you?" I focused on getting us away from that room.

"You're a princess."

I slowed to a stop. I looked at my daughter, at her wide eyes, at the dimples she'd gotten from her dad. My breathing steadied. I kissed her forehead, lifted her into my arms. She smelled of shea butter and applesauce, of airplane, and of skin. I pressed my cheek against hers. Our breathing synced.

"It's okay, Mommy."

They were the words I used whenever she cried. Hearing them from her mouth, I felt guilty, like a bad mother. I said, "It's just hard for me to be here. It reminds me of my parents."

"You don't love them?"

"I did love them."

"So why . . . ?"

But I didn't know how to explain to her the walls inside my head. I didn't know how to tell her that they formed a perimeter around this place, these people. How, once they'd gone up, they'd become load-bearing, connected to everything. To tear them down would be to threaten too much.

I pulled out my phone to see if Eric had texted. But all that looked back was a photo from a year ago. Simone on Eric's shoulders. Eric meeting my eyes.

"Come on," I said, looking away. "Let's go see our room."

5

Sunday, November 5

THERE WERE TEN OR SO DESKS INSIDE THE COPPER FALLS
police station. They weren't gunmetal and gummy, scratched by
bored cops or puckered by years of slammed fists. They were
heavy, shined as if on display. The whole place smelled like that,
waxy and oiled.

Where the photos of crime scenes should have been there
were framed pictures of brides and chubby-cheeked toddlers, of
infants dressed as pumpkins for Halloween. Instead of legal
pads with sloppy writing and witness statements needing to be
typed, there were crayon drawings held up with Scotch tape:
HAPPY FATHER'S DAY, I HOPE YOUR BIRTHDAY IS GREAT, I LOVE
YOU DAD. They made me think of my daughter.

Simone was at the house with Uncle Eamon and Uncle
Frankie. She was safe with them, just as I'd once been. Even if I
hadn't been happy. Yet in a dark corner of my mind, I was still

thinking of the promise I'd made to Eric, the promise to protect her. In that same dark corner I worried, irrationally, that I'd already failed.

Ronan was seated at a desk with a pile of mail fanned out in front of him. He was finishing a cinnamon bun, and icing dotted his fingertips. "Sorry we didn't bring out the welcoming committee." He motioned to the empty bullpen. "The chief didn't realize we had the Sunday rotation this week."

"What's all that?" I motioned to the pile of mail.

Ronan held up a sheet of stationery with a floral border. "Bernice Reynolds is reporting Alfred Cooper for not curbing his dog." Ronan lifted a postcard next. "An anonymous citizen is reporting Alexander Larsen for public urination." He held up a folded sheet of notebook paper. "Adam Talbot accuses his neighbor of weeding in the nude. He has photos if you want to—"

"You really open all the mail? That's not the job of a police officer."

"I asked to do it. It's my version of the tabloids." Ronan grinned. "Now, some people like to use a letter opener, but to me, that ruins the whole aesthetic, you know? I like to just go for it. Rip and ride." Beside him sat a pile of mangled envelopes. I eyed the gun and shield beneath them.

"Those for me?"

Ronan handed me a stack of papers. "Just give your John Hancock here and here, and they're all checked out to you."

The pen was sticky, and I dashed off my signature without reading anything. I lifted the gun.

It was a Colt, heavier than the Glock 19 I'd used in New

York. The grip was harder. I doubted the trigger was set to the same load. I checked the chamber. I pumped the cartridge with a click. I slid the piece into the holster beneath my jacket. A stitch released from someplace deep between my shoulders, a place I hadn't even known had been tight. For the first time in months, my breath reached the whole of me. "Which one is my desk?"

Ronan stood. He slapped the desk beside his own. "That way we can pass notes without the teacher seeing."

I started to pull out the chair, but stopped. "Where's my computer?" I looked around the room. "Where are *all* the computers?"

"The chief doesn't believe in them. Likes to keep technology out of policing. Simpler times and all. But the secretary has one."

Ronan pointed to the desk closest to the entrance. The computer was big, boxy. Clearly not from this decade.

"If we need a VIN number or something, she runs it through the system. The chief didn't see the point in wasting all that money on computers if we barely use them. He doesn't want to tax the taxpayers, you know? Plus, he thinks they're ugly."

"What about police records? Personnel files?"

Ronan motioned to the stairwell. A sign above it read REC-ORDS OFFICE: AUTHORIZED PERSONNEL ONLY. There was an arrow pointing to the basement. "You'll get used to it. Everybody does." Ronan lifted a patrol jacket off the back of his chair. He was wearing a navy Class B with a thick utility belt. A radio sat on his shoulder. It made him look stocky, cliché. He said, "The first thing we do each day is stop by some houses. You know a lot of people here are elderly. It's our job to make sure they're doing okay."

I slipped off my suit jacket and draped it over the back of the chair. I sat at the desk.

"I know, I know. With you it's all dead bodies all the time. But things are different here."

I opened the top drawer to find a stash of pens and a yellow legal pad. I looked behind me. "Is there a coffeepot somewhere?"

"Actually"—Ronan's keys jangled as he picked them up—"before you start looking into those deaths and everything, we have to go on our rounds. Together."

My smile said, *I don't think so.*

His replied, *But wait, there's more.* He stuck a piece of gum between his molars. He looked uncomfortable. "I'm actually not allowed to go alone. It's a matter of protocol."

"You're not allowed to go into people's houses by yourself? You just said, they're elderly."

Ronan smacked his gum. I expected him to be smiling. Yet his mouth and eyes were flat. "That doesn't make it safe."

6

RONAN KNEW THE ROUTE BY MEMORY.

I followed his instructions as I drove. I slowed for the 90-degree turns, pumped the brakes as we coasted downhill, and stopped when a wild turkey chose that particular moment to cross the street. Ronan had led us away from the center of town, down back roads and into areas that, as a kid, I'd never gone. I'd never had reason to. There was nothing out here but dirt roads, half-covered in wilderness, and skinny trees so close together they grew tall but not wide.

The houses were clapboard, propped up by bowed stilts or sinking cinder blocks. Spiky plants busted through cracks in the concrete slabs where trash cans baked. The smell was everywhere. Burnt rubber and leaf rot. It made the back of my throat raw.

As we drove, knobby branches clawed at the cruiser. "Are you sure this is a road?" I asked.

"Keep going," Ronan said. "We're almost there."

We trundled over a puckered metal bridge, barely wide enough to fit the cruiser. At last we pulled up to a house as small as a hunting cabin. It was surrounded by unruly bushes. A warped wooden porch jutted out over a ditch. Flies buzzed around it. From somewhere in the distance came the crack of an axe against firewood.

"This is it," Ronan said.

"I was beginning to think you were taking me into the wilderness to shoot me."

"Nah," Ronan said. "If I were going to shoot you, I wouldn't do it here. Too many witnesses."

"Is that the comforting tone you use with the elderly?"

He showed me his teeth. "Some charms I reserve just for you."

I parked and started to open the door. But Ronan put a hand on my arm. The playfulness in his expression was gone. "We can't go in."

"If this is a stakeout," I said, "then bringing the cruiser was a mistake."

"This is Ted Ferguson's house. He doesn't like sudden movements."

"And if I promise to open the door slowly?"

"Don't worry," Ronan said. He leaned back. He tilted his head as if resting his eyes. "Ted will come out."

"When?"

"You in a hurry?"

"Now that you mention it, I would like to see about some dead bodies."

"You mean dead people."

Ronan was still chewing the same piece of gum he'd had at the station. I didn't like this about him, the same way I didn't like it when someone chain-smoked or was always refilling their coffee cup. But my little brother had always been fidgety. "I was surprised," Ronan said at last, "that you came back for them."

"The dead bodies?"

He didn't look at me. "I mean, Bear had that stroke a few years ago. You didn't come back for that. Not to mention my wedding."

"You know about the case I was working. I told you."

"And Bear?"

"He was fine," I said. "There's nothing I could have done."

"And there's something you can do here?" Ronan's voice was soft, pitched too high. He said, "That's the only reason you're back?"

I could tell he wanted me to say more—about him, about family, about the things we turn our backs on only to find we need again. I looked out the window, toward the empty porch. Ted Ferguson wasn't on it. Again came the crack of axe on wood.

Ronan said, "After what happened in New York, I don't know, I just thought maybe you'd be ready to come home. For good."

What happened in New York. This was, of course, the perfect way of saying it. As if New York had been the problem. As if New York had compelled me to draw my weapon on my partner. The city-appointed psychiatrist had called my actions *an acute emotional breakdown in which the detective's judgment was temporarily suspended.* But that didn't mean anything. Not to me. It had been my hand. My gun. My voice. My judgment. Yet it's like it hadn't been me at all.

I pushed the scene from my mind. I said, "I can change people's minds. This case can help me do it."

I thought back to the story I'd heard a long time ago. About a cop who'd stabbed his partner. He'd been suspended. Indefinitely. Like me. But seven months later, he'd found an abducted girl in the basement of some creep's house. She'd been missing for three years. The guy came back to the NYPD with a Medal of Honor.

I said, "I need to rebuild my reputation brick by brick. This is how I start."

"Brick by brick," Ronan said. He rolled the words around in his mouth. "Mom used to say that. She said every building, every skyscraper, began with a single stone."

I kept my eyes on the porch. I didn't like that I'd quoted her. I didn't like that I hadn't remembered she'd said that.

"Okay," Ronan said. "So, say you pull it off. Say you build back your reputation. Then what?"

I flashed to Eric, to the way he'd looked at me when I'd turned in my shield, like I was on the wrong side of the law now, the wrong side of his heart now. I said, "Then I get back my life."

"You really think you can go back to how things were?"

In the distance, a log cracked into two sides of itself. I listened as the pieces landed on top of each other. At some point, the woodpile would be great enough to outlast the cold.

Forty minutes later, Ted Ferguson emerged from behind the aluminum door. As it wheezed shut behind him, Ted sidled out onto the porch wearing a heavy flannel and a baseball cap too small for his head. He was in his seventies, maybe a little older. At first I thought he had a limp. "Y'all don't got nothing better to do than clog up my drive?" he said. It was then that I realized what made his gait uneven. It was the bolt-action rifle against his hip.

Ted made his way around the porch, keeping ahold of his firearm.

Ronan poked his head out the window, apparently unfazed. "Just checking in on you, sir. How are you doing today? You doing okay?"

"Besides the fact that I got Big Brother up my ass?"

I glanced at Ronan, watching for his reaction.

Ronan's smile weakened. "You need anything, sir? Anything inside the house we can help you with?"

Ted slapped his hand to the barrel of the rifle so the gun formed a bar across his chest. "Go to hell."

Ronan motioned for me to start the cruiser. As the engine caught, he said, "Good seeing you today, sir. You have a nice day. Stay out of trouble." Ronan said this last part as if it were a joke between them. Ted didn't smile.

I reversed, and the gravel crunched beneath the tires. Ted drew back his face to spit. By the time I put the cruiser into drive, Ted had shot a loogie in our direction. He wasn't exactly aiming toward us. He wasn't exactly not.

"Tell me I'm overanalyzing," I said, "but I don't think Ted Ferguson wants us looking in on him."

We viewed Ted out our side mirrors. He still had both hands on his gun as he watched to make sure we left.

. . .

By the time we reached the last house of the day, the sky was smoked in purple. It was a sky that had you sealing shut the windows, that had you feeling your face for droplets of rain.

We'd been stopping at houses for more than four hours. While some of our visits had been to the elderly, the majority had not. As with Ted, they spoke to us from their porches. As with Ted, they held hunting rifles as if we were out-of-towners and this was the Wild West.

Clearly, these weren't wellness visits, not as Ronan had described them. We weren't checking in to see how these people were doing. We were there to monitor them. I just didn't know why.

I could have pushed Ronan to tell me the truth, to tell me why the taxpayers of Copper Falls would pay to send two armed officers to keep tabs on these people every day. But it didn't concern me. The same thing happened in New York, a version of it anyway. The beat cops checked in on known criminals to make sure they weren't committing crimes. The criminals tolerated this because they had no choice. If Ronan wanted to pretend these were wellness visits to ease his mind, it wasn't my place to judge. We all lie to ourselves, when it suits us.

We were at the edge of the woods now, at a house that was too big to be like the country shacks we'd come from and yet too derelict—chipped paint, shin-high grass, balusters like broken teeth—to be among the candy-colored Queen Annes from on top of the hill.

I turned off the engine. Ronan cranked the handle of the door.

"Oh, now we're getting out?" I said.

"This is Maude Hummel's," Ronan said.

"Maude?" The word came out flat, like I'd hit the wrong note and now was stuck with it.

"She's not like the others. You'll see."

"Does she also have a rifle?"

Ronan shut the door.

We climbed the brittle front steps with missing boards like booby traps. As Ronan knocked and we waited, wind swirled through the leaves behind us. A truck gave a low-pitched growl from someplace far away. At last, Ronan creaked open the door. He let himself inside, and I followed.

The tiled foyer was littered with frayed ropes and cracked leather shoes, several decades out of date. Tangled fuzz collected in the corners in clumps. We stepped over a threshold and then at last we stood in a deep hallway. Flames glowed inside oil lamps attached to the walls. They flickered with the draft. "Mrs. Hummel?" Ronan shouted. His voice came back an echo.

We stepped carefully over a scatter of Persian rugs, which were gnawed at in some places and in others worn to their threads. We walked past shelves cluttered with tarnished silver and toppled figurines, of boys with sailor caps, of flowers with broken stems, of porcelain animals that had the eyes of humans. I caught a flicker of movement. "Wait," I said.

Ronan stopped, turned to face me.

I reached inside the toppled vase on the shelf beside Ronan's shoulder. I pulled out a garter snake. I lifted it by its head. Its scales chugged across my skin. Its heartbeat tapped against my wrist.

Ronan shuddered.

The snake curled between my arms. It sensed the air with its tongue.

"I forgot that about you," he said, examining me. "How you do things like that. It's fucking creepy."

I'd forgotten it, too. Yet, my body had remembered. Here, it remembered. I placed the snake onto the hardwood floor. It zigzagged away from us, but I still felt it on my skin. I followed Ronan deeper inside the house.

The farther inside we went, the messier the house became. Its energy grew more chaotic. We stepped across the threshold of an empty room with half-fallen curtains and brittle-paged books flung open as if thrown.

On our right was a dining room piled with terra-cotta rubble. On our left was a closet with rusty wire hangers from which hung nothing but cobwebs and fluff. "Mrs. Hummel?" Ronan said. "It's Officer O'Donnell. Mrs. Hummel?"

A bang. Loud, like a firecracker.

Ronan flinched. He lurched back.

I unclipped my Colt from its strap. I pressed its weight against my palm.

"Leigh," Ronan said. He tripped over his words. "That's not necessary. I'm sure it's just the water heater or something. These old houses, you know?"

But I'd seen the rifles at the other homes we'd visited. I knew what could be lurking in darkness, even at an old woman's house. Sometimes instincts keep you safe.

I moved Ronan out of the way. I pressed forward.

Rats scuddled in a dark corner up ahead. The scents of fresh soil and rain filled my chest. I held my calloused finger tight to its home trigger.

I spotted it.

Out back, past the porch. A figure, hunched in the shifting darkness.

I crept across the kicked-up rug. I stepped lightly. My breath was steady. I hinged open the storm door. Its creak was plaintive, pleading. I kept going.

A glint flickered up from the figure's hand. I aimed my gun. I cocked back the hammer. Felt the metallic click. Blood pumped everywhere.

The woman's joints cracked as she turned to look over her shoulder.

Maude Hummel sat in an old-fashioned wheelchair. A dusty afghan was draped over her lap. Knotty fingers, all veins and liver spots, rested on something metallic.

I opened my mouth to say, *Hands up*. But she wasn't holding a gun. A pair of binoculars hung on a collar of linked metal rings, like a chain of office around her neck. I searched the seams of the blanket. Smooth. I searched the lines of her housedress. Same. I reengaged the safety. I lowered my weapon. I released my breath.

"Detective O'Donnell," I said. "I apologize for the fright."

But Maude Hummel didn't look frightened. She turned away from me just as the air pressure shifted and my ears popped.

Maude's voice was far away, the way the chime of a bell can feel distant even if it's right in front of you. "You're too late," she said to me, to no one. "Every last one of them is dead."

The sky blackened as the rain approached. Yet I followed the line of her eyes, past the wheat-colored arcade, past the scattered pines and the rocky crag. Out there, deep in the wilderness, the shadows bled across the expanse like ink.

Then my gaze was upon it. So serene from here. So calm. Yet I knew the lie.

To get up close would be to see the conflict. To see the rush of water as it sped over rocks. The crash at the bottom. The impossibility of return. The inevitability of descent. The fear, the flee, the consequences of its own terrible momentum.

Here was Copper Waterfall.

Maude Hummel wheeled herself into a small, attached greenhouse. Ronan didn't ask the usual questions about how she was doing. I didn't ask the questions on my lips, either. Not yet.

The air in the greenhouse was thick and tropical. The walls were scalloped and foggy. The ceiling mushroomed over us. It should have seemed vast, that room made of glass. Instead, it was overgrown and choked. It was cramped with every shade of green.

Tangled vines draped over hooks and papery leaves winged out from too-small pots. Tiny flowers with pink and white buds sickled over terra-cotta lips. From the ceiling hung drooping succulents and dark green plants like strings of pearls. The floor—a dirt-speckled mosaic—was crowded with end tables and wiry stands, with wooden pallets and tilting stacks of waterlogged books. On every surface sat verdant tendrils. They reached for a sun they could only sense. It was embarrassing, how little they could hide their wanting.

"Ronan," Mrs. Hummel said. "Would you please . . . ?"

Ronan said something obliging. He traced his fingers through a cluster of metal watering cans. He headed back inside the main house. Seconds later, the rain began to fall.

There, seated in the center of things, Maude tilted her chin up to the ceiling. She closed her eyes. Her mouth fell open. Her whole body relaxed against the patter of water on glass.

"What do you think it is?" Maude said. She opened her eyes and fixed them on me. They were iced blue and startling. "What makes some people cultivate life and others court its destruction?"

I teetered, as if off balance. "You want to know why I'm not a horticulturist, you mean?"

Her smile made me feel I'd admitted something I hadn't meant to say. "They're the same thing," she said. "Life and death. Two sides of the same coin. You flip it, you get one. Eventually, you get the other. Only, you can't know ahead of time how the toss will land."

There was something contrived about the way Maude spoke. It made me think of palm readers. Of mediums. Of the women I'd interviewed at Bellevue who'd claimed to be a coven. I said, "One week ago, three men died on that waterfall."

Maude wrapped the tip of her tongue around the edge of her lips. Sour seeped down my throat, into my stomach, where it stayed.

"Outside," I said, "when you said all of them were dead, you meant Duncan Schott, William Houser, and Neil Mayer, didn't you?"

The rain sprayed against the ceiling. It ran down the creases of the glass, smudging the light.

"I meant my brothers, of course," Maude said.

I searched her fleshy face. Duncan, William, and Neil couldn't have been her brothers. They were younger than she was by half a century, at least.

"It'll be sixty-five years next month," Maude said. "It was supposed to be a family reunion. Instead my brothers burned while they slept."

Ronan had reminded me about this over the phone. The family reunion where everyone burned alive. "I'm sorry for your loss," I said, because it was part of my script, because I didn't care.

"Don't do that," she spat. "Don't condescend to me."

As we held each other's eyes, Ronan's words came back to me, about how just because these people were elderly, that did not make them safe. I knew he hadn't meant Maude Hummel. I knew he should have meant Maude Hummel.

For a brief moment, I entertained the idea that Maude had done it. She'd killed those three young men for reasons I had yet to uncover. But no, that was impossible. Maude was in her eighties. She was in a wheelchair. These were three grown men.

Intellectually, I knew this. Yet the feather hairs on my neck disagreed. I said, "Outside, when you said they were all dead? Were you *only* talking about your brothers?"

Maude's eyes pinned mine. You couldn't look at those eyes and not see the life in them. You couldn't look at that body and not feel its rush toward death. "You're quite the hunter."

"I'm a detective."

"That's not what I meant."

"Then what did you mean?"

She ran her fleshy tongue across her lips. She appraised me, considered. "I meant the young men, of course. Duncan. Neil. William."

"You knew them?"

Maude pressed the tip of her finger to the tip of a thorn. Her finger did not bleed. I waited, for blood or for words, as though either would've satisfied me. "To fight against death," she said, "is to fight against the tide. In the end, they didn't allow death to come for them. They fought against it."

Again, that feeling that her lines were scripted, like she was acting out her part in a play. My lips tasted of salt, of wax. I said, "Are you saying you saw the three men go over the falls? That you saw them fight?"

Maude's voice was hard, like a rock against a windowpane. "No."

Her eyes keyed in to mine. Her pupils were tiny. I felt each heartbeat in the socket of my throat.

"I only saw the bodies. The people in them were gone before they ever began to fall."

7

Monday, November 6

THE RECORDS ROOM IN THE BASEMENT OF THE COPPER FALLS
Police Department smelled strongly of wet cement. Overnight,
the rain hadn't let up. The noise of it thrummed like the inside
of a seashell, endless, shushed.

It was seven o'clock in the morning. I sat at a long wooden
table with three case files spread out before me and a cup of coffee that had long ago gone cold. Around me were tall cedar cabinets with hundreds of tiny drawers. In them were index cards
with call numbers referencing the boxes of files at the other end
of the room.

It'd taken me hours to work out the convoluted filing system.
But now that I'd found the records I'd been looking for, I knew
why Ronan had thought there might be something suspicious
about these deaths. I also knew why he thought there might be
nothing there.

Duncan Schott. William Houser. Neil Mayer. Or, as Ronan had put it, the good-looking one, the nice one, and the musician. All twenty-five. All white. All unemployed. All found in the plunge pool of Copper Waterfall on the same crisp morning at the end of October by a middle-aged couple out on their morning run.

It could have been coincidence, all three dying like that. But as soon as I'd laid out the autopsy photos on the table, the patterns became obvious.

None of the bodies showed any signs of strangulation. No signs of blunt force trauma. No broken bones. Not even postmortem bruising. There'd been enough water in their lungs to be consistent with acute cerebral hypoxia—fatal loss of air. As a result, the medical examiner had ruled all three to be drownings. There was no indication of foul play. They were what, back in New York, we'd have called paperwork cases.

Yet, as I stared at their autopsy photos, a feeling started at the base of my neck and spread down my arms. I brought coffee to my lips, but I didn't register its taste. Just like at Maude Hummel's house, there was something here commanding my attention. It was a long time before I understood what it was.

Over the years, I'd grown accustomed to dead bodies, to gnarled faces and smashed-in skulls, to knocked-out teeth and lacerations that never bled. I'd seen gunshot wounds and broken kneecaps. Flayed wrists. Eyes hanging on by their threads. Yet, these bodies weren't anything like those other bodies. It's not just that they were undamaged.

They were pristine.

No scars. No pockmarks on chins from old acne. There

wasn't even a torn cuticle among them. Their hair had been freshly cut. Their fingernails had been freshly trimmed. Even their ears had been scraped of wax. These weren't bodies as I'd known them: messy, unselfconscious things. These were cleaned in preparation for slaughter. Ritualized.

It'd have been unusual enough to see *one* body in this state. But three?

Then there was the question of how exactly they'd drowned. This hadn't been a drug-induced dive over a cliff. Their tox screens were clear. There wasn't bruising from being strangled or being hit over the head. No broken fingernails from where they'd clung to dirt or rock. It was as though they'd simply entered the water and not come out.

Then there was the other thing, what Maude Hummel had said about seeing them go over the falls. If she was right, if the three men *had* been lifeless by the time they'd fallen, then that meant they hadn't drowned in the plunge pool after all.

They'd drowned somewhere else, somewhere that still might hold evidence of a crime.

I unlocked my cell phone and dialed the Wood County Medical Examiner's Office. I wanted to make an appointment to see the bodies for myself. But the call went straight to the machine. Dr. Aliche, it said, was out of town for the next three days. *Anyone unfortunate enough to meet their maker whilst I'm away,* the voice chirped, *should be sent to Lucas County instead.*

I swiped to end the call.

Above me, the door to the basement swung open. Rubber-soled feet came barreling down the stairs. A woman in jeans and a red flannel stood on the landing. She brought in with her the smell of Ivory soap. Her shirt didn't reach her wrists. Her hems didn't reach her ankles. It took me a beat to recognize her. "Janice?" I said. "What are you doing here?"

Janice laughed out of her nostrils. Her face retrieved its familiar expression. Wry. Amused. A little bit smug. "I could ask you the same thing." She held out her hand. I stood and shook it.

Janice had been in my grade in high school, technically. Sophomore year, however, she'd started taking college classes in Toledo. By senior year, she was taking college classes full-time. I only saw her at graduation, as we tipped our mortarboards to each other like fellow cowboys who'd only been passing through. We'd both been so determined to get out. We both were here now.

"I'm consulting on some possible homicides," I said, releasing her hand. "It's just for a little while."

"I heard you were a detective now."

"And you're a librarian?"

"Archivist." Janice's voice was a little sharp. She shrugged. But it didn't look casual. "The town needed someone to put their archives in order. I fit the bill. I guess you've noticed this place isn't big on digital files."

Janice pushed a strand of hair behind her ear. It didn't stay.

"When I got here," she said, "they didn't even have a card catalogue. Just a bunch of boxes that were vaguely alphabetical. That computer out there? It hadn't been updated in like a year."

"*You* did all of this?" I motioned to the long room. There must have been hundreds of files. Even from the few I'd pulled, I could tell how meticulously they'd been catalogued. I couldn't imagine having that kind of patience. I couldn't imagine being as smart as Janice and wanting to spend my time that way.

"I riffed on the Dewey decimal system. I combined it with the system the NYPD used at the turn of the century." Janice adjusted her glasses on the bridge of her nose. "I only had to make some minor adjustments to account for crimes that weren't in existence then, like digital fraud. I published a reference volume for how to do it. Not that it's sold more than a few hundred copies. But two and a half years later, here we are. A complete catalogue of all twenty-four hundred files."

"There are twenty-four hundred criminal records?" Even if everyone in town had committed a crime twice, there would still be too many.

Janice smirked. "These aren't just criminal records. They're everything. House deeds. Marriage licenses. Birth announcements. Daguerreotypes. Family trees. A lot of it's junk, but at least now it's organized junk."

"But the files I pulled were bare," I said. "Just death reports, background checks, phone records, autopsy photos. That sort of thing. Certainly no daguerreotypes."

Janice gave a sideways grin. "Do you know the history of the word *archive*?"

She walked around me. She touched her fingertips to the table, looking over the photos of William Houser, Duncan Schott, and Neil Mayer. She didn't shrink at the sight of their bodies. But then, I guessed these weren't the first autopsy photos she'd seen.

"It comes from the ancient Greek, *arkheion,* meaning 'house of the ruler.'"

I nodded. "And these guys were from the Sticks."

"I always liked that about you. You're quick. Now if only you had a sense of history."

She opened William's file and touched his senior photograph. It had a blue, cloudy backdrop and gold lettering on its bottom corner. Painfully generic.

She said, "If you want your immunization record commemorated in the annals of history, be rich. If you can't be rich, be influential. Because if you aren't either of those things, your legacy will be consigned to the family scrapbook. Even then, it will only last a generation before it gets thrown out with the trash."

"When you put it like that, your job sounds very glamorous."

"Hey, we can't all spend our days with decomposing corpses."

At once, I felt defensive, irked. It must have shown on my face.

The playfulness dropped out of Janice's expression. She touched her fingers to her lips. Her eyes went soft. "The bodies would be the easy part for you. It's the family interviews you hate. All that grief. It must be triggering."

Just for a flash, I saw it: the glaze of my mother's eyes as she told us that Dad strapped to a gurney would be the last memory of him we'd have. But just as soon as that image appeared, my thoughts shuttered shut, as if sealing off a draft. I felt for the closest file I'd pulled. The one I'd grabbed on impulse. "There's a thick file on Maude Hummel." I made my voice hard. "Maude isn't rich or influential. So by your logic, her file should be bare."

Janice startled. In the glow of the overhead lights, I registered the stoop of her. It was a barely there hunchback, like she was raising her shoulders to her ears, but not evenly. She said, "What do you want with Maude Hummel?"

I clocked something in the air then: a tightening, like a change in barometric pressure.

"I mean, I could see the appeal, as a detective," Janice said, straightening.

Her voice was lighter now, like a stone skipping across water. She walked around me and finger-stepped over the files I'd pulled, reading the tab of each one.

"All three of her brothers burn alive in a fire that Maude mysteriously walks away from? Accelerants everywhere. Clearly arson. Before that, her parents die in a freak car accident? Suspicious, right? You'd think there'd be something there. A cold case you can sink your teeth into? But it's cold for a reason. You're not going to find anything about her. About either of them, for that matter."

Janice's gaze flicked up at me. She watched to see how this last part would land. I took the bait. "Either of them?"

Behind Janice's eyes, there was a shift, small, like a blip in a recording you're not sure you really saw. "Not many people our age are aware of this. You know how small towns are with secrets." She drew in a breath. "But Maude Hummel is actually a twin."

"She has a sister?"

Janice smiled.

"Why is that something people wouldn't know?"

"Estella is—I don't know how to say it. *Touched,* some might call it."

"Mentally ill?"

"You can imagine that's not a topic people here discuss," Janice said. "Especially since we're all related. So instead, they've parked Estella far away from our collective consciousness. The older generations don't talk about her. Most people don't even know she exists."

"But Maude can't pretend her own sister doesn't exist."

"Well, that's the thing. When they were sixteen, Estella married a Wagner and left Maude to rot in that old house. Maude never forgave Estella for leaving. Estella never forgave Maude for not visiting after her psychotic break."

"So the sisters aren't on speaking terms?"

Janice nodded. "But come on, Maude had to have known her sister couldn't refuse a Wagner. Their dad dug sewers for a living. It was basically the Copper Falls edition of Cinderella."

I mentally added this to what I already knew about the Wagners. We'd studied them in grade school, years before I'd learned about the Founding Fathers. Archibald Wagner had left Germany in the 1800s amid fears of persecution. He and his family had embarked on a treacherous journey in covered wagons until they found abandoned land. Archibald had named the town for his wife, Agnes "Kopper" Wagner, so called for her golden hair. He'd declared this place would be prosperous, and it was.

I couldn't believe I still remembered all that. But there it was. Right next to the lyrics to "How Great Thou Art" and the Pledge of Allegiance.

"If most people don't know about Estella," I said, "how do you know about her?"

Janice smiled. She palmed the card cabinet. "Turns out we're both in the business of uncovering secrets."

"When you put it like that, our jobs actually do **sound** glamorous."

"Maybe they really are."

I said, "I want to see the file on Estella Wagner."

Janice's mouth flattened. "I told you there's nothing there."

And maybe there was nothing. But my skin told me differently. Sometimes instincts keep you safe.

"I'll pull it for you," Janice said at last. She motioned to the stairs. "But you'd better get up there before the chief catches you here. He'll flip his shit if he sees you going through this stuff."

I thought she must be joking. But her expression didn't break. "He has to know I'm looking at police records."

"Oh, he doesn't care about that," Janice said. "It's the historical records that matter to him. He's paranoid someone's going to misfile something and erase whole family histories. I know it's not the same for you since you're not really from here." She paused. "But here, history is everything."

Janice stepped past me then, toward the rows of open shelving stacked with bankers' boxes and plastic bags. She withdrew a pair of cotton gloves and disappeared behind a row of cabinets.

8

FROM ACROSS THE TABLE, SIMONE WIGGLED IN HER BOOSTER
seat. "Mommy, they have spaghetti!" She pointed to the picture
on the menu.

Simone was happy to be doing something familiar. We'd had
to drive fifteen minutes to find an Italian restaurant, but it was
worth it. Even if just for this smile. "Is that what you're having?" I asked. "Spaghetti?"

"Maybe," Simone said. She held the menu in front of her face
as if she could read every word. "I need to de-lib-er-ate."

Deliberate was one of her new words. She liked the way people smiled at her when she said it, like how I was smiling at her
now. "Don't deliberate too long. I only have an hour for lunch."

Simone stuck out her bottom lip and tented the laminated
menu around her face.

Back in New York, I'd had lunch with Simone whenever I'd
wanted, for however long I'd felt like eating. It was only my
second day at the Copper Falls Police Department, but already

I knew that leisurely lunches weren't going to fly. We had rounds in the morning. A strict hour for lunch. Traffic stops all afternoon. Paperwork starting at four, which included watching Ronan open the mail. Only then could I work on the case.

It was becoming increasingly clear that if I wanted to investigate these deaths, I'd have to bend the rules to make the time for it. Here, as everywhere, social hierarchy mattered, and William, Duncan, and Neil were from the Sticks.

As Simone continued to *deliberate,* I took in the restaurant. Above us, Chianti bottles dangled from straw baskets. Fading Italian prints hung from wire fixtures. Heavy brass frames held sepia photographs, though whether these were family photos or picked up at a yard sale, I couldn't say.

In one photograph, thick-middled men in undershirts with slicked-back hair sat at a round table. In another, an old woman in a housecoat stood in a doorway with a cigarette dangling from her lips.

In the oval one up top, two young women had their arms slung around each other. They had pin-curled hair and secretive smiles. It was impossible to look at those women, who could have been sisters, and not to think of those other photos, the ones I'd seen that morning in Estella's and Maude's files, before I'd had to leave with Ronan on the rounds.

First, it was the family portrait. Maude and Estella's father and mother sat in the back. Their three older brothers knelt before them. The identical little girls sat cross-legged in front. They wore old-fashioned dresses with ruffled collars, and their hair was split into braids.

Then it was the photo of their parents' Oldsmobile, U-shaped

55

as it wrapped around a spiky pole. The scene was all shattered glass and hunks of metal. A dark stain spilled over the dashboard. Blood.

Then there was the photo of their three brothers, their bodies lain out on the grass like slabs of charred meat. In the background stood the cabin, now just a carcass, boiled down to its bones.

The on-scene photos of Estella and Maude, who were then sixteen, showed them smudged and dirty. Yet they had no burns that I could see. Their faces weren't tearstained and puffy. If anything, they looked defiant.

Then, dated six months later, came the wedding photo of Estella Hummel and Carmichael Wagner. Estella, by now, looked very different from her sister. She had a figure that belonged on a stage, spinning in endless circles but never going anywhere. She wore a tea-length dress, gauzy, with a scalloped veil. For the first time, I saw how much her name suited her. Estella. Sparkling. Like the stars.

Maude was in the background, thicker now than her sister, her waistline barely distinguishable from her hips. She clenched a small bouquet of dahlias. She looked away from the camera, toward a figure in the shadows. Yet I could still make out her scowl.

I'd kept turning the pages, wanting to know about Maude and Estella. I wanted to know what it was about Maude that had commanded my skin's attention. I wanted to know what kind of illness forced Copper Falls to pretend Estella didn't exist. I couldn't figure out how any of this was relevant to my case.

By all logic, it wasn't. But I couldn't make my brain and my body believe the same thing. I needed to understand why.

Yet as doggedly as I searched, in the end, the twins' files were useless, like Janice had tried to tell me. Just deeds to land on the properties they owned and wills naming each as the other's beneficiary. There were no photos of Maude Hummel as an adult. No baby announcements from Estella Wagner. No invitations to grand parties. It was as though after that wedding, they'd ceased to exist.

"Mommy!"

A teenage waiter was standing at our table. He held a silver pitcher between his hands. "Are we ready to order?"

I gave Simone the go-ahead.

She sat tall in her chair. "Spaghetti for me," she said. "Mommy wants beef."

"The beef tenderloin?" He scribbled. "How would she like it cooked?"

"Rare," I said. "With the heart still beating."

"Got it." The waiter rolled his eyes. "Beating heart. On a platter." He clicked his pen and disappeared behind a high-backed booth.

From across the table, Simone giggled. "Are you going to eat that?"

"A beating heart?"

She nodded.

"I'll make you eat it, obviously."

Simone's mouth opened wide as she laughed. Her large eyes crinkled. Just like that, I didn't see the old photographs in front of me anymore. I didn't see the dead bodies of Duncan, William, and Neil, the charred bodies of Estella and Maude's brothers. I didn't see the photo of Estella happy and Maude scowling. I simply saw my little girl. She was radiant.

All during the rest of lunch, we joked and laughed and threw pieces of breadsticks at each other. We talked about Ohio, what she liked—the quiet, the colors—and what she missed about New York—the carousel, her dad. We made plans to make massive plates of pancakes on the weekend. I gave her bites of my green beans. She slurped spaghetti loudly through the gap in her front teeth. She rubbed her belly and said she was full. The waiter offered us dessert. She insisted she had room.

Simone had vanilla ice cream trailing down her wrist. She smiled so that both her dimples emerged. It was the crest of a wave. She said, "I like Daddy's new friend. She's nice."

"His friend?" I sipped coffee from a porcelain cup. It was unusual for Eric to make new friends. He knew who he liked. He stuck with them.

"She was there before," Simone said.

Coffee pooled in the wells of my cheeks. I swallowed. "When I dropped you off?"

"And before that. She touches Daddy a lot. She smells good."

The wall clock behind Simone ticked, deafening. For a moment, it was the only thing in the room that moved.

Simone held her spoon against her ice cream dish. Her eyes registered something in mine. Just like that, her smile vanished. Her hand slackened against her spoon.

I swallowed back the bitter. I said, "I'm glad you like her."

Simone's eyes moved between mine.

"I like her, too."

"Really?" There was that smile again. I worked to match it.

"Now, come on with that ice cream." I looked at the clock. It was too blurry to read. "I have to get back to work."

Simone clinked her spoon against the bowl, but the sound was miles from me. All I could hear was the blood rushing in my ears, and the thump of a heart that was, impossibly, still beating.

9

"LET ME DO IT," SIMONE SAID.

We were in the parking lot. Simone was in her car seat. A bag of leftovers languished beside her. She always wanted to clip herself in. I never let her. But this time, I helped her take the plastic buckles into her small hands. I guided her as they snapped shut. "I did it!" she said.

"Yes, you did," I replied. I bit back the urge to add, *Now tell me everything you know.* "It's fifteen minutes to get to the house. You need to try really hard to stay awake, okay?"

I handed her Arnie and pressed the door shut. I took my seat behind the wheel. Yet I didn't lift the key to the ignition.

"I'm awake, Mommy."

"I know you are, baby."

Still, I didn't lift my hand. Instead, the scene in Eric's lobby played out before me. The way he hadn't wanted me to come up to his apartment. How he'd barely looked at me. It was so obvious now. There was someone with him he hadn't wanted me to meet.

"Hey," called a voice in the distance.

But all I heard was Eric's voice, low like a cello, on the day he'd proposed. He'd told me that before we could get married, I had to promise him one thing.

My mom cheated on my dad, he said, his steady voice cracking. And I knew this was big. Eric never talked about his family. His mom was out of the picture. The few times I'd met his dad, he'd mostly sat in front of a television and smoked himself senseless. *She took his self-respect, Leigh. I can't go down that path. I won't be who he became when she did that. I can't do this unless I know we will be faithful. For all of it.*

Sweat dripped from Eric's palm onto the ring, making it slippery. His whole face seemed slippery. He was never like this. He said, *I need you to promise.*

And I had. I'd thought we had.

"Hey!" called the voice again. "Hey, Wildcat!"

Something about that voice, that word, that name, pulled me back to the present. Out the window, the sun was beginning its downward climb. It blurred the lines between the lit parts of the pavement and the shade.

From the shadows strode a man, tall, blond, broad. He was wearing distressed jeans and a thin red sweater. A smile wended its way across his face. I stepped out of the car. I let the door hang open like an unfinished thought.

"Mason Vogel?"

"Hey, you." Because of my sidearm, I never let anyone hug

me. But this time, I didn't react fast enough. Mason curled his arms around me, over my back, to my ribs. Then my arms found the breadth of him. I inhaled.

Mason smelled like expensive department store and that scent he'd had since childhood, earth and moss and something else. Then it wasn't just chest touching chest anymore. It was the whole line of us, our bellies, our hip bones, our necks. I drew him in and something caught in my throat.

At last, I released him. But I still held Mason's warmth in my body, in the way of cold-blooded things stealing heat. I scrambled for words. I said, "You look different. What are you now, a spokesman for J.Crew?"

Mason laughed. It exposed his throat to me. It was the exact opposite of Eric's laugh, which was always reserved, always half-hidden. Eric never let his vulnerable places show. I used to say his self-control was pathological. Mason said, "It turns out Goth didn't suit me beyond the early aughts. Not enough angst to sustain it."

"Let me guess." I took in the muscles that curved down his neck, that knit his shoulders together. "You discovered fitness instead?"

A flame lit the back of Mason's eyes. He looked away. In a flash, I saw the man-child I'd once known, the one who'd worn tattered shirts and tried to pierce his ear with a needle only to end up on antibiotics for a week, the awkward Mason, who was nothing like this polished man whose shadow took up so much space.

Mason's gaze returned to me. He dragged it over my length.

"And what about you?" he said. "You look like you have

your own crime show. The kind in syndication, you know, but still."

I was surprised to find myself laughing. I was surprised at how easily the tension spilled out of me and became something else. I had on a gray suit with an open jacket, heeled boots. I was conscious of my body. I was conscious of his body. The way they had once fit. "I'm a homicide detective. In New York."

"A Montague and a Capulet." Mason motioned to himself. "Journalist. Though I guess that metaphor only works if we're in love." There was that glint again. Only, this time he didn't look away. His lips separated as he smiled. It sent hot oil slipping inside of me.

"I hear you're working on a magazine story," I said. "About the deaths."

"I hear you're working a case. About the deaths."

I registered this, that he already knew I was a homicide detective, that he let me tell him anyway. Yet I already knew he was a journalist and I'd let him tell me.

"Sounds like we should share notes," Mason said.

At last, a muscle memory kicked into gear. I crossed my arms. "Typical journalist. Always thinking information goes both ways."

"Typical detective. Playing things close to the vest."

"Have you found out anything I should know about the case?"

"That depends." He smiled. "Have *you* found out anything I should know about the case?"

I could have threatened him with obstruction. I could have hauled him in and made him talk. But if he had anything worth sharing, he'd have used it as leverage by now. I had access to files that he did not. He didn't need to know there was nothing in them. I said, "My daughter is in the car." I motioned to her. She was asleep. I said, "I'll see you around."

Mason stepped toward me then, as if to give me a parting hug. I outstretched my hand. My elbow was straight, like a bar.

The side of Mason's lip curled up. He wrapped his large hand around my fingers. He didn't shake. Instead, he flipped my hand over so its palm faced the sun. He clicked open his pen.

There was a moment when I could have pulled away, when I could have stopped him from doing what I knew he was about to do. But his heat spread over my fingers. It made its way to the deepest part of my chest. He wrote his phone number on the lines of my hand.

Mason clicked his pen shut. He released my hand to me. "Just in case you change your mind. About exchanging notes."

I worked my jaw. "I'm sure I won't have time."

"We could make it a quickie."

I shot him a look. He hadn't had that wry smile back in high school. Or if he had, he hadn't used it like this, so that it curled up on one side like a hook. "Goodbye, Mason."

"Goodbye, Wildcat. Or should I say, Detective Wildcat?"

I turned away from him completely. But even with my back to him, I could still feel the pull of something, the way the tide syncs up with the moon, something old and familiar.

10

THE UNCLES HAD BARELY MADE ANY CHANGES TO THE HOUSE since I'd left. The dining room was exactly as I remembered it. Large bay windows filtered in buttery light. A burnished credenza, veneered in a marquetry picture, sat against the wall. A lead-cut chandelier cast rainbows over everything. Glass cabinets held crystal goblets. Heavy gilt frames hung level, their pictures always capturing the same view.

Uncle Eamon, Uncle Frankie, and I sat at the lacquered table before the same plates we'd always eaten from. They were covered in pot roast. The juice made their pastoral scenes into swamps. In the background, amid the sounds of chewing, of forks clanging, there was only silence.

I glanced to the chair at the end of the table, where Dad would quiz us on Bloody Sunday in his Belfast brogue. I glanced to the other end of the table, where Mom would launch her legendary wit, her Cleveland accent making her vowels twang. My stomach turned over, and it was like an engine flooding.

My uncles had loved my mother, maybe even as much as I had. According to lore, my grandfather had beaten the shit out of them when they were kids until, at last, my grandmother left him. She would do doubles at the glass factory just to keep the four of them fed. My mother, being the oldest and the only girl, took over all the cooking, all the tucking in, all the homework, all the hugs. She'd been the only mother my uncles had ever known. Before they'd moved in, at least one of them had called her every day. It'd been like that my whole life. Now they were just shipwrecked sailors who, unable to navigate without their captain, had made this strange island their home.

"Hey." Uncle Bear stood in the doorway. He was round and hairy, like an animal on his haunches. Gray hair bushed out from under his rolled-up sleeves. He smelled of cigarettes, gasoline. "Where's my plate?"

Eamon blinked up at him. "You're not even going to say hello to Leigh?"

Bear glanced at me. His Cleveland accent was just as strong as Mom's had once been. "Have you got my plate?"

"I didn't check the bottom for a name," I said, "but when I'm done eating you can take a look."

"Still deferential to your elders, I see?"

"And you're still as punctual."

Bear grunted.

Eamon sighed. Since I'd known him, Eamon had never had an accent. Mom said he'd lost it during his time in Ireland, when he'd gotten his doctorate in Irish literature. Bear said he'd lost it because he had a stick up his ass. Eamon said, "Did you check the dishwasher?"

Bear left and came back with a plate with a chip out of its edge. All at once, I remembered that plate. My mother had dropped it years ago. It was an heirloom. She'd been so upset. But Bear had picked it up and ate off of it without a second thought. As Bear thumped into the seat of his chair, Frankie pinched something green out from the back of his teeth. Eamon cut his meat delicately so as not to splash.

"How's Simone settling in?" Eamon asked.

"She's fine," I said. "Just tired. It's been a long couple of days." It was seven thirty. Simone was already asleep.

"What's with the armadillo?" Bear said.

I cut him a sharp glance. It unnerved me that he knew this about my daughter even though I hadn't introduced them. "Arnie," I said. "He's a transitional object." I looked back at my plate. I still didn't know why he was called that, if it meant Simone was transitioning from being a kid to being less of a kid, or transitioning from needing her parents to needing other people. Maybe, I suspected, it just felt good giving ordinary things labels, building a taxonomy of human needs, as if that meant we understood them.

"Yeah, but why an armadillo?" Bear asked.

Frankie interjected. "You mean to say, your kid loves an armored animal that inside is all squish?" He slurped his can of Coke loudly and looked directly at me. "Yep. No idea why she'd be primed to love *that*."

"You know," Eamon said, his dulcet voice pitched high, "we could arrange for Simone to have her own room. We do have the space. It can't be particularly comfortable, sleeping in the same bed as a four-year-old."

"No need to bother," I said. "It's not going to be a long trip."

"She's just here to solve those murders," Frankie said. He pointed his fork at me. "Isn't that right, kid? Then you're outta here?"

Bear said, "*If* they're murders. Sounds to me like everyone else thinks the guys offed themselves. When my time comes, I want one right between the eyes. None of this diving over a waterfall shit." Bear scooped up a mound of pot roast and chewed as he spoke. "A lot of hoopla for the same damn result."

"If Leigh thinks they're murders," Frankie said, "I believe her. I have faith in you, kid. Besides, she's the only one of us who has seen the bodies. You have seen the bodies, right?"

"Actually . . ." I said.

Frankie grew animated. "What did they look like? Like water balloons, right?"

Eamon winced.

Bear growled.

"I know this may come across as an extreme request," Eamon said. His voice was at the tip of his teeth. "But I would prefer not to talk about dead bodies at the dinner table, if at all possible."

For a long moment, Frankie's expression was somber. Eamon was the oldest and Frankie was the youngest. So on occasion, Eamon did have the power to make Frankie close his mouth. At last, Frankie nodded. He said, "You're right. I get it. I really do."

Frankie pushed his chair out from the table and picked up his plate. His knees creaked as he took a step toward the windows.

"Leigh, now that I'm not at the dinner table, tell me about

these dead bodies. They go swimming with their concrete shoes on or what?"

"Jesus, Mary, and Joseph," Eamon said. His fork clattered.

Bear spat, "What are you, twelve?"

"Actually," Frankie said, "I'll be sixty in June. Don't worry, Leigh. I'll make sure you're invited to the party."

"Please," Eamon said.

"Sit the hell down," Bear barked.

Frankie, at last, set his plate on the table. He tucked himself in with two loud scoots. Eamon cringed at each of them.

Eamon picked up his fork.

Frankie said, "I'm just saying."

Eamon's fork clanged to his plate.

"Naw, I mean it. Since Leigh's here we should take advantage, you know? Ask her all our burning questions. Besides, you'd think if anyone would want this case solved, it'd be you." He was looking directly at Eamon.

"Frankie!" Bear said. "Knock it off."

"Why you?" I asked Eamon.

Eamon's sigh was heavy and pleading. His look asked me to take pity on his nerves.

I asked, "Did you know them?"

"Not all of them," Eamon said. He shook his head. "Just William Houser."

I knew precious little about William Houser's life from his file. Only that he'd lived in the Sticks with his father, that his mother had died when he was young. I'd seen his birth certificate and a graduation photo. I had Ronan's unhelpful character sketch that he was a *nice guy*. But what I knew about William

Houser could fit on a note card. I said, "How did you know him?"

Eamon kneaded his brow. "He came to one of my talks. Though why we must discuss this now is—"

"Yeah, Leigh." Bear leveled me with his gaze. "You're being insensitive."

I ignored him. To Eamon, I said, "William Houser came to one of your talks at the Historical Society? When?"

Eamon stared at a painting on the wall, the one of the lone fisherman gathering his nets in a storm. "The day before he died."

I lifted my notebook from my jacket pocket. "Did he ask any questions? Did he talk to you after your presentation?"

"Leigh, please."

I shifted to face him. "Anything at all? Anything you can remember? It might help."

Eamon took off his glasses. He rubbed his eyes. "William wanted to know about the falls."

I didn't blink. "What about the falls?"

"It wasn't after my talk," Eamon said, still rubbing at his wrinkles. "It was mid-lecture, which I consider to be quite ill-mannered. I was talking about how the ancient Celts didn't believe the gods were above us in the sky, but below us, in the ground.

"I was explaining how this was the reason the earth is holy to the Irish, why they had sacred mounds and hills. They believed the way to access the gods was not by climbing mountains, but by diving to the bottoms of lakes, or in seas, or in caves. William asked if I knew how to find the shrines in the caves underneath the waterfall."

"Shrines?" I knew about the caves. Everyone did. But I'd never heard about any shrines.

"Naturally, I didn't know what he meant." Eamon removed a cloth from his pocket. He wiped it across his lenses. "I directed him to my colleague, who specializes in local history."

"What's the colleague's name?"

Eamon returned his glasses to his face. "Please, Leigh. Can't you find out some other way? It wasn't easy for these people to accept me. It took a lot of convincing to make them see that the Irish pantheon could be of use to their history, too. I've just settled in."

"It's been seventeen years."

Eamon was silent for a long time. He could have forgotten the question, or his mind could have drifted off to some ancient era, when things were settled and knowable, where there were no pots to be stirred, only facts to be uncovered, facts that hardly mattered to anyone. Frankie and Bear exchanged looks. Eamon cleared his throat. "I sent him to the president of the Historical Society." He exhaled. "Dr. Calvin Wagner."

Bear's palm slapped the table.

Frankie held up his watch. "That's time!"

Bear leaned toward Frankie. "What we at?"

"Give or take a few seconds for timekeeper's delays . . ." Frankie examined his watch, cocked his head. "That puts us at exactly seven minutes and ten seconds, which means you owe me twenty big ones."

"Horseshit," Bear said. "Let me see that."

"Really," Eamon said, throwing his napkin on the table. "You two are children."

"Here." Bear chucked a crumpled twenty on the table. "Buy some sense."

Frankie crisped the bill in front of his face. "I told him you'd get the information out of Eamon in under ten. Bear thought it'd take you longer." He winked. "Like I said, I have faith in you, kid."

Eamon took his plate into the kitchen. Bear plucked a cigarette from a soft pack of Marlboro Reds. Frankie came around to my side of the table and clapped me on the back. "Just like old times, right, kid?"

Eamon clanged pots in the kitchen. The front door banged shut. Frankie jogged to catch up with Bear. I turned to the empty table.

Yeah. Just like old times.

11

Tuesday, November 7

IT WAS A LITTLE AFTER EIGHT IN THE MORNING WHEN I parked on the gravel in front of Duncan Schott's house.

Duncan's home had a white picket fence. Not the kind with thick wooden posts, nailed together at perfect angles. This one was made of plastic, like something bought online and erected in a spirit of wishful thinking. Mounds of bright pansies, crimson and yellow, bloomed along its base, enclosing a green lawn and a single-wide trailer with white shutters, made jaundiced by the sun.

I had unwrapped Simone's hair that morning, buttered her toast, and left her under the care of the uncles. I hated leaving her for the day, but I was also glad for it. Glad for the reason to clip my shield to my belt and slide my arms through my holster. Glad, at last, to be working on getting us back to our normal rhythm.

I climbed the cement front steps and rapped on the door the way I always did when I wanted to invoke the authority of the police. Normally, this had people patting their pockets and smoothing their hair. It had them drawing back their shoulders and answering the door with a cautious *Ma'am?* Normally, it gave me immediate command.

Only, this time, a woman's voice yelled back through the door, "Yeah?" She gave the word three syllables.

I knocked again. Then again, harder.

"Who's there?" she snapped.

I knocked harder still.

Through the fiberglass door, I heard everything: the woman's under-the-breath mutterings about the early hour. Heavy footfalls and an exaggerated puff of air through her lips. When she came to the door, I'd expected a heavyset woman, all twisted features and messy hair. Yet a slender face appeared in the slat. The woman was wearing red lipstick. She was smiling.

"Angie Owens?" I asked.

But even before she responded, it was obvious this was Duncan Schott's girlfriend.

Angie had one of those faces that made you ashamed of any inclination you had toward vanity. Disney princess eyes. Perfect skin. White teeth. Blond hair in cascading waves. It was no wonder Duncan Schott had ended up with her. Beautiful people always had a way of finding each other, like bugs drawn to the same light.

"Listen," Angie said, not opening the door more than she had to. "I appreciate you being out here at the crack of dawn and beating on my door 'cause you're so mad about Jesus." Her words stretched out like taffy, cloyingly sweet. "But we're full up on Bibles, okay? Have a blessed day!"

I held up my badge. "Detective Leigh O'Donnell. I'm here to talk to you about Duncan Schott. May I come in?"

Her face betrayed nothing. It made me think she knew exactly who I was when she'd seen me at the door. She pursed her lips. "Isn't that just precious? You guys are looking to clean up your own mess now that you got three dead souls on your hands? I'm afraid I don't have time for more Copper Falls bullshit at the moment."

As she spoke, I nodded sympathetically. Over the years, I'd met with plenty of families who'd had good reason to distrust the police. It was my job to convince them I wasn't like those cops who'd roughed them up or humiliated them simply because they could. I was homicide. Even *they* had to see that meant something different.

Angie went to shut the door.

I pressed my hand against it. "Ma'am," I said. "I understand your distrust. And truly I'm sorry to hear that, but—"

"No." Her fake smile vanished in a heartbeat. "You ask Christ to forgive your sins. 'Cause it sure as shit ain't gonna be me."

I barely had time to yank my hand back before Angie slammed the door and bolted it. The floor creaked as she settled back in whatever part of the trailer she'd come from.

I took a step back. I chewed my cheek. I pulled a business card from my jacket pocket and slipped it under the door. But I knew she'd just toss it.

If I wanted Angie to talk to me, I'd have to lure her out, like something wild.

. . .

I was surprised at how close their homes were, Duncan Schott's and Neil Mayer's. They both lived in the newer part of the Sticks, where the homes weren't old or patched together with coats of paint like layers of sediment. They weren't separated by skinny trees that provided privacy if not shelter.

Out here, the houses were mass-produced replicas of one another. Mostly single-wides in neutral tones, done up in aluminum siding and festooned with plastic shutters. Some, like Duncan's, had patches of green lawn. Others had front porches with hanging plants and lawn chairs. Everything was cheap but striving.

I crunched across the gravel, which filled in the places that weren't lawn, and walked up to one of the few double-wides in the lot. Most of the other trailers had white lattice plywood to hide their foundations, but not this one. This trailer sat on heavy cement blocks. As I climbed the front steps, I thought of the fleet of tornadoes that threatened Copper Falls every summer. I thought of how easily any one of these homes could be thrown to another part of town.

It took several minutes of me banging my fist against the door before a neighbor came out and told me that Neil's roommates worked nights and slept like the dead. If I wanted to talk with them, I'd have to come back in the afternoon.

As the neighbor shuffled back inside, clearly avoiding any questions, I knew I'd have no choice but to head to William Houser's house.

.   .   .

William Houser's father lived in the old part of the Sticks, where the homes were clapboard and sagging. On the rickety front porch, I took a moment to collect myself. I was 0 for 2 so far. I needed to squeeze something useful out of someone today. Yet I hovered, not ready to knock. Roommates and girlfriends were one thing. A grieving father was something else.

I pictured the slow release of Dale Houser's tears as he spoke about his son. How his fingers would quake as he grasped to recall facts that still didn't feel true. How he'd bring up his wife, who'd died ten years ago, and point out that his whole family was gone now. I saw his hand reaching for my hand, asking for a comfort I couldn't give.

Over the years, I'd done enough family interviews to know how to power through them. I'd sit as far away as possible so there could be no potential for touch. I'd recite my questions with the precision of a surgeon whose job it is to extract one thing. I'd make my voice strong, blunting every emotion that threatened my focus on the case.

I'd get through this. I'd talk to William Houser's dad. I'd get my win.

As I gathered my courage, the front door swung open. There, filling me, was the scent of apples. Warm cinnamon, mixed with nutmeg, mixed with clove. All at once, the memory bloomed from out of nowhere. My dad with those oven mitts shaped like paws. Apple peels littering the floor. The apple pies Dad loved, lined up on the counter so there was enough for everyone. Dad used to joke that apple pie was his favorite thing about getting his green card and living stateside. Every holiday, every birthday, he worked to perfect his recipe. The crusts were always rubbery and the apples were always soggy and flavorless. Yet we ate them smiling. In all my memories, we were smiling.

Dale Houser's voice was loud. "I said, can I help you?" He had white hair and the slackened features of someone overtired who wants you to know it.

"Yes, I'm. It's . . ." But I couldn't find my words.

"The apples," Dale said. His smile was shadowed. "They have that effect on people."

I shook off a chill. I held out my hand. "Detective Leigh O'Donnell."

At my words, Dale's eyes, which before had seemed large for his face, now squeezed tight.

I let my hand fall. "I'm here to talk with you about your son, William."

Dale crossed his arms. "What for?"

I should have said something vague about doing due diligence, something that didn't raise his hopes that there might be someone to blame for his loss. But I didn't want to come back here. I said, "I'm exploring the possibility that William's death wasn't a suicide."

Dale didn't miss a beat. "What makes you think that?"

But I couldn't reveal the details of an ongoing case. I said, "The same thing that told you I paused just then because of the apples. Instinct."

Dale's face had dark spots that shifted as he thought. At last, he said, "Bear said you were like that."

"You know my uncle?" I couldn't believe it, that Bear hadn't told me he knew William's father—especially after what a big deal he'd made about Eamon knowing William.

Dale nodded. "Bear has been known to loan a car or two out to folks free of charge. People wouldn't accept help if he made a big show out of it. But that uncle of yours, he knows better. He's a good man. He talks about you from time to time."

"Does he?"

"He says you're a pain in the ass."

I set my mouth.

"He also says you've got your mother's heart."

Just like that, something hard lodged in my throat. I held my breath even though I didn't want to, even though every inch of me screamed to get back in the car and drive away and feel nothing.

"Come on," Dale said, creaking open the screen door. "The pies are already in the oven. But if you're not too good for skinning game, I could use the extra hands."

The inside of Dale's house was nothing like it was on the outside. Whereas on the outside, it was derelict and crumbling, inside it was polished and neat. Original hardwood floors spread out over the large living room. They were adorned with a braided rug along with two reclining chairs, angled toward each other, and a teetering pile of books. Half-moon glasses sat on a side table on top of a newspaper with a marked-up crossword. Photographs hung on the walls in handsome clusters: Dale with oversized retro glasses and a turtleneck. William's mother with feathered hair and a polyester dress. William as a toddler in overalls, smiling.

At the end of the room, a simple archway opened up to a kitchen with a yellow tiled floor. Heavy wooden cabinets with small brass fixtures hung low on the walls. The countertops were lined with crinkle-edged pies on cooling racks. A stockpot simmered over a gas range. Above it, an old-fashioned cat clock ticked out the seconds with its tail.

Dale motioned to a knobby chair at a round, wooden table with a pile of limp rabbits on it. He brought over a cutting board and a wooden-handled cleaver. He sat them both in front of the chair. "You know how to skin a rabbit?" Only after searching my face did he allow himself a smirk. "Okay. I'll do the first one. The rest are up to you."

I watched soundlessly as Dale sat in front of the cutting board and brought the cleaver down over each of the rabbit's paws, then its head. He drew a pair of heavy shears across the skin between its hind legs and then yanked until its skin came off in a tube of fur. With his bare fingers, Dale drew out the innards and slopped them into a ceramic bowl. He held up the carcass to show me. His expression made me feel hazed.

"Think you can handle that?" Dale stood and dropped the skinned body into a Styrofoam cooler. I took his place.

I should have been resistant. Yet I didn't hesitate before picking up the cleaver with one hand and a fresh rabbit with the other. As the blade thwacked down over each paw, I felt the pressure in my chest release. I felt calmer still as I ripped the skin to pull it up over its neck like I was taking off its shirt. The innards were warm as I dumped them. I held up the body for inspection. Dale quirked his brow.

"A natural."

I dropped the carcass into the cooler. I picked up the next rabbit. "Tell me about William."

Dale sat in the chair beside me and leaned back.

He rubbed his thumb across his wrist so hard that the skin blanched and then reddened, like it had no circulation. One of the admins at the precinct used to rub her hands like that. She had terrible carpal tunnel. So, I realized, did Dale.

He said, "Will was your usual twenty-five-year-old, though in my opinion, he was better than most. He hung around with Neil Mayer and Duncan Schott. Nobody else that I know of. He wasn't the type to need a big group of people around him. Not like some people."

I brought the cleaver down over the rabbit's head.

"Will convinced the two of them to go with him to some of these houses every weekend, to help folks out. Mow their lawns. Pick up their trash." Dale tried to swallow, but he couldn't quite seem to manage. "His mother and I, we taught him that." His voice was scratchy. "You get out of a community what you put into it. No government is gonna help you. It's up to you."

I continued cutting. So far, this jibed with what Ronan had said about William being *the nice one*. I said, "Who did they go to see each week?"

"Antonia Beck. Maude Hummel. Richard Kimmer. Maybe others."

I was pulling the skin off the rabbit but stopped. "Did you say Maude Hummel?"

Dale rubbed his wrist again. Nodded. "Will always liked Maude. She'd tell him stories about the people in town. Will was a good soul—his mother and I raised him right—but I'll tell you, he loved his gossip."

I dropped the fur onto the pile with the others. "What kind of stories did she tell him?"

The shadows deepened Dale's wrinkles. Grief did that to people, I knew. It made the darkness root out their tucked-away places. Dale said, "You got to understand, we got farmer's markets every Wednesday and Saturday. We make fifteen pies for each of them. And we sell whatever game we catch. That's a lot of prep time for Will to talk my ear off." Dale shook his head. "After a while, I'd just tune him out. Hell if I don't miss it now, though."

I tossed the skinned rabbit in with the others, harder than was necessary. "Did he have any enemies that you're aware of?" I picked up a new rabbit and got to work. "Anyone who'd want him dead?"

Dale blew air through his lips. "No."

"Was William suicidal?"

"Absolutely not. He wouldn't do that to me. Not without so much as a note."

"Did William keep any notebooks or letters? Anything that could indicate his state of mind when he died?"

Dale glanced at the pile of dead rabbits. I could see him weighing his desire to keep me working with his desire to have me gone. It was only a matter of time before the balance switched.

It was a long shot, but worth trying. I said, "Did William ever talk about the caves underneath the falls?"

At this, something shifted in Dale's expression. His shoulders, which before had been hunched forward, now flexed, just an inch. His eyes, which had been so tired, now searched the foreground. He held up a finger. The floorboards creaked. He left the kitchen.

I heard Dale in a room behind me, rustling papers. Something heavy fell to the floor. He didn't pick it up. After a few minutes, Dale emerged holding a folded sheet of paper. He held it out to me.

I set down the cleaver. I wiped my hands on the towel beside me and retrieved my cotton gloves from my jacket pocket. I slipped them on before lifting the sheet from Dale's hands.

It was a map of the caves beneath the falls.

12

THERE WASN'T GUEST PARKING ON THE GROUNDS OF THE
Historical Society, so I had to park on the steep, winding road
leading up to the hill. Earlier that morning, Bear had loaned me
a '95 Chevy Impala that made a rattling noise whenever I
touched the brake. I parked it underneath an aging willow tree,
whose feather-veined leaves canopied the car.

Beside me sat two skinned rabbits wrapped in layers of newspaper. Dale had sent me away with them, shoving the rabbits
into my hands and making it clear that while he appreciated the
help, he didn't want to owe me anything. I shook my head, looking at the bundle. They'd just have to keep.

As I opened the door, my phone buzzed. It was the fourth
time that morning. This time, I picked up.

"Hey, it's me, Ronan."

"I know," I said into the phone. "We've been over this." I
punched down the lock and stepped out of the car.

"Hey so, um, I just wanted to know? Um, when were you

planning on coming in this morning? It's almost ten now and . . ."

I shut the door. The wind blew my hair across my face. I set the phone on the hood. I tugged my hair into a quick ponytail. When I picked back up, Ronan was still talking.

"Once you work here for a couple of years, you know, you can roll in whenever you want. But it's day three, Leigh. You need to kiss the ring, okay? The chief asked if you're avoiding him. I hate to say it but he's got a point."

I'd expected this phone call, but I also needed to work my case. I said, "Just tell him we got our wires crossed and that you're meeting me in the Sticks."

"Okay. Okay great." Relief flooded his voice. "So I'll see you in ten?"

The lane up ahead was all brick. On every fifth row or so, there was a stamp with the name of the bricklayer: H. S. Vogel. I looked at the faded numbers on my palm. I closed my hand. "You get started without me. I'll join you when I get back."

"When you get back?" Ronan lowered his voice. "Leigh, I told you. I'm not supposed to go out on my own. It's not safe."

At the top of the hill, I spotted Dr. Calvin Wagner. He looked just like in his picture on the Historical Society website: same oiled gray hair, same pink skin, same three-piece suit. He was wearing a straw hat and held a metallic cane.

I'd seen Dr. Wagner several times over the years. Onstage during the Copper Falls annual fair. Cutting ribbons at homes that were being deemed historic sites. From those quick glimpses, I knew him to be pompous and prone to long speeches, self-important in the way of high school quarterbacks, of homecoming kings, of branch managers. Yet his family had founded this town. He knew every inch of it. He might be able to tell me what William was looking for the day before he died.

Into the phone, I said, "You'll be fine."

"How can you say that?" Ronan said. "You saw those rifles."

"I'll call you later."

I hung up and set the phone to silent. I slipped it into my suit pocket. I suppressed a pang of guilt. I told myself this case was more important than Ronan's feelings.

Then I took a deep breath and climbed the long drive.

Dr. Wagner stood at the edge of the grounds, between the labyrinthian hedges and the arcade of cherry trees, which, even out of bloom, were like bodies frozen in dance. "Detective O'Donnell," I said, holding out my hand.

"Eamon's niece," Dr. Wagner said, shaking it. His hand was warm and brittle. "I recognize your face."

Up close, I could see Dr. Wagner's features more clearly. One of his eyelids drooped lower than the other, and dark spots stippled his temples and forehead. His lower lip disappeared into his mouth. He was softer than he'd seemed to me all those years ago. Yet his eyes were restless, alert. "Eamon keeps all your press clips from your days as a swimmer," he said. "Right there next to an artist's rendition of Fionn MacCumhaill. It's quite the juxtaposition."

But I wasn't here to talk about my family. I said, "I'm looking into the circumstances surrounding the three deaths on the falls. I understand you knew William Houser."

Dr. Wagner moved his cane first and then his feet, stepping carefully over the pink and blue cobblestones. He walked us away from the giant marble mansion with its arcaded white porch and its round windows that, even from behind me, were like eyes watching.

The Historical Society was at the center of town, the way some old towns are built up around a church. It was a fact I'd never thought too much about. Only now, as we walked away from the building, I recalled Janice's words, that here history was everything.

I said, "How did you know William?"

Dr. Wagner didn't hesitate. "It's a small town. Everyone knows everyone."

I didn't know everyone. But then again, my family wasn't included in this blanket statement. To them, we were just barnacles attached to someone else's ship. "According to my information, William came to see you the day before he died. What did he want to talk about?"

Dr. Wagner's cane paused mid-stride. Just for a moment. Then it continued its course. "My memory isn't what it used to be, Detective. But I believe William wanted to discuss local history. Many do, you see, because of my expertise. They lose touch with their roots. They want connection. I help them find it."

"What do the caves beneath the waterfalls have to do with William's roots?"

The cords of Dr. Wagner's neck tensed. He turned and focused on the path. He took us up a shallow brick staircase. He held the banister as he made a show of concentrating on his steps.

When we got to the top, Dr. Wagner sat on the marble bench, catching his breath. He laid his cane across his lap. I stayed standing.

He said, "Do you know, Detective, that part of the reason the Wagner family was able to settle here was, in fact, because of those caves? Early settlers didn't want to be near them. Many cultures—across Europe and in the New World as well—believed the caves were connected to the underworld. Some even believed there to be a hellhound at the gates. My family, however, has never been swayed by such flights of fancy. They were not afraid of darkness. The lands here were fertile and the water was clean. That's what mattered to them. And just look what we have built."

From the vista, I viewed the rosebushes, which were now just brambles. They were everywhere, patches of thorns. The hedges and cherry trees were gloomy, casting spindly shadows on the grounds. Even the Historical Society stood in shadow. "You must know what's down there," I said. "In the caves."

"Cave scientists," Dr. Wagner said, still admiring the view, "talk of two parts. There is the *twilight zone,* which denotes the parts illuminated by diffuse light. Then there is the *dark zone,* where you can't even see your hands if you hold them before your face.

"In the twilight zones, we've found pottery, inchoate drawings, what you'd expect. But a lot is still unknown. You have to understand, there are miles of caves beneath Copper Falls. Many are completely submerged. It's very much a shadow town, one none of us will ever truly know."

Dr. Wagner looked away from the vista and stood. He searched my face.

He said, "You can see now why the caves were appealing to a lost young man like William." Dr. Wagner drew in breath. "He wanted to believe in mystery."

I didn't like how Dr. Wagner turned subjective impressions into facts. My voice was sharp. I said, "So which was it? Did William Houser want connection? Or mystery?"

Dr. Wagner smiled. Not warmly. He turned and started us back down the steps. He said, "You cannot have a connection unless you are in on a secret together. It forms a bond to know what others don't. Surely, you must have found that in your own relationships." He glanced at my wedding ring. "In your own marriage."

My words came out tight. I said, "It sounds like you and William were close."

"Not especially," he said. We were at the bottom of the steps now. "I'm just very old. A lot of young people have come through my door. Eventually, you notice the patterns."

I was surprised that Dr. Wagner spoke to me with so much candor. He was so unlike the people in the Sticks, who believed, even before I'd opened my mouth, that I would use what they said to make their lives worse. Yet, it didn't seem to occur to Dr. Wagner to be afraid of me. This automatically made me suspicious. I thought to the map Dale Houser had shown me. It was all I had to go off of. I said, "Did William have plans to explore the caves?"

"He didn't express that intent to me."

"Was there something specific he was looking to find?"

"I couldn't say."

I thought back to my conversation with Eamon, decided to take my shot. "Would he have been looking for the shrines?"

It was at that moment when Dr. Wagner's cane hit upon a raised cobblestone. He stumbled forward. His straw hat flipped off. I caught him by the arm. A tuft of hair fell over his forehead.

Dr. Wagner pushed to his feet.

"You'd think," he said, straightening his vest, "I would know my ancestral home well enough to avoid that stone. Yet I hit it every time."

I dusted off his straw hat. I handed it to him. When he reached for it, I met his eyes. I felt a wall come up between us, one that hadn't been there before. I knew that feeling. Every solve started with it. It told me there was something he was hiding, even if I didn't know exactly what. I said, "I'm told that the day before William Houser died, he asked you about the shrines."

Dr. Wagner looked away from me. His lips pressed together. He stepped with more deliberation. He was taking us on the direct route back, the one that avoided the curved footpaths. After a long while, he said, "William never mentioned anything of the sort to me."

Just like that, we were in front of the mansion of the Historical Society, square in the bloom of its shadow. Dr. Wagner shook my hand. He begged off. An appointment, he said. He was of course disappointed he couldn't stay and chat. With a great deal of flourish, he added, "Do let me know if there's anything I can do to help your investigation."

"There is one thing."

His thin eyebrows drew up his face.

I thought about what Dale Houser had said about the three dead men visiting Maude. I thought of what Janice had said about Maude's sister being a secret. I said, "I understand Estella Hummel married your brother."

The smallest flinch, then total blankness.

"Do you two keep in touch?"

"She's my sister-in-law." Dr. Wagner's voice was hollow. "Of course we keep in touch."

"I'd like to speak with her."

"I don't see why you would. I'm sure she didn't know William."

"I thought you said everyone knows everyone."

Dr. Wagner did not so much as blink. "If you want to speak with her, you don't need my permission. But I will warn you. She is not always coherent."

"You mean because of her mental illness?"

"I really do have to be going."

"There isn't a phone number in her file. Or an address."

Dr. Wagner set his jaw. A war played out behind his eyes. At last, he pointed to the road down the hill. "Eight or so miles north. Take a right at the Archer barn. Then another right when you get to the road by the creek."

I pictured the route in my head. I said, "Do any of these roads have names?"

"Not out there they don't."

13

IT WASN'T QUITE ONE O'CLOCK BY THE TIME I REACHED NEIL Mayer's trailer, yet I knew his roommates were home because the hood to their Pontiac Sunfire was open and two bodies leaned over the engine.

I pulled the Impala up behind them, and even at the rattle of my engine, neither straightened. Their neighbor must have told them to expect me. Yet they hadn't fled. This I took to be a good sign.

"Detective Leigh O'Donnell," I said, shutting the door. But before I could get out the next part, their full bodies came into view. They both were women.

They were young, in their late teens, dressed in more or less the same outfit, one in buffalo check, the other in gingham. They each wore mismatched earrings and high-waisted jeans that stopped at their ankles. As I approached, they watched me in the appraising way young women could look at women in their thirties, as if trying to decide if self-possession really could matter more than beauty.

"I'm looking to speak with Neil Mayer's roommates," I said, searching behind them. "Are they home?"

The girls exchanged a look. Immediately, I realized my mistake.

"Ronnie and Mel," I said. "*You're* Neil Mayer's roommates."

The girl in gingham bent back over the engine while the one in buffalo check crossed her arms. "We don't have time for this," she said. "We have to get to work."

"I thought your neighbor said you work nights."

"And before our night job, we clean houses."

I nodded, registering this. "I won't take much of your time. I just want to ask you a few questions about Neil."

The young woman's stance was hard, yet fear spilled off her like a draft. If I wasn't careful, she'd clam up entirely. I had to make her relax.

I looked over the items strewn across the gravel. Plastic tubes and a pump. A dirty bucket and a jug of motor oil. I said, "How long has the *Check Oil* light been on in your car?"

Neither girl spoke.

"And Neil would always change it, right?"

"We can do it," Buffalo Check said.

"Are you Ronnie?"

"She's Mel," said the girl in gingham. "I'm Ronnie."

I sighed. I stepped past them and looked under the hood.

The girls had bought an oil pump extractor online, which, I guessed, is what Neil had always used instead of emptying the oil from underneath. The device consisted of a plastic pump that connected to the car's battery on one end, and the other had tubes that siphoned oil out of the tank. From the looks of it, Mel and Ronnie had tried to hook it up. They'd turned on the car. But the oil hadn't ever traveled through the tubing. That's when they must have turned off the car while they tried to figure out what they'd messed up.

I said, "I can tell you what you did wrong."

"And in exchange?" Mel bit her bottom lip. At my silence, she nodded. "Right."

Ronnie, who I took to be the friendlier of the two, nudged Mel and whispered something that sounded like *We're gonna be late again* and *What's the big deal?* At last, Mel threw up her hands. I motioned for Ronnie to start the car.

"You're wasting gas," Mel barked from her place on the front steps. She had her elbows on her knees and her head in her hands.

"You have to wait for the engine to get to temperature," I said, "or the oil's too thick to go anywhere. Trust me. Just wait."

The engine sounded terrible, even to my untrained ears, and I wondered how old the car was, how much longer it would last. When at last the oil began to flow, Ronnie and Mel exchanged a smile.

Ronnie climbed out of the driver's seat and came to hold the bucket. Mel directed the tubing. When the oil at last puttered out, Ronnie turned off the engine and came around to my side. Freckles dusted her nose and cheeks. She said, "How did you know to do that?"

"My uncle fixes cars. I picked a few things up." The truth was, Bear had shown me more than a few things. He'd made me learn how to take care of a car before letting me own one. At the time, I hated him for it. I couldn't understand why he had to make everything so hard. Now Dale's words came back to me, that Bear had said *you've got your mother's heart.*

Mel uncapped the lid of the new jug of oil. Her voice had lost its edge. "I don't suppose you know how much we should put in?"

I slipped off my jacket and rolled up my sleeves. I held out my hand and she handed over the jug. I weighed the bucket of discarded oil and then started to pour. I said, "How did you two end up living with Neil?"

I was surprised that Mel was the one to speak first. With her arms not crossed, she looked different. Not angry so much as tired. She couldn't have been much older than eighteen. Yet she had the eyes of someone older, someone on the verge of being worn down. "We're friends with his little sister. We were all in band together. But Trista—that's her name—she was better than either of us. She started school at Eastman in September. That's in New York."

I knew of the Eastman School of Music, if only by name. It's where people went when they didn't get in to Juilliard. "What does she play?"

"The harp," said Mel.

"Sounds expensive."

Ronnie pushed a strand of brassy hair behind her ear. "Neil was a musician, so she wanted to be one, too. And he loved Eastman, so . . ."

"Neil also went there for school?" I remembered what Ronan had said about him playing the trumpet.

Ronnie nodded. "He worked under the table. Cleaning

houses during the day. Janitor at night. We'd drop him off on the way to our jobs."

"Why did he work so much?"

Mel shrugged. "I guess no one told him what the interest rates on his student loans were? Or like he never did the math? He just figured he'd get a big orchestra job and be able to pay it all off. But it wasn't enough. He couldn't pay rent and pay off his loans. It was one or the other."

Ronnie added, "He started claiming unemployment, but his loan deferment period was about to end. He was due to start a job at the Cleveland Orchestra this winter. It was his dream. But it wouldn't be enough to make the monthly payments on his loans. He didn't know what he was going to do."

I recapped the jug of oil. I found the lid to the oil tank and screwed it on. "Did you see him the night he died?"

Ronnie looked at Mel. "He wouldn't tell us where he was going. But . . ."

Mel held my eyes. "He took my waterproof flashlight. It was the monogrammed one my dad gave me before he was deployed."

I said, "Neil knew it was special to you?"

"He swore he'd bring it back."

I shook my head. "People break promises all the time."

Mel didn't flinch. She lifted her chin. "Not Neil. Not when it came to things like that."

When I pushed open the front door to my parents' house, I expected Simone to come running toward me, the way she always did when she'd been with the sitter all day. Instead, I heard voices from the kitchen. I followed down the side hallway until I found them, Frankie and Simone. They were wearing trash bags with holes punched out for their heads and arms.

"Mommy!" Simone said. Her feet pounded against the rug as she zoomed over to me. I shifted the package of rabbits in my hand as I lifted her up. On the counter lay a carton of eggs, filled now with sinewy eggshells, spotted with wet. Flour dusted the floor in bursts. There were butter wrappers stuck to Frankie's trash bag like scout badges. The windows were open, but still, I could smell it. Burnt chocolate and smoke. The kitchen reeked of it.

Uncle Frankie flipped his hand as if holding a tray. "See, when I asked the young lady what she liked to eat, she told me cookies. Seeing as how we didn't have any cookies, I thought we'd whip some up. Simone here said you didn't like it when she messed up her clothes. So, well . . ." He scratched the back of his head. "We improvised."

Simone pressed her hand against my ear. She whispered, "We've been here for hours."

Frankie held up a finger. "I told you. The road to success is paved with failure. This is the winning batch. I know it!"

To Simone, I said, "Have you eaten anything?"

As she shook her head, Frankie interjected, "She will soon. This is the one!" As if to prove his point, he creaked open the door to the oven. He grimaced and gently closed it.

"Here." I tossed him the package.

He pulled up the edge of the newsprint. An eyebrow lifted. "What's this?"

"Lunch."

. . .

An hour later, we'd all eaten what Frankie had christened *Thumper Stew,* and Simone had gone down for her nap. Frankie went down for his *siesta* as he called it, since according to him, grown men didn't take naps.

I'd cleared off a spot on the kitchen island and started a pot of coffee. I had the case files spread out before me like tarot cards, whose messages had to be interpreted to be known. I sat at a bar stool as I added my notes from the day's interviews while they were still fresh in my head.

I didn't have much to go on so far. Yet it wasn't nothing. I knew that William, Neil, and Duncan had gone around their neighborhood helping people out, including Maude Hummel, who'd told William stories. I also knew that William had recently gotten interested in the caves beneath the falls. He'd even gone so far as to acquire a map, though whether he'd been looking for shrines or something else, I still couldn't say for sure.

Even though Duncan's girlfriend wouldn't talk to me, she did accuse me of coming round to *clean up your own mess,* which meant Duncan had had beef with the police.

Then there was the fact that the night Neil died, he'd taken a sentimental flashlight and promised to bring it back. It seemed probable, in my mind at least, that he had plans to explore the caves with William, and that they really had thought they'd be returning.

I swigged coffee from a china mug and examined the autopsy reports for what felt like the hundredth time. I took in the men's shorn hair, their smooth faces, the careful trim of their nails. I thought of a mass suicide that a colleague had investigated years ago. A cult leader had convinced seven disciples to drink poison with him, only the leader had lied and hadn't poisoned himself. He was convicted of seven counts of murder in the first degree.

Those, too, had been manicured bodies. Those, too, had been people prepared to die.

I turned to the last page of my files, to the map from William Houser's things. It was hand-drawn, with crinkled edges. It had a crease in the middle where it'd been folded. A dark spot at the top was labeled *sinkhole,* and below it jagged tunnels spread out like the spikes of a splatter of blood. In various sections were tiny, dark drawings, of bats, of spiders, of snowflakes, of steam.

As I examined the map, my pulse steadied. My breath came in full and deep.

The caves looked totally normal. There was no indication of any shrine.

14

"RONAN," I SAID. "CAN WE PICK UP THE PACE?"

It'd taken me most of the afternoon to finally track down where William had gotten the map of the caves so I could get that person to explain it to me. Just as Simone and Frankie were waking and I was about to leave the house, Ronan had caught up with me in the foyer. He'd insisted on driving. Now, forty-five minutes into the hour-long drive to the University of Toledo, we rolled along Route 20 as traffic sped around us.

Ronan shook his head and released his breath in puffs. His foot eased off the gas, slowing the cruiser to a crawl. "I just can't believe you did that to me. I can't believe I *let you* do it to me again. I vouched for you, Leigh. I put my reputation on the line."

"The speleologist said she has fifteen minutes before her next lecture." I felt for the map of the caves in my jacket pocket. "All I ask is that we go the speed limit."

"Then, instead of meeting the chief like we're supposed to, you have me driving you to Toledo to meet a cave scientist for god knows why. You don't even care how much trouble you could get me in."

"You didn't have to drive me."

Ronan's knuckles were white on the wheel. "You lied to me. You said you'd come help me with the rounds, but you never came."

I watched the clock on the dash. It ticked to 3:28. Behind us, the cage rattled. "Ronan, let's get to the university first. Then we can—"

"No." His voice was indignant. "Not until you explain yourself."

"Explain myself?"

He clenched his jaw.

Anger spiked through me. "Okay, you want to talk? Let's talk. How about you start by telling me what those rounds are really about?"

I shifted in my seat to face him.

"I know you want me to believe you're the good guy here. That you're this sweet Sheriff Taylor figure and Copper Falls is some Mayberry knockoff. So tell me, why do the people in the Sticks greet you with their rifles?"

Ronan set his mouth.

"Why was Duncan Schott's girlfriend so angry with the police?"

I thought of my encounters with William's dad and Neil's roommates.

"Why doesn't anyone in the Sticks trust the cops? Why don't you explain that to me?"

Ronan glanced out the window. For a moment, I thought

he'd deny everything, that he might still try to play at this all being an innocent act of public service. Instead, he adjusted his hands on the wheel. He pressed down a little harder on the gas. The russet fields on either side of us blurred into streaks. I released my breath. He said, "I'm not saying they're wrong."

"You're not saying who's wrong?"

Ronan blew air through his lips. He seemed to be figuring out a way to say this next part. "Remember when I told you about that guy who tried to build a meth lab?"

I vaguely remembered this from that day on the phone. I'd told Ronan I wasn't interested in catching drug dealers.

"Well, there's a little more to the story."

Ronan scrubbed his hand through his hair. Flecks of silver were just coming in. They caught in the low-hanging sun.

"Some months back, the chief conducts this secret investigation into the meth problem in the Sticks.

"I didn't even know we had a meth problem. But that's what he's like, the chief. He gets his hunches and goes after them. Sometimes without telling anybody what he's up to. He's like you in that way."

Something told me not to be flattered by the comparison.

"Anyway, the chief learns that about a dozen or so households out there were involved in selling drugs. So he gets some help from the sheriff's office and they do some raids."

"Why didn't the DEA handle it?"

A sheepish look from Ronan. A shrug. "I don't know."

"You didn't ask?"

"I did ask. The chief gave a reason. I just—"

"You wanted Chief Becker to like you." I looked away from him.

"You don't know how it is here," Ronan said. "You can't make waves in a small pond. You just can't."

I sighed. "Then what?"

Ronan's voice was chastened. "The sheriff and these deputies go on this drug raid. They find meth obviously, but they also find just stacks and stacks of cash. I guess the people out there don't believe in banks. You know the type, right? Anyway, the chief says it's all drug money. He confiscates it."

"All of it?"

"Yeah." Ronan glanced at me. "The meth, the money, all of it."

The technical term was *civil asset forfeiture*. It meant that cops could seize assets they believed were gained through criminal means. But that belief could be based on anything. Actual evidence, or even just a hunch.

"I guess there was a problem with the chain of evidence or something," Ronan said. "So nobody was charged."

"They put all that manpower into meth raids and didn't make a single arrest?" That sounded like a grade-A fuckup to me. No wonder no one had mentioned it.

"Now, you'd think," Ronan said, "since these guys aren't being charged with anything, they'd get their money back. But that's not how it works. The law says they have to prove this wasn't drug money, or else their cash is gone forever."

I nodded. The law was the same everywhere. In other words, cops taking advantage of civil asset forfeitures was a problem everywhere. Departments could use it to get rich. I said, "And now every day, the police department sends two armed officers to visit the houses of the people targeted in the raids? Why?"

Ronan fiddled in his pocket. He found a pack of gum. He unwrapped a piece and chewed it loudly. "The chief wants us to see if they're still making meth. He says we're supposed to check their eyes for dilation. Look around for anything suspicious. He wants to try again to make arrests. He doesn't want to go in unless he's sure we'll find something we can use."

Ronan's signal ticked as he turned off the highway. He slowed as we curved along the exit ramp. There was a stop sign at the end of it. He looked both ways before moving forward.

"Why didn't you just tell me this?" I said. "Why all this bullshit about wellness checks?"

Ronan was silent until we got to the traffic light. There was a Taco Bell on one side of us and a Wendy's on the other. A Starbucks a little farther on. "I thought if you knew the truth, you wouldn't want to be a part of it. Everything's so black and white with you. This is gray."

Ronan shouldn't have lied to me. But he was right. I didn't want to be a part of it.

The light turned green. Ronan accelerated. We passed an Applebee's and a Texas Roadhouse. It smelled of gasoline and frying grease. He said, "But now you understand why I needed you there today? These people we're checking in on, they think we're going to arrest them. If we spot drugs or paraphernalia, they may get scared and start shooting. I mean, what do they have to lose?"

"Were Duncan's, Neil's, and William's houses targeted in the raid?"

Ronan shrugged. "They've never been on my rounds list."

"Why Maude Hummel?" I couldn't picture her running drugs. Especially not from a wheelchair.

"I don't know," Ronan said, leaning back as he drove. "The chief said it was confidential." He chewed his gum with his mouth open. I felt the crack of it under my fingernails. "All I know is when they got to her house, they hit the jackpot."

Ronan's eyes were shining. They shifted to meet mine.

"In a trunk upstairs," he said, "they found a half a million dollars."

I thought back to her derelict house, its chipped paint, its broken tiles. "Where did she get that kind of money?"

"I don't know," Ronan said. "But the department confiscated every last cent."

We parked in the fire lane in front of the geology building and climbed up the cement staircase that led to the second floor. At last, we arrived at Dr. Ortiz's classroom. The door was open, so we let ourselves in.

Spelunking helmets and waterproof overalls hung from hooks on the walls. A side table held an open backpack, with ropes and a pick. Stainless-steel lab desks stood scratched and shining. It smelled of hard water and dirt and, faintly, of candles.

Paintings hung on the walls around Dr. Ortiz's desk: of a black-haired woman in a fringed jacket with an eagle over her head, of a Native woman wrapped in a colorful robe searching the moon. There were woven blankets, too, with blocky designs and saturated colors. There were scientific representations of rocks.

I cleared my throat. "Dr. Ortiz?"

Dr. Ortiz was brown skinned, with a thin frame. She wore a cable-knit sweater and smelled of lemon verbena and sage. She stood as we approached.

"I'm Detective O'Donnell," I said. "We spoke on the phone."

Ronan stepped in beside me. "*We* did *not* speak on the phone." He held out his hand. "But it's a pleasure to meet you all the same."

Dr. Ortiz quirked her mouth at Ronan. "Well, aren't you a ray of sunshine in a dark place?" Her bangles clanged as she shook his hand.

"I go by that sometimes, sure," Ronan said, smiling. "You can also call me Officer Ronan O'Donnell."

"Two O'Donnells?" Dr. Ortiz sat. She looked from me to Ronan. Her heavy glasses made her face seem small. "This is where you say *but no relation*."

Ronan eased onto the seat beside mine. "Ah, but I don't like to lie. Not when I can help it. This is my big sister. She taught me everything I know."

"That must be interesting," Dr. Ortiz said, shifting her gaze between us. "Working with family."

As they made small talk about the heavy rains this year and what we could expect for winter, I scanned the papers on Dr. Ortiz's desk. There were a handful of maps as well as graph paper with penciled-in numbers, puckered and torn at their edges, some still a little wet.

There were tools I didn't recognize and others that I did—an L-shaped ruler, a protractor, and a graphing calculator. A compass with a pencil attached to its arm. Then my eyes found it, a single drawing, black and white, like something from an old book.

It was the size of a tarot card, with heavy shading and smooth lines. It showed a woman, naked except for her long hair, which waved over the length of her. With one arm, she dipped a gourd-shaped jug into a ravine. With the other she tipped a gourd-shaped jug over her head. A galaxy poured over her. She had one foot on land, the other in the water. She balanced between two worlds.

"The Hunter," Dr. Ortiz said.

I blinked up. My mind cast back to Maude Hummel. She'd also used that word.

"She's part of the traditions of a First Nation that lived in Copper Falls. That is, before the colonizers wiped them out."

I recalled the history I'd memorized as a child. I said, "You're saying Copper Falls wasn't abandoned when the settlers arrived?"

"Of course not," Dr. Ortiz said. "That land was sacred."

That word *sacred* snagged on something in my head. I thought of the shrines William was looking for, of the ritualistic state of his and his friends' bodies. I said, "Do you know anything about the shrines beneath Copper Falls?"

"Yes," Dr. Ortiz said.

A stirring in the room settled.

"In fact, they're the same shrines that interested your young friend."

"William Houser?"

Dr. Ortiz nodded.

I took out my notebook. My skin had the familiar buzz that

came from a promising lead, that feeling that this could be the interview that cracks open the case. I went through my initial questions quickly. I confirmed William had come to see Dr. Ortiz the day before he died. I asked what they spoke about. She verified he'd asked about the shrines.

"Tell me about them," I said. "Where are they? What are they for?"

Dr. Ortiz looked at her watch. "I'm sorry but I have to go to my lecture."

"Dr. Ortiz," I said. "We need just a few more minutes of your time."

"I can't—"

Ronan interjected, "Professor, do you like music?"

Dr. Ortiz furrowed her brow. The question was out of nowhere.

Ronan leaned forward. "Neil Mayer, one of the men who died, he was a really talented musician. And here." Ronan scrolled through his phone and held up a picture of Duncan Schott. It looked like he'd pulled it from a social media site. "Have you ever seen such a handsome face?"

Dr. Ortiz opened her mouth.

"And William," Ronan continued. "You met him. You must have seen immediately what a good person he was."

Dr. Ortiz started to stand.

"Please," Ronan said. His eyes were large. His face was open. "Three young men in our community are dead. Their families need to know why."

I was embarrassed at Ronan's earnestness, at the rawness of

his emotions. Yet I also felt the shift in the air. Dr. Ortiz's body slackened. Her nostrils flared as she sighed.

"Ten minutes," she said. Her wooden chair creaked as she sat. "I only have ten minutes."

Dr. Ortiz told us how, in that area of Ohio, there were at least three dominant Sovereign Nations: the Kickapoo, the Erie, and the Shawnee peoples. In the 1700s and 1800s, the United States formed a number of treaties with the Nations, most of which were signed under duress. These led to the Ohio Removal. That is, the indigenous peoples were supposed to leave Ohio. However, many refused. "It was the land their families had lived on for generations," Dr. Ortiz said. "They would not give it up."

Dr. Ortiz leaned back in her chair. She folded her hands over her lap. I kept writing.

"The government declared that the people who stayed were *no longer Indian,* ensuring they'd never be what we call *enrolled members* and so would never have access to federal help.

"These people were given the choice of either assimilating to white culture or going into hiding. Those who went into hiding formed their own Nations. One of those Nations relocated to the area now known as Copper Falls. They were the ones who first discovered the shrines."

Dr. Ortiz folded her glasses on the desk. She framed them with her hands.

"The shrines had been built by a Nation even older than the one that migrated there, yet the displaced Nation kept the shrines sacred, the way a Christian might consecrate an abandoned church even if it was of a different denomination.

"But when the Wagners settled in Copper Falls, they murdered the Nation that was living there. In doing so, they destroyed all connection to the shrines. Those shrines might have been lost forever if it hadn't been for two little girls.

"Years ago," she said, "the girls were playing in the caves underneath the falls. The caves are treacherous. There are sinkholes and cavities. The girls could've been swept away by an underwater current. They could have died. But you see, neither of the girls did die."

Dr. Ortiz leafed through the papers on her desk. She pulled out a map identical to the one in my jacket pocket.

"Right here," she said. She pointed to one of the deeper caves. "They broke through a false wall. They found a room filled with ancient pottery. Handmade beads hung from the walls. Semiprecious stones were carved into shapes. They were arranged around an altar. Around a body."

Dr. Ortiz's eyes shifted color. They became glassier, more amber.

"The body had long ago decomposed," Dr. Ortiz said, "so it was only a skeleton. Yet it was not *only* a skeleton, if you understand me. When the girls shone their lanterns upon her, she glittered in the light. She was covered with calcite. It made her bones plump, sparkling."

Dr. Ortiz edged forward in her chair. So did Ronan. I kept writing.

"This was not just a bunch of pottery. Not just a skeleton. This was a shrine. The skeleton was a human sacrifice. This was the shrine to the Hunter."

My heart, my breath, my pen stilled. I felt the pieces come

together in my head, in the way of magnets, attracted by the other's charge. Maude had called me a hunter. The shrine William was looking for might have been the shrine to the Hunter. William's dad had said that William liked to visit Maude because of her stories.

I thought of the uneasiness I felt with Maude, the way my mind kept calling me back to her, the way my body insisted that, despite all evidence to the contrary, she was connected to my case.

I said, "Do you know the names of the girls who found the shrine?"

Dr. Ortiz shook her head.

"And there were other shrines, too?"

"Over the next few years," Dr. Ortiz said, "crews found evidence of a shrine to the Shaman and one to the Creator. But we've never been able to actually find them. Unless there's a serious drought again, we likely never will. As you know, the rains this year have been exceptional."

"Do people know about these shrines?" I asked. "Are they a secret?"

"We've been in touch with the Historical Society in Copper Falls about continuing our excavation. But they shut us down. Some nonsense about preserving the Wagners' heritage. As if the First Nations had anything to do with them."

I ran my tongue along the inside of my mouth. I swallowed. Dr. Wagner had sworn he hadn't known a thing about the shrines. But he had known the whole time.

Yet, I still didn't know why William and his friends wanted to find the shrines. What did they think the shrines could give them? Did it have anything to do with the ritualistic way they died?

I said, "The Shaman, the Creator, the Hunter, these are gods? Beings people pray to?"

"Not exactly," Dr. Ortiz said.

Ronan said, "They're archetypes, actually."

Dr. Ortiz and I both stared at him.

"You know, frequently used symbols in mythology. Carl Jung writes about them." Ronan shrugged. "I've been taking online psychology classes. They're free, you know. Anybody can take them."

Dr. Ortiz continued. "To the Nation that lived here, these archetypes—the Hunter, the Shaman, and the Creator—were also real beings. They were eternal, but they could die and be reborn. Yet unlike many Western religions, which since the Athenians have placed their eternal beings in the sky, many First Nations believed that they—"

"—resided in the earth," I said.

Dr. Ortiz's expression was nettled. "Don't tell me you're taking online classes, too? Can this shift to online learning wait until I retire?"

I thought of Eamon talking at dinner about the ancient Celts. Of the sacred hills all over Ireland. It finally made sense why William had gone to Eamon's lecture. He'd wanted to learn about accessing the sort of eternal beings that lived in the earth. He'd wanted to know it badly enough to visit Eamon, Dr. Wagner, and Dr. Ortiz all on the day before he died.

There was a connection here. I felt it, even if I couldn't say exactly what it was.

Dr. Ortiz pointed to an enlarged photograph on the wall

behind her. In it, an archipelago of grassy hills rose up over a prairie.

She said, "That's why all across the Midwest—especially in Ohio—there are so-called Indian mounds. It's also why many Sovereign Nations put their altars not on the tops of mountains but deep in the earth. It's one of the many reasons the earth is sacred to them."

"Was there anything specific people used the shrines to pray for?" I asked. "Anything that could help us understand what William and his friends might have been looking to find?"

"No," Dr. Ortiz said. She put on her glasses. They made her eyes owl-like and searching. "But as I'm sure I told William, the caves are treacherous. If you're traveling that deep into the earth, there's something you want very much. You're willing to risk your life for it."

15

Wednesday, November 8

THERE IS A DREAM I HADN'T HAD IN YEARS, NOT SINCE BEFORE Eric, not since before the NYPD. But after eating dinner standing up in the kitchen and then checking in with Simone, after twisting and wrapping her hair and tucking her into bed, the dream arrived again. My own message in a bottle, one I'd long ago tossed, forgotten, into the sea.

I am gliding across an icy lake. My skates make a sound like knives sharpening. Fluffy snow curls around me in the way of snow globes, in the way of magic. I smile up at the deep blue sky and think of nothing.

Then a crack like thunder. A fall and a descent. A cold so deep that it grips my chest. It chills my blood. In the dream, I am thrashing.

I have no air, only the crush of ice around my body. It freezes everything.

I am sure I will die.

I brace for it.

Then, before me, there it is. A gleam of red so bright as to be imagined. A snake. It waves across my vision.

A switch flips inside me. At the improbability of it. At its beauty. At its life and my destruction. The quiet overtakes me.

I stop thrashing. I stop fighting the cold. I yield to it, to the life that will continue without me. I yield to the inevitability of my death.

I am still.

The snake slides above me, up, up, like a flag, like a kite. Light shines through the dusty pane of ice. I think of church. Of prayer. Without meaning to, without choosing it, my body rises up.

I rise up toward the snake, up toward the place where the water is not still and frozen. The wind punches it down in dents.

I break the surface. My mouth finds air.

I am alive.

I broke from the dream.

I blinked.

My eyes adjusted to the dim light. I squinted from it, blinded.

My childhood bedroom shocked me. Simone beside me shocked me. I looked at the bedside clock. It was almost four A.M. Goose pimples ran up and down my arms, over my chest, up my neck. I went to rub them, to scrub the bone-chill from my limbs. But when I lifted my arm, my hand was full.

I held open my palm. I removed the crushed paper from inside it. It was still in its evidence bag. I laid it across my lap.

It was the map of the caves, the one Dale Houser had found in his son's things, the map Dr. Ortiz had given him.

I studied it. This time, I honed in on the tiny drawings that before had seemed irrelevant. A cluster of bats at the edge of one cave. A snowflake in another. I drew in breath.

There, right near the entrance to the false wall that gave way to the Hunter's shrine, was the unmistakable coil of a snake.

It was still dark outside when the tires of the Impala spun uselessly in the mud. There would be no driving back. When the time came to head home, I'd be going on foot.

I cranked the emergency brake. I lifted the backpack I'd dug out from my closet. I tucked my hand underneath my sweatshirt and ran a thumb over the shoulder of my swimsuit. I couldn't tell if it was tight now because my body had changed, or if it'd always hurt to breathe and I'd simply learned not to mind.

I kept the headlights on as I picked my way across crisped leaves and snapped twigs and roots that grew up from the ground like tentacles. I inched over a slippery patch where the mud clumped. From someplace high above me, an owl gave a throaty whoop. Farther off, a coyote bayed at the taunt.

As I walked, I searched the ground in front of me, careful to keep an eye out for any trace of the victims. William Houser might have traveled along this path. Neil Mayer might have shone his roommate's flashlight at the place I was shining mine now. Duncan Schott might have been trying to talk them out of it, this hunt that would end their lives.

The higher I got, the more treacherous grew the terrain. The mud up here was so wet that I could only climb the hill by hanging onto saplings, by pulling at the heavy branches of nearby trees, by keeping low to the ground. As I worked my way up, the wind fluttered the leaves above me. In the distance, water gurgled and crashed against rocks. The mud became rocky. The rocks became smooth. The scarred birches stood like glowing sentinels, like protection.

At last, I came upon the spot. The moonlight found the limestones and made them bright. I pulled out the map. I turned in a circle. I stopped when I saw the entrance to the caves. The steam rose out of the fissure like fog.

I stood above the crevasse looking down. I told myself all I'd wanted was to find it, to see if, outside the caves, there was any trace of William, Neil, or Duncan. Yet I was wearing my swimsuit. I knew what I was going to do the same way that coyote knew it would hunt.

I undressed with the efficiency of someone trying not to think. I tied one end of a long rope to a thick-trunked tree. I belted the other around my waist, pulling it tight. I tied the knot the way my mom had taught me when we'd go camping. I brushed aside fronds and saplings. Mud flecked my thighs, my wrists. I grabbed the Maglite. I sat at the edge of the sinkhole.

As the steam covered my legs, my face, Eric's voice was in my ear: *Don't be reckless.*

My body's response was in my blood: *This is safe.*

I'd left a note on the kitchen table. If I climbed down and couldn't get out, someone would come and find me. It was low tide. If I wanted to search for traces of William, Neil, and Duncan, it had to be now.

I held tight to the flashlight. I eased myself down through the crack in the limestone.

I closed my eyes and held my breath.

Mud slicked my back. Bubbles formed around my face. Water rushed over me. My stomach slipped to my chest. I closed my mouth. Five seconds. Ten.

My feet at last gained purchase. My knees scraped rock. I landed in a pool of water and blew out my breath. I pushed to stand.

I'd made it.

The water here was waist-high, bathwater warm. I wiped my face and beamed the flashlight all around me. What I saw stole my breath.

Stalactites hung like teeth from the high ceiling. Water dripped into a pool of black. A cloud of bats flapped out from a crevasse and swept through to the faraway tunnel, toward the one that, if the map was right, led all the way to the Hunter's shrine.

I kicked as I swam toward it. My breath mixed with sulfur, mixed with steam. My skin hummed at each sound: of water lapping, of ceiling drips, of breath. I should've been worried about the darkness. I should have been scared of the unknown. Yet my skin and my blood kept telling me there was nothing to fear. Not here.

I climbed over a ridge of stalagmites, then through another tunnel. Stone scratched the bottoms of my feet. Water dripped onto my forehead. My shoulders relaxed down my back. I'd just started to look for the crawl space when the beam of my flashlight shortened into a stump.

In front of me stood a wall.

I pressed my palm against the stone. I searched with the flashlight.

It was no use. This was a dead end.

In a matter of seconds, the darkness of the cave blackened to pitch. The space around me closed in. I had nowhere to go but back.

I swallowed. I rubbed my arms to suppress a chill. I started back toward the entrance. I was sure I'd missed something. I was unsure what that could be.

At the far end of the tunnel, I felt my neck. The fine hairs there were raised in warning.

In one swift movement, I turned. I shone the flashlight across the darkness. Slowly, the light captured the wall, inch by inch.

When I found it, my stomach clenched.

There, higher than any single person could reach, was a hole just wide enough for one person to squeeze through.

I held my flashlight high above my head. I tried to plumb its depth. But there was only darkness.

16

BY THE TIME I ENTERED THE POLICE STATION, IT WAS NINE o'clock in the morning.

My pants were knee-high in mud and the soles of my boots tracked clods. At the front desk, Janice stared at me from over her glasses. An officer walking out from the kitchenette stopped at the threshold, a breakfast sandwich half in his mouth. The precinct was closer to where the Impala had stalled than the house. I needed to borrow Ronan's van so I could go back and change.

Up ahead, Ronan was deep in conversation with a man whose back was to me. He said in a voice like a shout, "See, Chief? What'd I tell you? Car trouble." But as he said this, Ronan didn't look relieved. He was pulling at a tuft of his hair like he was going to yank it out. He used to do this when we were kids and our parents were fighting. It didn't signal anything good.

When I arrived beside Ronan, Chief Becker turned to face

me. He was small, built like a runner, with wraparound sunglasses that hung from his neck. He wore a Class B uniform, like everyone else. But unlike the others, his entitlement was everywhere, from his wide stance to the assessing way he took me in.

"We meet at last," he said, holding out his hand. A flash of a smile. A wink of yellowing teeth. "I was beginning to think Ro invented you."

I cocked my head at my brother. *Ro?*

Our parents had been the only ones to call him that. Not even Cathy had crossed that line. Ronan shrugged.

"Ro said you had a problem with the car?" Becker said. "An issue with the brakes?"

Something about his tone made me think of slapped wrists and denied hall passes. Something about how close he was standing to Ronan made me think of fathers-in-law who insist on you calling them *Dad*. "I tried to take a '95 Chevy Impala off-roading," I said. "I'd say the brakes were the least of my problems."

Ronan stiffened.

The smile fell from Becker's face. "In this mud?" He crossed his arms. "That seems like an error in judgment."

I crossed mine, too. "It's only an error if there was something I needed to get back for."

Becker shot Ronan a *What the actual fuck* look. Ronan's eyes gave a *She's never like this* reply. Becker zeroed in on me.

"I understand you have a big personality," he said. "That it caused you some problems at your last job. Ro assured me that's not going to be an issue here."

"It won't be, sir," Ronan said. "It's only her fourth day. She's still adjusting."

Becker chewed his lip.

I knew I was being unreasonable—Becker had given me a job, hadn't he?—but a wire had tripped in my head. I did not like this man. I didn't care he didn't like me.

"Ro says you're good," Becker said at last. "I trust him. When you were late again today, I called your former captain. He vouched for you, too."

The anger slipped out of me. Something sharp cut into my throat. *My captain?*

"But actions speak louder than words, Detective. Your attitude may have won you some pissing contests in New York City. Maybe you had something to prove, you being a woman and all. But it doesn't have any place here. Do I make myself clear?"

Blood drained from my face. *Eric. He spoke to Eric?*

"You have to show up on time. You have to show up clean. And dressed appropriately." Becker looked down at my jeans and muddy swimsuit. "And you have to show up ready for duty. No more *errors in judgment*. Understood?"

My voice came from the pit of my stomach. "What did Eric say?"

"*Captain* Walker you mean?" Chief Becker's eyes were unbelieving. "I should have done my due diligence before you came. But for better or worse, I'm the trusting sort." He cupped his hand over Ronan's shoulder. "Especially when it comes to those I consider family." Becker gave Ronan's shoulder a squeeze. "I'm due at Calvin Wagner's in ten. Take the day, Leigh. Get yourself sorted. I'll expect you here tomorrow. Ready to do your job."

An air bubble lodged in my throat.

It was still there when, a minute later, Becker's cruiser pulled away.

Ronan stepped toward me. His face was a mess of emotion. He started to chastise me. Ask what the hell I was thinking. All of it was a jumble of words. None of it was comprehensible.

I grabbed Ronan's keys from his desk. My legs were heavy as I ran to his minivan.

I drove like an old woman, like someone who no longer trusts her ability to see the road. I didn't trust it. I didn't trust the road to still be there for me. I didn't trust the van to take me over it.

Eric knew I'd lied to him about coming here just to visit. We were in last-straw territory as it was. This could be his.

17

WHEN ERIC AND I HAD FIRST GOTTEN TOGETHER, HE'D BEEN my lieutenant and I'd been less than a year with the gold shield. There was something between us right from the start. It was there at that very first briefing, when Sergeant Bailey had said I was wrong to assume our killer was female, and Eric had cut him off mid-sentence with a simple "Detective O'Donnell is right."

It there when, weeks later, we celebrated a high-profile solve at McSorley's and Eric handed me a pint. Our fingers touched. It was only for a few seconds, but it was like a plug finding its charge.

It was like that every time we were in the same room together, that extra pulse that made even the softest sounds—the pushing in of a chair, the latch of a door—into something loud and electric, like our bodies had tuned in to each other's frequencies, waiting for the signal from the other one to go.

Then came the case that made Eric cross the line.

A young woman had been stabbed to death while on a night-time run in Battery Park. She was a student at NYU. Her phone was missing. The on-the-scenes made a big deal out of it being a mugging. Even my partner agreed, saying how, with no witnesses and no murder weapon, there wasn't a chance in hell we'd catch them, not unless the mugger was stupid enough to sell the vic's phone.

I shouldn't have had an opinion. Or, if I did have the audacity to have *thoughts,* I should've known to defer any judgment to my partner. He was older, more experienced, better liked. Yet, from the moment I'd stepped under that crime scene tape, I'd stopped being able to think with my brain.

We'd gotten to the body within an hour of the time the guy on State Street had heard a woman's *bloodcurdling scream.* She was two miles from her apartment in the East Village, in running clothes and sneakers. Her keys were tucked into a little pocket in the back of her pants. Her headphones were hanging from her ears, attached now to nothing. Clearly, my partner concluded, she'd been on a run when she'd been caught by a mugger. She'd resisted and ended up dead.

As he recited his theory to me, I looked at the rose of blood that had bloomed at the victim's chest. It covered her hands, as thick as gloves. My eyes traced her forehead, her neck, her armpits. Yet for all the mess of her, I couldn't see so much as a bead of sweat.

In the time between when she'd died and when we found her, her sweat could have evaporated. I certainly wasn't an expert on any of that. Yet her hair wasn't wet, either. It wasn't even damp at the nape of her neck. Not even in those wispy hairs along her forehead, the ones that cling to my face when I walk fast.

Before I consulted my partner, before I so much as asked the techs if what I was about to do was okay, I got down on my hands and knees beside her body. I smelled her.

In the background, the techs said how I was getting fresh with the corpse. My partner joked about being teamed up with a K9. I let the edge of my nose hover against the tip of her jaw. She smelled of rusted pennies, face wash, and gum, but not even a hint of sweat. Instead, I smelled perfume.

And I knew.

Hours later, I stood in Eric's office. I told him what I'd done. How I'd pulled in the boyfriend right then, before he'd even had a chance to clean the blood from the soles of his boots. I'd nailed the interrogation. Even then, I'd had a knack for them. The boyfriend had signed his confession before the food carts so much as rolled up on Fifth Avenue.

When I was done speaking, Eric just sat there, staring. It was like I was that faceless person on the subway who opens her mouth to sing and you stop because, no matter how long you've lived in New York, you still are capable of awe.

"I've been working this job for ten years," he said, his voice a deep cello. "I don't know that anybody has ever solved a case before by scent. Not like that."

I sat on the other side of the desk from him. The bullpen behind us was empty. It was Sunday morning. The church guys were at church and the non-church guys were sleeping off last night's mistakes. It was just Eric and me. I wanted to impress him. I wanted a reason for him to pin me with his gaze and not release me until I screamed for him to stop. I said, "You'd be surprised what you can know about people from the way they smell."

He raised an eyebrow. "Is that so?" I couldn't tell if he was humoring me. But I didn't need certainty. I just needed a chance.

I said, "Detective Harris spends every morning in his little greenhouse. With his tomato plants. He grows them, even in winter. He dreams of living someplace with land."

Eric's eyes didn't leave mine.

"Detective Rosin is losing his hair. He used to scratch his head when he was thinking. Now he stops himself. He takes the smell of minoxidil everywhere."

"And me?" Eric's voice was soft now. "What do you smell on me?"

It wasn't the question itself but the way he said it. I knew we were crossing a line. It was a line I could have backed away from. A laugh to ease the tension. A shrug to say I really hadn't thought about his smell at all. Instead, I kept my eyes locked on his.

"You've gone this far," he said. His lips separated. His chest rose from underneath his suit. "Don't stop now."

"In the mornings, like now, you smell of Dove soap and Listerine."

Heat bloomed up the length of me. I sat taller.

"In the afternoons, when you come back from the gym, you smell like eucalyptus and mint."

My heart hammered up my throat. My body leaned toward his. My face was hot.

"At night, when you come in after being on call, you smell of rooibos and Old Spice."

I thought to the musk and wool scent of his skin, how just a trace of it could heat the coils inside me. Like now.

I said, "But you never smell of alcohol. Never any cologne."

"And what does that tell you?" Eric said. "That I have good hygiene?"

I didn't second-guess. I just spoke. "You believe you have to be perfect. You're afraid of being seen as sloppy or poor. You're afraid of showing weakness."

I was out on a ledge now. I couldn't step it back. I didn't want to.

"You do everything you're supposed to do," I said. "You hold on to that bundle of *shoulds* like it's a ballast. You're afraid of what will happen if you do what you want."

The tip of Eric's tongue touched the inside of his lips. I felt its warmth on mine. The soft fullness of it. "That's quite a lot of assumptions," he said at last.

The words came out fast, like the kickback from a shot I had to take. "So tell me I'm wrong."

But Eric didn't speak. He simply breathed. So deep. So heavy. He spread his large hands over his lap. He said, "I must be out of my mind."

I didn't look away from him. He didn't look away from me.

He said, "They'll smell it on us, you know."

A flutter in my chest. An explosion. "You said it yourself. Ten years on the job. No one has sniffed out a case yet."

"There's been nothing to smell."

"Is that how you want it to stay?"

His words surprised me, the way a mountain can surprise you by its magnitude when you get up close. No pause. No hesitation. "Hell no."

My body ached to rush him then, to let the straight lines of his body find the curves in mine, to let him open and fill me. I stayed in my seat.

He said, "You have to know, if people find out, it'll hurt you more than it hurts me. Anytime you do anything of note, any promotion you ever get, people will say you slept your way to the top."

"No, they won't," I said. A pause as I confirmed in his face what my body had already told me. "You'll defend me."

There was pleasure behind Eric's eyes. "I will," he said. His voice was strong, unflinching. "With all my might."

I'd felt the force of his words in the back of my throat. I'd known—*just known*—that this thing between us was real. For the rest of my life, any man who came after him would always have to measure up to what we'd been.

Yet I hadn't wanted there to be a man after Eric. Even then. Even still.

18

THE MINIVAN SLID OFF THE ROAD. INSTEAD OF FIGHTING IT, I put it into park. I dialed. Eric picked up on the fourth ring. He didn't say hello.

"I know you're angry," I said. "I should have told you before, but there's this case. Ronan asked me to look into it. That's it. That's the whole story. We'll be back as soon as it's done."

A pickup truck passed on the road beside me. I didn't even register it until the trail of its exhaust bled through the open window.

"That's not what this Becker says. He says he hired you. He says you've moved back into your old house. For good."

"He's confused."

"Because you lied to him, too?" Eric's tone verged on eruption. "Just explain to me one thing. Where's Simone? While you're *looking into this case,* where is our daughter?"

I didn't know what I'd expected Eric to say. It wasn't this.

He said, "You swore you would protect her."

"She's with the uncles," I said. "She's fine."

"How do you know when you're not even with her?"

"What do you mean how do I know? They're my uncles. I trust them."

"Oh, and that gut of yours is always right?"

I gripped the steering wheel until I couldn't feel my hand. "Once, Eric. I screwed up once."

"That's your problem, Leigh. You always think you get a second shot. Life doesn't work like that. Not for you. Not for Simone. Not for any of us."

It was the tone that did it, that ugly, guttural tone that said, *You're too reckless for us,* that tone that said, *We needed you to be perfect.* That tone that said, *You failed us, and I can't forgive you.*

"You're right," I said. My cheeks burned. "It was thoughtless of me to bring Simone here. It was thoughtless to have her spend time with her *family* while I looked into an important case. All this time, she could've been there with you and your new *friend*."

Bile rose up my throat.

"You know, the one Simone says *touches you a lot*? The one who *smells nice*?"

"Leigh."

"Tell me." My voice made a sound I hated. Shrill. Girlish. Pleading. "Tell me it's not what I think."

My blood was loud in my ears. My face was sweating. The phone slipped down my cheek. We were drowning. I was holding on so tight. Eric wasn't even trying to save us.

"Do you love her?" Those words sent a crack through me. I didn't need him to be faithful. But I needed this. Even if it was only this. I said, "Do you?"

"Leigh," Eric said again. His voice held no emotion. "We'll talk about this when you get back."

I didn't know what a seizure felt like. Maybe like this. Like the skin was shaking off me. Like I'd lost control of my body. My lips, my fingers, my eyelids trembled.

Of course he couldn't just say it. Of course he couldn't admit he'd been lonely and he'd been weak.

I wished that made me hate him.

"Forget it," I said. I spoke loudly to fight the quiver. "I don't need you anyway." What I meant was *I need you so much it hurts.* What I meant was *I'd die for you and that means nothing.*

The sweat made the phone slide down my cheek again. Only, this time I didn't try to hold on. My thumb fumbled until I swiped the screen to end the call.

That's when I touched my face. It wasn't sweat on my cheek. I was crying.

Maybe I had been for longer than I'd known.

19

Thursday, November 9

THE WOOD COUNTY MEDICAL EXAMINER'S WAS BLINDINGLY white. It was the white of places never dulled by smudges of smoke or oil, where spills are scrubbed over with sinus-clearing bleach. It smelled like disinfectant and cold freezer. As I walked past the equipment, all stainless steel, I tried not to inhale.

I was only a few steps in when I caught sight of my brother.

Ronan was circling the equipment as if this were a museum and he were trying to look thoughtful. He seemed to have recovered since yesterday's dustup with Chief Becker, enough to have figured out when I was due to meet with the M.E.

"You must be Detective O'Donnell," Dr. Aliche said. The medical examiner swept into the room with a file in his hand. He was in his fifties, Black, with the quick eyes of someone who gets high on caffeine, and the clipped voice of someone who demands you keep up. "Your partner and I were just getting started."

Dr. Aliche opened one of the refrigerated lockers lining the wall. He unzipped the body bag to reveal a face and shoulders. Dark hair. Strong jawline. Eyes open, as the dead's usually were. I recognized him immediately. The one Ronan had called the *good-looking one*. This was Duncan Schott.

Duncan Schott's file had been a little more filled out than William Houser's, but not by much. He'd been living with his girlfriend, Angie, at the time of his death, though I still couldn't get her to talk to me. He'd done some community college, studied IT and then business. He'd never gotten his degree.

"He is attractive, isn't he?" Dr. Aliche said, gazing at Duncan. "I can assure you, he's just as handsome on the inside as he is on the out. Not a clogged artery among them. A heart like a stallion's." He touched Duncan's face. "Such a shame."

Ronan fidgeted.

I said, "Have you ever seen a body like this before?"

"A healthy one?"

"Cleaned up like this." I motioned to his cut fingernails, his fresh haircut, his smooth face. "Pristine."

"It is tickling, isn't it?" Ronan and I both flinched. "As I'm sure you're aware, things like facial hair continue to grow after one expires. But not with our dear, sweet Duncan. Not with the other two, either."

I asked, "Does that mean someone shaved their faces after they died?"

"Oh, we do have an active imagination, don't we?" Dr. Aliche's hands danced in front of him. "It's possible, of course. It's also possible that they were simply the unlucky sort with insufficient testosterone to support adequate plumage."

Dr. Aliche put his face close to Duncan's, as if studying it. Then he shook his head, stood erect.

"I worked out of Lucas County before coming here. A woman there shot herself with her husband's revolver. Right between her eyes. She'd also cleaned herself up before her suicide. Shaved off her pubic hair even, which I understand can be quite uncomfortable for women."

Ronan shifted between his feet.

"But in her case, obviously, we had the luxury of a wound," Dr. Aliche said. "Whereas with our new friends here, the bodies were as immaculate as virgin gifts. Not a bruise or scrape on them. It really was a shame to defile such clean canvases. Truly, a shame."

Ronan put a fist to his mouth like he was going to cough. But he just held it there, dry swallowed.

"Could the men have taken anything to prevent blood clotting?" I asked. "So they wouldn't bruise?"

"Detective O'Donnell, what a delight you are. I haven't had such a mental workout in ages!"

"So, no?"

"While I do applaud the out-of-the-box thinking, the answer is no. It's unlikely that anticoagulants would've had a substantial impact on the development of postmortem bruising, unless perhaps taken in extremely high doses. But then if that'd been the case, those would've shown up on the tox screens, which, as I'm sure you know, were clear. Not even a hint of liquid courage."

It was unclear why Duncan was still between us, except that

Dr. Aliche seemed to derive genuine pleasure from looking at him. He was like a family photo album, brought out for company and enjoyed, for the most part, by the host. I asked, "Is there anything your reference lab doesn't screen for?"

"We can't test for every compound known to man, as I'm sure you're aware," Dr. Aliche said. "As you're also aware, a negative tox screen simply means that none of the compounds we tested for were at high enough levels to be detected. It doesn't necessarily mean they weren't present.

"However, in a case such as this, when these were clearly drownings, one does find it difficult to justify comprehensive testing simply to satisfy one's curiosity. However robust."

"Are there any drugs you didn't test for that might have impacted the victims' ability to orient themselves underwater? Methamphetamines? Psilocybin?"

"You're wondering how they managed to drown if there was nothing to knock them unconscious?"

"It is the obvious question."

"Not to crush that beautiful imagination of yours, but I believe the answer is the obvious one as well." Dr. Aliche touched a gloved finger to Duncan's lips. "When they jumped from the falls, they opened their mouths."

He paused, smiled.

"Simply put," he said, lifting away his finger, "they took in so much water that they couldn't recover. It's like the old Sherlock story. The one where the man is found with a hole in his chest but without a murder weapon. It was an icicle, you see. Even something as life-giving as water can be dangerous in the right context."

I was used to having my ass handed to me by medical examiners. It was their job to assess the plausibility of stories, just as it was my job to invent scenarios. But Dr. Aliche was having too much fun with this. He looked at me like I was a child riding a carousel thinking it was a racehorse. I wanted him to eat my dust.

I pulled out my notebook. I checked my numbers. I said, "In your report, you noted the pH levels of the water in the men's lungs was at a 5.1. That's very acidic for aboveground water. The water on the falls is closer to a 6.5."

Dr. Aliche touched his hand to his face with the same finger that had just touched Duncan's lips.

Ronan winced.

"Why, Detective! Your questions do give me such delight. If you're ever looking for a second career, I would gladly encourage your pursuits. Although in the medical field, one is restricted by the facts, which the more inventive among us might find to be stifling."

I closed my notebook. "So why are the pH levels in their lungs lower than the water they supposedly died in?"

Dr. Aliche folded his hands in front of him. "When a victim swallows a large amount of water, his ventilatory function decreases due to gastric distention. He vomits. When the vomit is expelled and he tries to inhale again, as one does involuntarily, he breathes in his gastric contents."

"So the fluids in their lungs become more acidic due to stomach acid?"

Dr. Aliche gave a single clap. "Yes. Precisely."

There it was again, that carousel feeling. I wanted to make

him take me seriously. Of course, the most obvious explanation was the one most likely to be true. William, Duncan, and Neil had swallowed too much water when they jumped off the falls. They vomited and choked on it. The case was open-and-shut.

"Not to interrupt," Ronan said. His skin was white. "But could we . . . ?" He motioned to Duncan. I hadn't even remembered he was there. "Could we zip him back up? Or close his eyes or something?"

"Ah yes," Dr. Aliche said. "I brought out Mr. Schott because I wanted to show you something. Ah, what am I doing? It's not even here. Oh, I am getting old." Dr. Aliche gave Duncan one last smile and zipped him up. He pushed him back inside the locker. He clamped it shut.

Dr. Aliche snapped off his gloves as he walked. He motioned for us to follow. We came around to the other end of the room. Ronan was behind me. Dr. Aliche sat in a swivel chair. He opened a drawer of his desk, frowned, then opened another. At last he pulled out a pickle jar filled with clear liquid. He placed it on the desk in front of him. "Ta-da!" he said.

A fish the size of my thumb swam inside of it. It was almost translucent, with a pinkish tint throughout its body, as if someone had tossed in a red with the load of whites. "Isn't he neat?" Dr. Aliche said.

Ronan was still holding his fist to his mouth. I was still thinking about my husband fucking another woman. It's safe to say neither of us gave a damn about a carnival fish.

"Ah, you're unimpressed," Dr. Aliche said. His frown was playful. "That's because you don't know the whole story. Guess where I found him? Oh, never mind. I see you're tired. I'll just tell you. I found this little fellow swimming around in Duncan Schott's thoracic cavity. Still alive!"

I watched Dr. Aliche to see if he was joking. When his expression didn't change, I said unhelpfully, "He swallowed a fish?"

"He did indeed. I didn't mention it in my report because it seemed hardly to be of medical note. But he is a resilient little fellow, isn't he? Look at him go!"

I put my notebook back in my pocket. My ears were ringing. I wanted to get out of there.

"Where's that curiosity when we need it?" Dr. Aliche said. "Don't you want to know what kind it is? No bother, I'll tell you anyway. I consulted with an old medical school friend. She gave up medicine to study marine life, which really is a shame because she'd have been an extraordinary doctor. Now, this fish hasn't been known to reside in Ohio. So this really is exciting. She tells me that this is . . ." His fingers played a drumroll. "A northern cavefish."

I blinked at him stupidly. "A cavefish? A fish. Found in caves?"

"At last we succumb to the obvious. A loss of innocence, surely." Dr. Aliche's face became wistful. "I have to send him off to Fish and Wildlife because he's endangered. But when you called to talk about the bodies, I thought, why I must show her."

I knelt down to the fish's eye level and my whole body was buzzing. The fish didn't have any eyes. He didn't need them. He didn't live in a place where there was light.

20

BEFORE WE'D EVEN MADE IT OUT THE DOOR AT THE WOOD County medical examiner's, Ronan was talking fast, like Dr. Aliche's energy had sparked a surge in his.

Ronan wanted to know if the cavefish in Duncan's body meant he'd died in the caves after all, if it meant all three of them had.

And if they had died in the caves, did that mean they were murdered? But who would have been strong enough to force three grown men into a cave? Who would they have trusted enough to follow down there?

We were in the parking lot, halfway to Eamon's Honda, which I was driving while I waited for the Impala to be towed, when I cut Ronan off. "First we need to interview Duncan's girl-friend. She may know something the others don't."

"Actually," Ronan said, "yesterday, while you were taking some *you* time . . ."

"I would never call it that."

"I already interviewed her."

There was a crack in the pavement beneath us. I looked up from it to see Ronan grinning.

"Just wait here. Let me show you."

Ronan jogged to the cruiser, parked off at the edge of the lot. He came back with an ancient Trapper Keeper. He handed it to me with a flourish. I undid the Velcro with a rip.

I flipped past a plastic folder, neon green, and to a page of wide-lined paper. The top of the page read *Angie Owens.* Below the name were handwritten notes. There were pages and pages of them.

My mouth was open. I closed it. "How did you get her to talk to you?"

Ronan scratched the back of his head. "I felt bad. About not standing up for you yesterday. To the chief, I mean. Maybe I don't always understand you. But you're still the only sister I've got."

I didn't meet his eyes. "I shouldn't have put you in that position."

"Leigh O'Donnell." He squinted. "Are you actually admitting you were wrong?"

I thought of Eric, of his *You always think you get a second shot.* Ronan would always give me one. Eric never would. I moved to the hood of the car. I sat. I said, "Hush now while I read."

The more I read of Ronan's interview, the more impressed I was at what he'd found out. It wasn't easy to get people to talk, especially someone like Angie, who hadn't even opened her door for me. Yet, Ronan had.

According to Ronan's notes, Angie was pregnant. That would explain the heavy footfalls I'd heard. She was expecting their son any day now. Duncan was excited about being a dad. He'd bought the whole family matching pajamas, the flannel kind with footies and hoods with ears. Yet, in the months before he died, he was stressed out. He didn't know how he was going to get the money to support his family.

This was consistent with what I'd already learned about Neil and William. William, too, had been hurting for cash. Or else why would he and his dad peel all those apples all day, despite his dad's carpal tunnel?

Neil's roommates had said that Neil returned from school with a lot of debt, more than his new job at the Cleveland Orchestra would ever pay off. Neil's little sister was going to music school, too, following in Neil's footsteps. If I had to guess I'd say that she also had no way to pay off her loans.

I thought suddenly of Mason's story for *Rolling Stone,* of the three seniors who'd died on the falls. They'd tried getting out of here, too. But they could never actually leave. I rubbed my thumb on my palm where Mason had written his number. I looked up at Ronan, who was bouncing on his toes, watching for my reaction. "Did Angie say anything about the caves?" I asked.

Ronan shook his head. "She didn't mention them specifically. But she said that lately Duncan had gotten, I don't know how to say it, chill, I guess you'd call it. They needed money. But Duncan started talking about how things were going to work themselves out. *One way or another.* It wasn't like him. The Zen-ness of it all."

"Go back to her," I said. "Ask about the caves. Also ask about enemies, motives. Ask about any groups he might have been a part of."

Ronan's smile took over his face. "On it, boss."

I opened the door of the Honda. "I also want to know about the shrines. Dr. Wagner lied about them, and we know William was interested in finding them. Maybe Neil, too. Check online. Has anyone written anything about the shrines? Any academic papers? Any blogs? Is there a subreddit?"

I handed Ronan his Trapper Keeper. He held the side of his hand to his brow. "I won't let you down, sis." His salute was hideous. "And I'll clear it with the chief. I'll ask him to take us off the rounds for the next few days to help you get settled."

I nodded.

Ronan grinned. "You have to admit—"

"Don't say it."

"We make great partners."

I felt the edges of my mouth curl up. Then I ducked into the car, where Ronan couldn't see my smile.

21

I ARRIVED AT BEAR'S LOT JUST AS A SPRAY OF BIRDS FLEW across the sky. The flock contracted and expanded the farther south they went. Near the edge of my vision, one straggler spun out from the formation. The space between him and the group grew wide. They should've left him behind. He was too slow. Yet all at once, the flock swept over him. They swallowed him into their ranks.

Bear's Sales & Repairs sat between Copper Falls proper and the Sticks. It looked the same as in my memory: rows of out-of-date cars with smoothed-out dents. Prices on windshields painted in white. A faded pennant draped over the drooping double-wide. The gravel crunched under my feet.

As I approached the trailer, the front door swung open. Uncle Frankie appeared on the steps. His long arms bowed on either side of him. He punched his thumbs through the belt loops of his coveralls. Simone appeared beside him. Arnie the Armadillo was tied to a holster at her waist. She was wearing a red cowboy hat. She giggled. Frankie nudged her. She said, "Howdy, partner!"

Frankie spoke from the back of his mouth. "What brings you to these parts, darlin'?"

"Hi, baby," I said. At this, Simone came running down the steps to me. Her hands were outstretched in a hug. Her cowboy hat slipped off her head and hung down her back.

"No, no, no!" Frankie howled. He wagged a finger at her. "What'd I tell you about fraternizing with the enemy?"

I swept Simone up in my arms. "Did you get something to eat?" I kissed her on the head. She smelled of shea butter and applesauce.

She nodded. "This time I told Uncle Frankie I like sandwiches."

I smiled. "You catch on fast."

"Uncle Frankie taught me how to play Cowboys and Indians."

To Frankie I said, "Simone's not allowed to play with toy weapons."

"I told him, Mommy."

"And no live ammunition, either," Frankie replied, coming in closer. He swung a wrench around his finger like a gun. "When Ronan's boys get back from camping, we'll teach 'em that rule, too."

"Where's Bear?"

Frankie flipped the wrench into his pocket like he was holstering it. It slammed against his hip. He staggered back. Simone laughed. I set her down. Frankie recovered. He said, "Now, that's the thing, darlin'. Sheriff Bear is, uh, not available at this time."

"Wait. Mommy should be sheriff." Simone had her hands on her hips.

"Is he inside?" I asked.

"He is indeed," Frankie said.

"She's *the Law*," Simone said. "Sheriff is the Law. You said."

"But she's a lady," Frankie said. "Everybody knows ladies can't be sheriffs."

"I'm a lady. I'm a cowboy."

Frankie made a face like, *Kids these days.*

Simone made a face like, *I'm not letting this go.*

"In what sense is he not available?" I asked.

Frankie pondered this. Coming up blank, he quick-stepped back to the trailer. He rapped the back of his knuckles against the door. "Hey, Bear. Leigh wants to know in what sense you're unavailable."

Bear muttered.

Frankie nodded, jogged back to me. "He said to tell you he's *indisposed.*"

"Mommy, tell him." Simone tugged at my suit jacket. "*You're* sheriff."

"Baby, I know I'm sheriff. That's good enough for me." My tone changed when I spoke to Frankie: "Indisposed how?"

Frankie held up a finger, jogged back to the trailer. "She wants to know *indisposed how*!"

"I know, I know." Simone tugged at my arm. In a loud whisper, she said, "Uncle Bear is yoga-ing."

"*Yoga-ing?*"

From inside the double-wide, a thud like a tree falling. Then came low noises that sounded an awful lot like *God dammit shit all to hell in a handbasket.* Frankie stepped out of the way. Bear barreled through the door. "Jesus, Leigh. I've had crabs that weren't this hard to get rid of. This couldn't wait?"

Bear stood in the doorway. Gray tufts of hair curled out from under his muscle tee. Spandex pants squeezed his thighs into sausages. The pants did not leave nearly enough to the imagination.

"Yoga?"

"Told you," Simone said.

"It's supposed to help me quit smoking," Bear growled. At this, he pulled a flannel off a hook just inside the door. From its pocket, he pinched out a soft pack of Marlboro Reds. He extracted a cigarette with his teeth.

Frankie said, "You can see how well it's working."

"Fuck off," Bear said.

"Do you two always swear in front of my four-year-old?"

Bear flicked on his lighter and sucked on his cigarette.

Frankie shrugged.

"Mommy." Simone tugged at my suit jacket. "All the time you say bad words."

Frankie put his hands on his hips. He spoke like he had a cheek full of chew. "Why, young cowboy, are you picking a fight with the sheriff? You know what happens when you pick a fight with the Law." Simone ran over to him. She squealed as he chased her. They disappeared behind the trailer, giggling.

Bear puffed out smoke. "If you're here to see if I towed the Impala out of the woods yet, the answer is no. I've been occupied."

"I need something with four-wheel drive."

Bear coughed. "You want to trade in the *free car* I gave you for an *upgraded free car*?"

"Are you saying you won't do it?"

Bear grumbled something that sounded a lot like *Un-fucking-believable*. His cigarette bobbed on his lips. "Let me put on some damned pants."

I was buckled into the passenger seat of the 1989 G-Wagen Bear had chosen from the lot. It was army green, with headlights like search beams. Its square frame made me think of Humvees, of survivalists. According to Bear, he'd bought it cheap and fixed it up so it was in tip-top shape. Though the engine was as loud as a combine's, it ran fine.

Bear had replaced his cigarette with a square of nicotine gum. As we turned onto Sugar Ridge Road, he downshifted and the engine grinded.

I said, "Isn't the point of a test drive that I'm the one to drive it?"

"Here I thought the point of testing out a car was so afterward you'd pay for it."

"I offered to lease it from you."

"Don't insult me."

By now it was almost ten in the morning. We were driving away from the center of town, toward a blanket of rust red and hunter green and lots of nothing. I said, "Where are we going?"

"You're coming with me on my weekly errand," Bear said. "Every Thursday morning. I figured you wouldn't mind."

"None of those other cars on the lot are drivable? Bear, that's no way to run a business."

"I see living in the city has done nothing to curb that mouth of yours." Bear glanced at the rearview mirror. He shifted in his seat. "Though now that you mention it, this will give us an opportunity to chat."

"You're not coming out to me, are you, Bear?"

"Look who's feeling better." He gave me a sideways look. "Simone said that after you showered off the mud yesterday, you didn't get off the couch. Said you didn't eat anything, either."

I flashed to Eric, to those hands that were holding someone else right now. To that body that was wrapped around someone else's body. To those eyes that were fixed on a light that wasn't mine. I was glad then for the angry engine, for the way it filled the silence with its roar. My voice was like sandpaper. I said, "What did you want to talk about?"

Bear leaned back in his seat. He scratched his beard with his fingernails. "I hear you went to see Dale Houser the other day."

"And?"

He glanced out the window. "He said you didn't treat him like a criminal."

I waited for the *but*. When it didn't come I said, "Okay?"

"You'd be surprised what people round here are like with those folks. Take that brother of yours. Now, he's not mean-spirited like some, but that boy can be as dumb as a doorknob. Treats those people like they're parolees. Always coming round to make sure they're not getting in any trouble. Doesn't have any notion what that does to a man's pride."

"That's what half of police work is," I said. "Driving around. Letting people know you're watching so they don't try anything stupid."

"Yeah, but that's not the work you do."

I scrutinized Bear's face. I couldn't understand why he was suddenly being so civil with me, why he was coming dangerously close to paying me a compliment. "No," I said at last. "That's not the work I do."

Bear chewed hard. His mind worked. At last, he said, "I take it you don't know what those *rounds* are really all about?" There was no threat in his question, just a desire to know something about me, something my answer would reveal.

I thought of what Dale had said, about Bear telling him I had my mother's heart. The feral in me receded. I tested the waters. I said, "I think it's suspicious."

Bear met my eyes.

"They should have brought the DEA in on the meth raids."

Bear's gaze returned to the road. "Go on."

"And if they did really confiscate all those drugs, where are they? I don't see them storing them in the basement of the police department with all the rest of their files. There's not even a security camera down there."

Bear nodded.

I waited. When he didn't speak, I said, "So are you going to tell me what you know? Or do I have to guess?"

The path ahead had been passed over before, by other cars that had stamped down the nettles and weeds. Big tire tracks punched down the mud. Soggy leaves collected in the pools of the treads. The tree branches were shucked away. It was like driving through a tunnel. I didn't know where we were anymore. I couldn't orient myself.

Bear parked the G-Wagen and pulled on the handle of the door. "Hope those fancy boots of yours aren't afraid of a little mud."

I followed Bear toward a rocky path grown over with moss. Wispy plants had filled in the cracks. Tall grasses brushed either side of us. The air was damp and cool and smelled of wet leaves.

"See this tree?" Bear said. "This one's birch and this other one here? This is pecan. The Sticks is full of them. Along with maples, of course. But you drive a spile—it's like a faucet head but for a tree—into the trunk of any one of them, you get sap all the same. Problem is, the sap has to cook for a real long time. It takes something like forty gallons to make one gallon of syrup. Don't ask me how the hell I know that."

I wanted to ask why the hell we were talking about maple syrup.

"The thing is," Bear said, glancing over his shoulder at me, "when the sap cooks down, it steams up something awful. That's why most people who make syrup have to do it outside. On these big-ass burners. With these big-ass pots. You can see the steam for miles."

I still didn't understand why he was telling me this. Then, all of a sudden, I did. "Bullshit."

"It's true."

I stepped around Bear so we were facing each other. He was taller than I was but not by more than a few inches. I said,

"You're telling me those people in the Sticks who got busted for meth were actually cooking maple syrup?" I watched to see him crack, a smile, a twitch, something. But Bear's face was cast in stone.

"Tree sap syrup. Birch. Pecan. Walnut, I think. But yes. They were making artisanal syrup to sell to all them yuppies who don't have nothing better to do with twenty bucks. They probably pour it on scones and shit. But these guys were making a pretty penny. Then, what do you know? The CFPD brings out the SWAT gear."

"The police would've been able to smell the difference before they even got out of their vehicles."

Bear stepped around me. He kept walking. "Oh, they knew what they were doing all right. Becker had gotten some dumb-ass warrant from some dumb-ass country judge who didn't know his ass from his elbow. He'd even called in help from the sheriff's office with the raids.

"Now, they get there and everybody can see right away it's syrup. But Becker says it's all a front. Like Italian restaurants were a front for the Mob, right? He orders his men to pull in the beakers and spiles and those big-ass burners. He has it all tagged as drug paraphernalia."

"Ronan said they found meth."

"You can say that water's wine, but that don't make you Jesus."

I let this sink in. Becker had lied. To everybody.

Bear's legs bowed as he picked his way over the path. He said, "Then Becker raids every single house with syrup equipment and takes all their cash. Those people out there don't believe in no banks. So it was a lot, too. We're talking at least a few hundred grand."

This had to have been in addition to the half a million dollars from Maude.

Bear's voice was lower, angrier. This was the part that especially riled him up. "Now the townies say Becker's a hero, saving Copper Falls from drugs. What do you know? When we had to vote on police funding this year, the CFPD got more money. Winner winner chicken dinner, as the French say."

"Did the people in the Sticks file a complaint?" If there was a complaint, then I could at least verify something about this story.

Bear held a branch so it wouldn't snap back in my face. "What are they going to do? Complain to the sheriff, who knows what bullshit this whole thing is? Complain to the judge who set Becker up with the warrant to begin with?

"Besides, they can't prove they weren't distributing drugs. That's what the law says they got to do if they want their shit back. But tell me, how do you get evidence against a negative fact, huh?"

"Assuming what you're saying is true."

"Oh, it's true all right."

The ground under my feet was springy. I said, "You're saying Becker knew all along the people in the Sticks were running a legitimate business? You're saying he *knowingly* stole from them? Why?"

We were deep in the woods now, headed toward an opening in the trees covered by wildflowers. Up ahead, a web glistened in the sun. A tiny ladybug was wrapped in silk. A spider climbed toward it. I stood, watching it hunt. Bear shrugged. He bent down to gather flowers.

I recalled the civil asset forfeitures I'd heard about in New York. Cops usually took people's money as a way of applying pressure. People get awfully talkative when they can't pay their mortgages. "Is there something the people in town are trying to get the people in the Sticks to do? Something they want?"

Bear handed me a spray of flowers. He stood. He had flowers in his hand, too. They were blue and white. They had delicate stems and shrunken buds. They didn't smell like anything. "I'm telling you, you don't need to look for complex motivations. It's free money. The townies took it. It's the bully stealing the little kid's milk money. Ain't no point asking the bully why."

And yet my whole job centered on that *why*. I needed somebody removed from the situation to tell me the truth. In a flash, I thought of Eddie Cain, the man my father had won that house from in a game of cards. If anyone would break rank with the townies, it was him. I said, "Do you know how to get in contact with Eddie Cain?"

Bear squinted at me, then shook his head.

"Have you told Ronan? About Becker?"

"He's dealing with some other stuff right now. But then I'll tell him."

Before I could ask Bear what he meant, I registered where we were. The iron fencing. The sharp edges of tombstones the weather had made curved. Bear held open the gate. He waited for me to pass through. I didn't move. My voice was hollow. I said, "What are we doing here?"

"I told you," Bear said. The flowers brushed his leg. "I stop by every Thursday to see your mom. I say hi to your dad, too, but he don't get flowers. Now, you just going to stand there or what?"

I didn't move.

"Still afraid, I see. Ironic, don't you think?"

I turned away from him. Behind me, the gate banged shut.

I walked as fast as my legs would carry me. I pushed away the sight of my father's dead eyes. I pushed away the feel of my mother's bare ribs when I hugged her. Instead, I thought of Eric, of his deep voice soothing me. Of the way his chest would rise and fall as he drew himself up. My protector. My rock.

But this time when I thought of him, something churned in my stomach. Up my throat. Restricting my air. I slowed. I felt sick. I needed to hold on to something solid.

I focused on the broad oak in the distance, at the thousands of leaves its branches held. As I watched it, I conjured Mason's heavy muscles. I recalled their tight flex as they wrapped around me, unflinching. The thought of him held me upright. The constriction in my throat released. Without thinking, I dialed.

Mason picked up on the first ring.

22

IT WAS CLOSE TO MIDNIGHT WHEN MASON CAME TO THE DOOR
wearing a solid T-shirt that showcased his heft. I imagined the
weight of his body around mine. I imagined Eric and something
sharp slipped down my throat. Mason opened the door wider. I
stepped through.

I hadn't been in the carriage house behind his mother's old
Victorian since we were kids. But its contours were familiar. A
whole wall was made up of lattice windows under a wide arch
frame. The hardwood floor was blackened by age, patched in
places, and covered over with handwoven rugs. A winding staircase led to the loft. Rumpled sheets and balled-up socks lay at
the foot of Mason's bed. His glasses lay folded over a book.

"You still drink gin, I take it?" Mason asked with a smirk.

With that smirk came a flicker of memory. Us on his mother's
porch. Glasses clinking. The bite of pine needles. The tang of
lime. The fullness of his tongue.

Mason went around the carriage house and hinged open the

windows so that fresh air swept through the space. It was cold. He pulled on a sweater. "Just the way you like it," he said. He handed me a glass.

"You have a good memory."

"I was in love with you." His eyes were intense. A challenge. "I remember all of it."

I took a sip. The same fizz of bubbles. The same clean scent. My tongue skimmed the inside of my lips. It was a long time before I looked away from him.

I stepped past Mason to sit on the couch. He eased himself onto the other end so that our legs kicked up like bookends. I said, "You have this place all to yourself?"

Mason looked out the window, toward the main house. From behind sheer curtains, the shadow of his mother zipped from one frame to the next. She was unaware, it would seem, of the hour. She was either putting away dishes or getting dishes out, cleaning something or making sure something was clean. She reminded me of a doll, hurrying through her home at the whims of an impatient child. He said, "She still won't let me in the house. Can you believe it? It's been seven years."

Mason's mother had been the central image in the spread of *Rolling Stone*. "Is she angry about the photo or about the story itself?"

"I actually think she likes the photo." Mason ran a finger along the line of his lip. "Though she'd never admit it. The photographer, a buddy of mine, used a soft-focus lens. She looked great. But she took a lot of flak for being a part of the story. You know how people are around here."

"I don't actually. Tell me."

Mason narrowed his eyes. "Are you playing detective with me, Wildcat?" He winked. "I'm not saying I mind. You can get out your handcuffs, too, if you're into that sort of thing."

"Is that one of your journalism strategies? Flirting your way out of answering questions?"

"Is it not working?" He held up a hand. "No, don't answer that. I want to keep hope alive."

Mason adjusted his body on the couch so that his muscles contracted and released. He leaned back. His legs stretched closer to my side.

"The folks here? They're good people. But they're clannish at heart. It scares them, this idea that they should care about everybody. You can't protect the whole world."

I thought of my brain, of its compartments. Of the dead bodies that would never be people to me. I nodded. I understood.

He said, "If you feel a sense of shared humanity with the sweatshop workers in China, where are you going to get your electronics? If you feel compassion for the starving kids in Africa, before you know it, you're starving yourself just so you can feed them. I don't say I endorse that kind of thinking, but I understand it. How insular they are. It allows them to be selfish and to not feel bad about it. Come on, don't you remember high school?"

I told him I didn't. Mason looked skeptical, but it was true. Every celebration, every milestone, every argument that had ever mattered had happened with my family. Inside that house. We were our own island.

Then, after Dad's heart attack, when Mom stopped eating,

when she stopped sleeping through the night, when her skin became tissue thin and her eyes clouded over, that island sank.

Now my memories from those days were mostly darkness with flickers of light.

"The Wagners were always the class presidents," Mason said. "The star athletes. The homecoming kings. They made you think it was because they were the best at everything." He sighed. "It's just this culture, you know what I mean? This culture of not breaking rank. If you do, it's a betrayal."

"Omerta and all of that?"

He shot me a look. "See, now I know you're playing detective with me."

"So what if the town is angry about what you wrote? You can't please everyone. Your mom must know that."

Mason leaned back even more. His legs brushed against mine. I didn't shift back to accommodate him. A smile caught at the edge of his mouth. He said, "Maybe you don't know this because you're an outsider—"

"—whose family has lived here for almost thirty years."

"Whose family has *only* lived here for thirty years. But most of the businesses in town—the grocery store, the antiques market, the candy shop—they're all owned by the same seven families. The Wagners are the majority share, sure, but this town? It's all one big family business."

"That's insane."

"Not really. I'm sure it's like that in a lot of places. See, those seven families have never left. Some individuals left, sure, but most of them stayed. People give their houses to their kids or their grandkids. Sometimes nephews and nieces. But it's rare for them to sell to outsiders. Especially the houses close to the center of town. There are ordinances forbidding new construction. We don't get many new people here."

I said, "But Eddie Cain left." I knew his was one of the seven families without being told. Our house was almost two hundred years old. According to a plaque in the foyer, his family had built it.

"I told you, people do leave," Mason said. "It's just not that common."

"You keep saying that, but it's never made sense to me. Why do people think this place is so great?"

"It's beautiful. It's safe. It's got a great sense of community."

"Stop bullshitting me, Mason."

"Say my name again, Wildcat."

"Why do people stay?"

He sighed. At last he said, "It's the money, probably."

Now we were getting somewhere. "See how much easier this is when you stop flirting?"

"You say *easier,* I say *less fun.*" There was a glint in Mason's eye. He went on. "People always underestimate the value of generational wealth. But something like thirty-five percent of all wealth in this country is inherited. If invested wisely, it just grows itself, like a tree your great-great-grandparents planted that now fruits year-round. So long as you stay here, you get to eat that fruit."

"You mean, if you're one of the seven families."

"Which is why it was so outrageous that Eddie left."

"But he lost his house."

Mason shrugged. Took a sip of his drink. "Maybe it's that simple. I don't know."

"Do you know how to get in contact with him?"

"Why?"

"Just turning over every stone."

Mason examined my face. "I tried once," he said. "To find Eddie Cain. I wanted to talk to him about my theory, about how the inheritors of Copper Falls can never truly leave. But I guess his parents should have been more inventive. There were too many Edward Thomas Cains for me to find him."

I held my next question in my mouth. I knew what it would signal. A shift. From work to him. From him to us. Did I want this? I said, "Was it worth it? Selling out the town? Leaving behind that inheritance?"

Mason swirled the ice in his glass. "I don't know how to answer that," he said. "If I say yes, I'm heartless. If I say no, I regret my whole career."

He bit his bottom lip, released it slowly. His lips shone in the flickering light.

"Being a journalist, it's a shit job. I know that. Shitty pay. Shitty hours. Shitty job security. I put my heart on the line constantly. I hold it up for public scrutiny, which, as a rule, is never kind. I travel too much. I haven't had a good relationship in years. I never take a vacation. I'm always working or thinking about work."

He blew air through his lips. I sensed not so much defeat as resignation.

"But I love it. As hopelessly as I've ever loved anything. If I didn't write stories, I don't know what else I'd be good for." He met my eyes. "You know that feeling?"

I'd forgotten how emotional Mason could be. With him, sadness and anger and loss and fear and affection always sat just below the surface. The tiniest scratch could bring them to life. Mason was the opposite of Eric, whose emotions were like icebergs some days, on others, like a mirage.

I retracted my legs. I readjusted myself on the couch. I couldn't do this. Not with him.

I said, "I came here to ask about those three high school boys who jumped off the falls seven years ago. The ones you wrote about."

Mason didn't seem bothered by this shift in topic. His shoulders fell away from his ears. His glass relaxed against his leg. Maybe it was true for him, too, that a retreat into work meant a pivot away from dangerous shoals, from those places where messy things stayed messy, where emotions had the power of storms.

He said, "What do you want to know?"

"Let's start with what you uncovered in your reporting."

"Don't you have access to the case files?"

I did. But like the files of Neil, Duncan, and William, these were bare, which didn't make any sense. These guys weren't from the Sticks. They were from the town. They were, in the eyes of Becker and the others, *the people who mattered*. So why weren't their deaths investigated? I said, "Let's just say I have a tolerance for hearing the same story twice."

Mason got up and brought back the bottle of gin. He poured a measure into my glass and then a measure into his own. He stayed standing. "Rich was a swimmer. Owen was a math geek. Brett was a stoner. Completely different social circles. Well, to the extent that's possible at a school like ours.

"I kept thinking I'd find some *Breakfast Club* connection. Like they'd all been in detention together one Saturday morning. But I never did. They didn't have any classes together. They weren't in any of the same clubs or on any of the same teams. So, the death-cult angle was out."

Mason screwed the cap back on the bottle. He took a drink. It made him look taller, broader. My pulse migrated below my navel, spread out.

"As far as I can tell," Mason said, "they didn't know each other in any particular way. Before you ask, yes they were all descendants from the seven original families, but a lot of people are. Yet, they all drowned on the same night. Their bodies were all found in the same place."

As Mason sat, the sofa sunk like a mattress. The heat of his body spilled into mine. His department store smell filled my chest.

"Rich had a swimming scholarship to Case," he said. "He was one of *those* guys. Owen was headed to Harvey Mudd in California. Wanted to study math. Brett had plans to move to St. Louis with some girl he'd met on the internet. Classic. All of them were getting out. So why kill themselves? It didn't make sense."

"Did you ever come up with a motive?"

He sighed. "In the piece, which clearly you read thoroughly, I said something poetic and, in retrospect, extremely wordy about how this was a town that no one *of standing* could ever really leave. For Rich, Owen, and Brett, they could never cross the border. For many of us, our tethers are less dramatic. A typical boomerang town whose siren would always call. I even speculated I'd be back someday." He searched the bottom of his glass. "How prescient that turned out to be."

"That thing you said about all the businesses being co-owned by the seven families, did that include those guys, too?"

"Of course."

"At what age do they become owners?"

"When they turn eighteen."

"And they were all eighteen?"

Mason nodded.

I'd gotten out my notebook and was writing. It felt good, making big things small. "The night before they left town, when they died, what were they doing? Where were they?"

"This really isn't in the files?"

"I want to hear it from you."

"They were doing the woods thing."

"What woods thing?"

"You know."

I said, "What woods thing?"

Mason searched my face. He leaned back. "The night before anyone leaves, people sleep out in the woods."

"And do what?"

"Nothing. That's it."

"Why?"

"I don't know."

"Did you do it?"

Something flickered behind Mason's eyes. For a few brief

seconds, I could see the old Mason, the one who'd light cigarettes and forget about them until they were pipes of ash. The Mason who got thrown against the lockers when he'd made one too many sarcastic remarks. I saw the Mason who was full of doubt, anxious, irritated, a little depressed. It made sense to me that he'd left, too, that he hadn't wanted to be stuck as that old version of himself. "Yeah," he said at last. "I did."

"What was it like?"

"Like sleeping in the woods."

"Meaning what?"

"Meaning, I got stoned and wandered."

"That's it?" I said. "You're sure?"

"You can ask my mother if you'd like. She was driving around all morning looking for me. I had her in a panic, apparently. She thought I'd thrown myself over the falls out of grief I couldn't be with you."

"Really?"

A slow blink. A lazy smile. Heat between my ribs.

"I told you. I was in love with you. For entire years of my life."

I turned the page in my notebook. I said, "Did you get a look at the bodies? As far as I could tell there weren't any autopsies done. Did they have any scratches or markings on them? Anything?"

He sat forward. "You don't even care that I was in love with you?"

I bit my lip. "Everyone thinks I should care about the past." I flashed to my uncles. To my parents' gravestones. To Eric and his mouth. To that gold shield that said NYPD on it. "The past doesn't matter," I said. "All that matters is what happens next."

Mason's eyes were emphatic. "If the past doesn't matter, then I only have the present. I can never be satisfied."

"Is that what you want? To be satisfied?"

Mason's voice was a breath. He inched closer. "Oh, yes. Very, very much."

There was something about that voice that did it, that voice that made me think of early mornings and late nights, when the buzz is coming down but the hangover hasn't yet begun, that voice that made me think of foreplay, of how Eric would press his mouth against my hip bone, waiting to see if I'd spread my legs.

I held my glass on my knee. I moved toward Mason. His freckles were a revelation to me. There were so many more than the last time I'd been this near to him. My lips separated. Something caught in his chest.

"Then come with me." Just like that I was standing. Just like that, I was heading us into the dark.

23

Friday, November 10

IT WAS ALMOST TWO A.M. WHEN I PUT THE G-WAGEN INTO seventh gear and took the same path I'd taken days before. It was dark now. A part of me knew this was a bad idea. Yet another part of me was fucking breathless. To be able to reach the shrine this time. To be able to take the route I believed William, Neil, and Duncan had traveled on the night they died. To have Mason beside me.

The G-Wagen rumbled beneath us as I drove up to the fissure that was the entrance to the caves. I cranked the emergency brake. Before Mason could ask questions, I pulled my backpack from the rear seat and stepped out of the car. I climbed over the limestones and strode right through the steam. I didn't have to go searching this time. I didn't have to look around to see if this was the right direction. I remembered. I knew.

"There," I said, pointing down. "That's where we're going."

"The caves?" Mason said. He'd clearly had other expectations when I'd whisked him off to the woods at night. "But all the entrances have been closed off."

"I wouldn't be so sure about that." I kicked off my boots and slipped off my suit jacket. Mason was large beside me. Without my boots on, I was so much smaller.

"This is . . ." Awe filled his voice. "How did you find this?"

I pulled my blouse over my head. The air was cold on my skin, exhilarating. "Turns out, I don't just play a detective on TV."

But Mason didn't move. The shadows caught in the creases of his face. "You're sure you want to do this?" There was a heaviness to his words I hadn't expected. I paused with my hands on the button of my pants, just long enough to check in with myself one last time.

I kept my eyes on his. I slipped one pant leg over a foot. Then the other.

Mason swallowed. He shifted between his feet. He shook himself as if loosening his muscles. "Then I guess we're doing this."

Mason stood on one leg as he pulled off his shoe. In a matter of seconds, his sweater and jeans were in a pile beside mine. His body was half-hidden in the shadows, yet the pieces I could see—the bulge of his forearm, the cut of his hip—helped my mind to sketch the rest of him. His shape was different now, more animal-like than it'd been at eighteen. Heat bloomed at the root of me.

Mason held his fingers curled around the waistband of his boxer briefs. "On or off?" His eyebrows quirked.

I stepped to Mason with a rope between my hands. I drew it around his waist, yanked hard to make the knot, just below his navel, where the hairs were darker, trailing down. "You can do what you want. But the rope is scratchy."

I went to pull away, but Mason touched a hand to my waist. A shock tore through me. It split me into two impulses that did not believe the other's truth. "Shouldn't we both tie in?" he asked. "Together? I wouldn't want you to get lost down there."

"I'll stay close to you."

"You will, will you?"

I turned to walk toward the opening.

To my back, he said, "You must really trust me."

"It's not that." I pulled the Maglite from my bag and flicked it on. The light shone on his face, making him whiter, smudged. "If you wanted to leave me alone down there, you'd have to do it in the darkness. I have the only flashlight."

I turned away from him and sat on the edge of the fissure. Steam spilled out of it like smoke through lips. Sulfur-rich and mineral. The hair on my arms settled as my pores opened, preparing for release. My knees fell away from each other. I took a breath.

I pushed myself off the edge. I fell. My stomach slipped out of its casing.

A rush of warm water gurgled around me. A splash. My feet landed on smooth rock. The water was up to my waist. The sulfur scent had thickened now. My skin was softer, like a bloom opening. I heard the whoosh of Mason landing behind me.

He belly flopped, miraculously not hurting himself. He stood and swiped back his hair, lifting his large biceps, making his body Herculean, ridiculously proportioned. "Holy shit." His voice echoed on every side of us.

I circled the flashlight so he could see. Water dripped all around us. Bats flapped up ahead. Insects zipped through the steam.

"I can't believe I didn't know this was here." Mason's voice was softer now, reverential. "I mean, I knew about the caves, obviously. But not this. My god." There seemed to be more he wanted to say. Instead, he let his mouth hang open. For once, speechless.

I touched his arm. "This way."

Water rippled around us as we waded and then swam down the same tunnel I'd swum through days before. I wasn't afraid. Maybe I should have been. But I felt the water's pulse. I was attuned to its familiar rhythms. I didn't believe it would harm me.

Mason and I climbed over the same ridge of stalagmites as I had before. We passed through another tunnel. All the while, Mason was behind me. I was aware how I must look to him. My cotton panties were thin. My skin stretched and released as I moved my legs. He used to joke with me about how much he liked my ass. At some point I'd realized it wasn't a joke.

"There," I said. I shone the flashlight on the opening three feet above my head.

"What is it?"

"I need you to give me a boost."

Mason was incredulous. "You're really not going to tell me what we're doing here?"

"I told you. Information doesn't go both ways."

Mason came to me then. He had his back against the wall. I put the flashlight under the crook of my arm. I laid my hands on his hands.

"Interlace your fingers," I said. "Like this."

Just like that, he was there, Eric. That rush of him, hot and sharp like a possession. Wool and musk at the back of my throat. I was touching Mason's hands but they were Eric's hands. "You okay?" Mason said.

I stepped on the lock of his fingers. I wrapped my hands around his shoulders, wet skin to wet skin. Warmth finding warmth. The beam of the flashlight filled the space between our faces. Mason met my eyes. His chest rose and fell. My chest rose and fell.

"You're crying."

I touched my hand to my cheek. It came away wet. I swallowed. "You'll be okay on your own here with no flashlight?"

"Why are you crying?"

I said, "It'll be dark."

"If I boost you up, I can't get to you. Will you be okay up there on your own?"

My smile was wan. "I'm always okay on my own."

"You've never been okay on your own. That's just not how you were made." He held me with his eyes. I was the first to look away.

I pushed my bare foot on Mason's hands. He pressed me up until my fingers found the opening. My body shimmied through. The flashlight fell loose from my grip. Its light moved ahead of me, like the view from a window on a moving train. I tried to stand, but the space wasn't tall enough to let me.

"You okay up there?" Mason shouted.

The crawl space smelled of rock and roots and, inexplicably, of flowers, something sweet. I was headed toward something. "Fine," I yelled back. There were tunnels on either side of me, small ones, bigger ones. They spread out like fingers. I was kneeling on their open palm. The flashlight scraped against the limestone as I headed through the biggest one.

Something about the swim or the climb had made me dizzy. I had to focus on every movement, every press of my palm, every scrape of my knee to steady myself as I went forward toward the shrine.

The sweet smell was getting stronger now. I imagined flowers lain at an altar. I imagined the monuments of death. An under-the-earth garden. Neil's roommate's monogrammed flashlight.

My fingers dug into something sharp. I slipped as I touched the edge of a sinkhole. I stumbled.

I collected myself. I turned to go another way.

I made my way around the bend. I gasped.

All at once, it was six years ago. I knew because it was my and Eric's first vacation together at that lake house that smelled of salt spray and rosewater, where we'd tried to light the fireplace only to send smoke choking us out of the house. We'd taken a bottle of wine with us to the beach. We'd stripped and slipped under the cover of the lake. We were naked, panting, drunk. In the moonlight, we glowed.

"Ready," Eric said.

"Set." My voice was a moan.

Neither one of us said *Go*. Yet we swam as if running, our breathing rapid-fire. The water made us wild. Clawing. Speeding. So goddamned alive. Hair tangled over my face. I couldn't see where we were going, but it didn't matter. All that mattered was that he was beside me. I reached forward and Eric's fingers wrapped around my thigh. I pulled back and my body twisted to face his. We moved together, under the moonlight, our slippery bodies entwined.

Eric's fingers found their way inside me as I wrapped my legs around him. I felt his breath against me. Ragged. Guttural. Growling even as we bobbed. His mouth filled my mouth. His fingers slipped out of me. His body slipped into me. My back arched. My legs squeezed. Eric kicked to keep us afloat. To keep us from drowning. To keep us this alive.

We flipped onto our backs. Sweat beaded our faces. We drank mouthfuls of silver light. Ripples expanded around us. I took hold of Eric's hand. I let the others go. I let my parents go. I let my family go. I didn't need them anymore. Not when I had this.

All at once, the memory faded.

A new one arrived in its place.

I opened the front door of our apartment. A redheaded boy handed me an envelope. It was white with a plastic screen that showed Eric's name. Our address.

I was in the middle of something—reading? Cleaning? I wanted to get back to it.

I headed toward the galley kitchen, our kitchen, with those

yellow-green walls and the flowered backsplash I pretended to hate. I held the envelope out as if to toss it on the credenza. Then I saw the return address. Then my whole body seized.

The walls crashed down around me.

"Leigh!" From someplace far away, Mason was shouting.

I blinked. My vision was blurry. The side of my face was cold. I'd been lying down, asleep.

"Leigh, something is falling. We have to go!"

The cave. The tunnel. Mason. The present came back to me in pixels. I pushed up from the ground. I wanted to shout to him, to tell him I was coming. But my voice stayed locked in my throat.

"Leigh!" he called. "Leigh, come back!"

The crawl space was wide enough that I was able to turn around. When I did, I was still dizzy. The space before me moved in and out. My view was covered in haze. My hands, my legs were unsteady beneath me. I needed to move forward. I didn't know which way that was.

Mason kept shouting my name. Over and over. His voice bounced over the tunnels. I closed my eyes. I knew I shouldn't. But they were heavy. I was so tired. Everything was heavy.

I felt the weight of Simone in my arms. I bit my tongue. My mouth filled with rust. I opened my eyes. I had to stay awake. I couldn't remember from which way I'd come. I started to panic. My heart revved. My throat was swollen and hard.

Then, before me, a streak of red.

I flinched.

I stared, unbelieving.

A red-bellied snake striped the opening of the tunnel to my right. Long. Thick-bodied. Almond eyes. Its scales expanded and contracted as it moved.

It was not just any snake. It was *my* snake. The snake from my dream.

It slithered away. Down the tunnel. Fast.

Mason was calling my name.

In the distance, a boom like an explosion. I didn't have the luxury of disbelief.

I followed the snake's path. I fumbled to grip the flashlight. I couldn't feel my knees as they crashed against the stone. I couldn't feel the jagged rock as my chest scraped against it. My eyes were going in and out of focus. Mason's voice was getting louder. I could no longer understand his words.

Rubble hailed down from above. I tasted it in my mouth. Up my nostrils. I couldn't stop coughing.

There were rocks in front of me. My clumsy fingers smashed at sickening angles as I pushed them away. Mason kept calling.

I broke through the opening.

All at once, I was dangling out of it.

All at once, hands wrapped around me.

I was falling into Mason.

24

I WOKE UP NAKED, IN MASON'S LOFT BED. THE BEDSIDE CLOCK read 8:07.

Mason was lying beside me, mercifully facing away. I took in his bare arms, his bare back, the outline of the scorpion tattoo on his shoulder.

I touched my tongue with my finger. I felt the tender spot I'd bitten to stay awake. I felt between my legs for semen. I breathed out my relief.

My clothes hung over the back of a wooden chair. I slipped them on quickly. There were scrapes on my knees. They were on my elbows, too. On the heels of my hands. My thumbs were purple and swollen. A pain shot through my chest.

Eric. He'd been right beside me. Inside me. I closed my eyes. I searched. But the memory was already fading. Only, I knew now it wasn't just a memory.

I'd hallucinated.

I needed to understand why.

I moved quickly, quietly. I didn't want Mason to wake.

I finished dressing. I crept downstairs. I held my boots in my hand. In the kitchen, there were only four cabinets. Inside, plastic tubs of protein powder. Glass jars of quinoa. Artisanal nuts.

I dumped a jar of sprouted cashews into a bowl. I held it up to the light that streamed through the lattice window.

Yes, this would do just fine.

The medical examiner's office was just as bright as the last time I'd been there. Only, this time, Dr. Aliche was in full autopsy gear, bent over an abdomen split in the shape of a T. Clamps held back flayed skin. It smelled of disinfectant and mouthwash. The air was refrigerated, chemical, foul.

"Why, Detective O'Donnell," Dr. Aliche said. He cupped a stomach in the bowl of his hands. "Isn't this a pleasant surprise. Although I must say, you do look a bit worse for wear. Late night?"

I placed a mason jar of yellowish liquid on the silver cart beside him. "I need a drug test on this." My voice came out gritty. "At your earliest convenience."

Dr. Aliche looked between me and the jar. He was still holding the corpse's stomach. "Am I to understand you've just bestowed upon me a jar of your urine? So kind of you to offer. But I'm afraid I prefer tea."

"I'd like you to test this for Schedule I drugs, paying special attention to naturally occurring hallucinogens."

Dr. Aliche deposited the stomach into a silver bowl. His eyebrows knitted together. "Detective, am I to understand that someone drugged you?"

I opened my mouth to tell him no, it wasn't like that. But I hesitated. Mason had poured our first round of drinks out of my sight. He could have laced mine with something. But then why let me drive? Why let me go off in the caves on my own? I shook my head. "Last night, I was in the caves underneath the falls."

Dr. Aliche snapped off his gloves. He dropped them into the bin marked MEDICAL WASTE. "Looking to reunite our guppy with his family? Is that it?"

"I smelled something sweet," I said. "I suspect the drug was gaseous. I hallucinated."

"What did you see?"

"The hallucinations aren't relevant."

"They are if you'd like your urine tested."

I tapped my foot on the linoleum. If he said no, I'd have to drive all the way to the M.E.'s in Toledo and explain the story all over again. If I got this over with, I could shower. I said, "It was a snake. I saw a red-bellied snake."

Dr. Aliche's concern slipped off his face. He lifted a fresh pair of gloves from a box and returned to his cadaver. Its skin was bluish. Its edges were brittle. He snapped each glove on and wiggled his fingers to adjust their fit. He said, "You are aware that snakes do inhabit caves from time to time?"

"It was a snake I've seen before."

He picked up a pair of tweezers. "Would that not suggest it was real?"

"In a dream."

Dr. Aliche did a funny thing just then. His shoulders tightened and his face became serious. He set down his tweezers. He spoke in a soft voice. "Is this the first time a dream of yours has come true?"

I thought he was saying I was psychic. "Weren't you the one who said the medical field is constrained by the facts?"

"I believe I was the one who told you the most obvious explanation is the one most likely to be true."

"You think it's more plausible that I had a premonition than that the caves released a toxic gas?"

"Not a premonition, Detective." Dr. Aliche looked at me with sad eyes. His mouth wilted. It was like being punched in the jaw.

"You mean a mental illness."

"It is the obvious question to ask." The hairs of my neck bit against my collar. "Did you not suffer a mental incident when you were in New York? Isn't that why you were suspended?"

I blinked away something hot. "You aren't supposed to have access to those records."

"I'm a doctor. I can access any medical records I want."

"Why would you?"

He paused, considered. "Yesterday, Chief Becker asked me to look into your medical history."

I closed my mouth. I searched the lines of Dr. Aliche's face.

"He wanted to know if you were fit to serve."

My muscles, my joints, my skin stiffened. Ronan had assured me the chief trusted his judgment. But that wasn't true. Becker had agreed to take me on only so long as I wouldn't be trouble.

Now he was looking for an excuse to have me gone. I said, "What did you tell him?"

Dr. Aliche's eyes gave away nothing. "I told him there was nothing in your file worthy of note."

My phone buzzed in my pocket. I pulled it out. It was Ronan. I looked at Dr. Aliche square on. I didn't know how to say this. "Why did you lie for me?"

Dr. Aliche's mouth slid sideways. He reminded me of one of the trickster faeries from Eamon's stories, the ones who make sport of human life. He returned his attention to the corpse. "Let's just say, I have a fondness for interesting specimens. I'll have your urine ready at my earliest convenience."

I wanted to say something—thank you?—instead, I swiped the screen of my phone. The door clapped shut behind me. The air was warm as I entered the hallway.

"Hey," Ronan said. "It's—"

"Yes, I know who it is. You don't have to announce yourself every time you—"

"It's Estella Wagner."

I was in the middle of a beige-walled, beige-carpeted hallway. Baroque pictures of viscera hung from the walls. My thoughts were slow, underwater. "What's Estella Wagner?"

"You'd asked me to see who'd written about the shrines. There's Dr. Ortiz, who's mostly published academic papers. Then there's a woman named Estella Wagner. I found some references to her on a few blogs, some interviews with her."

My breath came back to me.

"She's like a local psychic or something. But listen, you'll never believe this," Ronan chirped. "She's Calvin Wagner's sister-in-law. The Historical Society guy. It gets better. She's also—"

I swallowed. "Maude Hummel's twin sister."

"How did you know? I've never even heard of her until now. And I've lived here longer than—"

"I'll meet up with you later, okay? I have to—"

"Go. Yeah."

"Ronan."

"No, it's fine. Really."

"Any luck with Angie Owens?"

But Ronan had already hung up.

It didn't matter.

I knew where I needed to go. If Estella Wagner really was the local expert on the caves, she might know how to help me find the place William, Neil, and Duncan had died.

She might know another way in.

25

I TRAVELED DOWN THE UNNAMED ROADS DR. WAGNER HAD told me about days before. The lane was so narrow and so long that there was no going back, only forward. I had the feeling, as in the caves, of being headed the right way.

The trees out here were different from the others I'd seen on my trip. Gone were the red maples and bushy oaks from the town. Gone were the scarred birches and the pinnate-leafed ashes from the Sticks.

Here, the trees were spaced evenly apart. Their branches fanned wide like hands reaching for hands. Their leaves were dark and round. Nestled between them, improbably, were bushels of apples.

They were ripe and bright. When I rolled down my window, the smell of them filled my mouth. They were so close I could have plucked one off its branch. I might have done this, but something—reverence or awe or something else—caused my hand to retract.

Up ahead, the trees gave way to an opening. Burrowed around garden beds and a stump with an axe on it stood a white cottage. It had a timbered facade and a round-top door. It was the sort of place that belonged in the English countryside where there was no electricity or indoor plumbing.

The wrought-iron fixtures rattled. The heavy wooden door swung open. There she was, Estella Hummel Wagner.

I pulled along the dirt lane, toward her. My first thought was that this had to be Maude Hummel. My next thought was this couldn't possibly be Maude Hummel. Estella wasn't wearing a musty housedress dragging its threads. Instead, she wore an A-line dress, a blushing shade of pink. Her hair was white, like Maude's, but soft and to her shoulders, not nested on top of her head. Then there was her smile.

I couldn't imagine Maude smiling, not like that, not so the white of her teeth sparkled as if they'd never encountered a stain. Estella was in her eighties, but she was still that radiant girl from her wedding photograph.

I got out of the car. I took the winding stone path to the place where Estella was standing. As we came face-to-face, I was startled at the familiarity of her eyes. The same shade of blue. The same tiny pupils. The same feeling up my spine like ice.

"Estella Wagner?"

"You must be Leigh."

"Detective O'Donnell."

"I'm afraid we don't use honorifics in this house. Calvin Wagner is just Calvin. You are just Leigh."

It was strange that she'd brought him up. I couldn't picture Dr. Wagner in this house. Yet he'd told me that he and his

183

sister-in-law still kept in touch. He must have told her I was coming. It was the only way she could've known my name.

"Have you had breakfast yet?" Estella smiled. "Oh, never mind. I don't care if you have." She put a hand to my arm. She squeezed gently, like a grandmother. "I'll make you eat with me anyway."

I was caught off guard enough to follow her.

Within minutes, I was sitting at a round, claw-foot table in a room lit by hazy sunshine. I smelled ink somewhere, and asters. Two place settings were waiting for us at the table. Estella had a silver percolator.

I was surprised that she'd been so welcoming, but then again, if what Janice had said was true, that this town really did pretend Estella didn't exist, she probably didn't have many visitors.

Estella poured coffee into our cups. She mixed in milk even though I didn't take any. There was a cake, too, scalloped with slices of apples. It smelled of cinnamon and caramel and cloves. She cut thick, decadent slices. They curled away from her knife. "Just coffee for me," I said. I covered my plate with my hand.

Estella slipped the plate out from under my fingers. "Nonsense. You need to get your strength up. Especially after wandering the caves all night."

There was that feeling again, up my spine. I didn't like it, for the same reason I didn't like unsecured scenes and hands where I couldn't see them. "Why do you think I was in the caves?"

Estella heaped a slice of cake onto the plate. She pressed her lips together for a long moment. "Were you trying to keep it a secret?"

"How did you know?"

A beat. Maybe two. At last she said, "I can smell it on you, dear. I've been going down there since I was a girl. It's the scent of an old lover, you see. I'd know it anywhere."

I was embarrassed at how obvious her answer had been. I did smell like the caves. It was on my skin. In my hair. On my clothes. In my mouth. Like earth and mineral. Like sulfur. Like steam. Incongruously I thought, *So we have this in common.*

I said, "Then you must know about the shrine to the Hunter."

Estella raised her thin eyebrows. She was still as she held my eyes. I thought she was going to deny the shrine's existence, as Dr. Wagner had. Instead, she said, "Is that what you were looking for? I confess, I didn't take you for the type."

"What type is that?"

A smile wended its way across her features, not just her mouth, but over her eyes, her cheeks. Even her nose lifted. She was so beautiful. She said, "The type who believes in things she cannot touch."

I could see it now, what Janice had said about her being an eccentric. I said, "I have reason to think three men died somewhere in those caves last month. I believe they were looking for the shrines."

Estella's gaze drifted out the window then, like a bird alighting on a new branch. "Do you notice," she said, "how seeds always begin their journey toward awakening when they're under the ground?"

I followed her gaze to land on her gardens.

"Years ago, I tried to plant elderflower bushes. Way out there.

But they weren't growing. At last, I trudged out there to check on them. But can you believe it? I'd forgotten to bury the bulbs. You see, every living creature needs darkness to grow."

Images flashed before me, of what the darkness had shown me.

Eric, our hands under moonlight.

The envelope from the redheaded boy.

The snake.

Me, falling.

Mason holding me in his arms.

I took a bite of the cake. I didn't taste it. I only felt the crumbs soften inside my mouth. I felt my tongue kick it back.

"When I was a girl," Estella said, "my sister and I would spend hours in those caves. They were our secrets. Maude and I lived in them. We built elaborate constructions inside them. We decorated them with colored strings and tin cups, tatting doilies, dolls made from pine cones and sticks. We didn't know it at the time, but we were practicing a ritual that has existed since the beginning of humanity. We were giving them offerings. That's why the caves chose us. That's why we found her."

Estella's eyes flicked away from the gardens. They focused on me.

"The Hunter."

That word from her mouth was like hands on my throat. I said, "You and Maude were the two little girls who found the skeleton?" They were the girls Dr. Ortiz had told me about.

"We climbed the rope ladder we'd built. We went down the long tunnel and then she was in my head. The Hunter. I could feel her."

Estella's blink relaxed her face.

"I was crawling, but I wasn't seeing the ground in front of me. You understand? Instead, I saw myself. Here, in a cottage just like this one. I saw myself as I would become. Having enough. Being enough. Thirsting but not being sick from it."

She focused on the tract of land outside the window. It was covered over with apple trees and a patchwork of gardens with fleshy cabbages and tomatoes in their final fruiting, bushy herbs, tender greens.

The clouds shifted over the sun and Estella's face darkened. "But Maude didn't see that future at all," she said. "To Maude, the Hunter showed decay, a life growing backward. She saw herself retreating back into the earth. She saw anger and guilt. Shame. Repudiation. She saw ruin.

"I look back now and I think this was the beginning of our split. The darkness had shown me renewal, whereas it had shown her destruction. We could no longer live parallel lives."

Estella sipped her coffee. The cup clinked against its saucer.

"We'd reached the final leg, where the large tunnel tapers into a hole. We kept going. At last, we saw her. The skeleton. The shrine."

Outside the clouds shifted again. The light through the window hit Estella's eyes more directly. Her irises became kaleidoscopes. I found myself staring into them, watching for the shapes to shift into another configuration. I meant to say, *What else did you find?* Instead, I said, "What did she look like?"

"Radiant." Estella's kaleidoscope eyes opened wider. "I fell to my knees. I relinquished myself to the Hunter, for I knew if I accepted her darkness, she would help me grow."

All of this was so crazy. Yet I couldn't look away.

"Unfortunately, Maude wasn't ready to relinquish herself," Estella said. "She wanted control. She fought to turn away from the Hunter's truths. She thought she could outrun her. But none of us can outrun fate. None of us. A bone snapped in Maude's foot. It forced her to the ground. It forced her supplication."

Estella swallowed. There were tears in her eyes. I did not blink.

"I wish I could describe to you the horror of my sister's scream. Inside those caves, there's nothing but your own body to absorb it. It stays with you. In your bones."

Estella rubbed her fingers together.

"We couldn't go back the way we'd come. With Maude's foot, it would be too dangerous. I begged the Hunter for a short-cut to get us out. I closed my eyes and let her lead us. It worked. Within minutes, we had found the surface again."

"How did you get out?"

Estella shook her head. Her eyes glazed over. "I told Maude to lie to our parents. I told her to say she'd fallen over a rock. But Maude told them anyway. Our parents sold her out. The Hunter."

Estella ran her fingernail across the gold edging of her plate. Her slice of cake was gone. Though I couldn't remember her eating it. Mine was gone, too.

"The caves were on their land, after all," Estella said. "It was within their rights to sell her. The university couldn't extract the skeleton, but there were artifacts down there, gifts to the Hunter. Our parents sold them. They became rich."

I thought of the half a million dollars in Maude's house. At last it made sense.

Estella lifted her lace napkin from her lap. She folded it into a square. She said, "The town was angry. They didn't think our parents should have kept the money. They claimed it should go to the town. Yet our parents had convinced themselves they'd earned it, like Cortés and his Aztec gold."

Estella grimaced.

"Three weeks after the first check arrived, our parents crashed the Oldsmobile. They both died. Yet Maude and I survived. It was fate.

"Maude and I told our brothers not to touch the money. We told them it was cursed. For a year, they believed us. But then their willpower ran out. They got it in their heads they'd earned it. By taking care of us. By surviving. Our brothers had an extravagant cabin built for themselves. They brought us out there for a big family welcome. But instead of bringing us closer—"

I said, "They burned alive."

Estella nodded.

"Because the money was cursed?"

"Some might say that."

"Some might say it was arson."

"The ultimate curse indeed." Estella's face, before so pliant, became unexpectedly stern.

Something about the set of her features made me imagine the scene, she and Maude with a can of gasoline. A single match, lit by one, thrown by the other. I pictured it, but I didn't know if it was true.

Estella said, "You don't have to believe me. Sometimes I think back to all that has happened, and I wonder if I've made it all up. I wonder if I'm simply an old woman trying to make sense of things she doesn't understand. But please listen, Leigh. Listen to what I'm about to tell you."

Estella took my hand in hers. I started to pull away. But her fingernails dug into my palm. Her grip was unrelenting.

"You need to stop searching for the shrine. The Hunter doesn't want to be found."

I said, "Three men are dead."

In a voice so deep as to send a chill under my skin, she said, "That should tell you all you need to know."

From the set of her jaw, from the stone in her eyes, from that dark voice, I knew. However much I pressed her, she wasn't going to tell me the alternate way to access the shrine.

She wasn't going to help me find the Hunter.

26

I PULLED UP IN FRONT OF THE HOUSE IN DESPERATE NEED OF a shower.

As I walked inside, I felt the weight of how little I still knew about the men's deaths. This was my sixth full day in Copper Falls and I still hadn't scratched the surface of this case.

My keys jangled against my thigh as I stepped into the foyer. It smelled of floor wax and dish soap, but nothing edible. A part of me was disappointed no one had made the house breakfast, the way that, on Fridays, my mom used to do. As soon as the thought occurred to me, I felt ridiculous. Of course they wouldn't.

I had my hand on the banister to go upstairs when, from the family room, came the high-pitched voices of cartoons. The door was cracked. I stepped toward it and eased it open. The room smelled of Cheerios and vacuum powder and of my daughter.

Simone's hair was wrapped in her favorite scarf. She was curled up on the sofa. Her little body snuggled a brocade pillow. But her eyes didn't leave the screen, even as I said hello.

I sat down on the velvet sofa. I moved her head to rest on my lap. I placed my hand on her head.

Cartoon dogs were scooting in front of us. I never knew what they were doing, only that, normally, they made my daughter smile. Simone was looking at them. But her eyes were glazed over. "How are you doing?" I asked.

"Fine."

"How was your morning?" She always got up early.

"Fine."

"What have you been doing?"

"Nothing."

I watched the screen with her. At last I said, "Where's Arnie?"

That's when Simone started to cry. Not slow, quiet tears, but big, fat, loud ones. Simone cried and her whole body heaved. Instinctively, I pulled her to my chest. I felt her sobs against my throat.

"What happened?" I said.

She shook her head.

"What's the matter?" My mind was racing through scenarios—something Frankie had said to her, a "joke" he thought was funny. Maybe Eamon had made her do chores and this made her feel bad for reasons she couldn't articulate. "Simone, tell me."

The words came out muffled through her sobs. "He's gone."

"Who's gone?"

Her eyes were filled with tears. "Arnie."

My shoulders, my arms relaxed. "It's okay, baby. We'll find him."

"I hate it here."

"It's okay."

"I want Daddy."

I held Simone gently, as if she were an egg and I was wrapping her up to keep her from breaking. I rocked her. I shushed her the way my mother used to shush me. I closed my eyes and felt Eric's fingers wrap around my own.

I should have told her everything would be okay. I should have reassured her. Instead I bit my lip.

"Me too, baby."

Me too.

We searched for Arnie the Armadillo well into the afternoon. Frankie scoured the lot. Bear combed the yard. Eamon opened every drawer and every closet as if Arnie were playing a game of hide-and-seek.

Simone and I tried to retrace her steps from earlier that morning, but it was no use. Eventually the only thing I could do was distract her and hope to redirect her emotions away from what she'd lost.

I found I still remembered my mother's pancake recipe. The gist of it anyway. I withdrew Mom's yellow Pyrex mixing bowl from the dusty back cabinet and got to work.

Simone and I made pancakes in funny shapes. She sat on the stool at the kitchen island, where I used to sit when my mom cooked. We talked about animals, about the difference between an aardvark and an elephant, a crocodile and an iguana, a giraffe and a leopard. "Rats and opossums both have hairless tails," I said, flipping a pancake I'd insisted was shaped like an opossum. "So they must be the same thing."

"Mouses, too!" Simone said, giggling.

I crossed my arms. I made a serious face. "I see what you mean. A mouse is clearly not an opossum. This must be a rat."

I flipped the pancake onto the plate, and we proceeded to our next set of animals, our next round of pancakes, our next act of pretending everything was fine.

Then it was time for Simone's hair.

After her bath, Simone sat playing with the trinkets on my old vanity—a music box, a locked diary I never wrote in—as I did her hair.

I combed. I separated it into segments. I combed again. I applied cream. I twisted and twisted and twisted. I applied more cream. My hands hurt, but I liked it. I liked my fingers on my daughter's scalp. I liked feeling the shape of the person who'd once lived inside of me, the person whose body was still so connected to my own.

During Eamon's search for Arnie, he'd found some ancient crayons that were dry and crumbling. A few were good enough to use. While Simone's hair dried, we sat on the Persian rug in my room. I sorted out the unusable crayons. Simone made posters for the walls.

Some were pictures of Arnie, which gave the display an air of a memorial. But the rest of the pictures were of Eric. Of the square of his jawline, of that dimple that emerged like a prize.

Of Simone holding each of our hands as we squeezed in on either side of her. Eric towered over us, taller in her memory than in real life. In all of the pictures, we were smiling.

It was late in the afternoon when a number I didn't recognize rang my phone. It was a Copper Falls area code. I answered on the second ring. "Leigh, hi. It's me, Janice." My classmate from high school. From the CFPD.

She wanted to meet that night for a drink. Was I free around nine? She sounded nervous, unsure of herself, a little scared.

I looked from Simone to the pictures of Eric that would stare back at me long after she'd fallen asleep, to his smile, to his dimple, to the mythical size of him. "Sure."

I didn't know what Janice wanted to say to me. But whatever it was, it was clear that a part of her was having second thoughts.

27

THERE WERE TWO BARS IN TOWN. THE INEXPLICABLY NAMED
Animal House, where the coasters were napkins and the glasses
were foggy and indestructible. Then there was the other bar, the
bar whose name had probably changed a half dozen times over
the years, where the cocktails were served in delicate coupes and
the beer came in shapely glasses, too small to hold a pint. This
was where I met Janice.

The bar, now called Zeitgeist, had plush seats and Restoration-
style furniture. The music was low and twangy, the voice singing, a little flat. It made me feel vaguely sad, contemplative, and
not at all in the mood for other people.

Janice was already there. She was seated in a porter chair
with a balloon back and a hook under the armrest for a lantern.
She was out of her usual flannel, instead wearing a high-necked,
sleeveless blouse, skinny jeans, and heels. I was also out of my
suit. I'd put on a V-neck, jeans, and boots. We should have

looked the same as everyone else, yet we were immediately recognizable as different.

The women around us were awash in burnt orange, fire-engine red, glittery gold, and electric blue. They wore heavy makeup and had intricately styled hair. Yet we were both in black, both with simple hairstyles and no makeup. Even our bodies were stretched thinner, like we'd traveled here from a different climate.

There, in the corner opposite to ours, sat Bear.

His thick, unruly hair was slicked back. His low-center-of-gravity body was stuffed into a collared shirt. He was sitting across from a woman I didn't recognize. She was older, pretty.

As I approached Janice, she caught the direction of my gaze. "Esther Schott," she said, motioning to the woman. "They've been together four or five years now. She's Duncan Schott's aunt."

I sat. I felt a pang the way I had when I'd found out some other detectives were on a group text. For all of Bear's overtures about reconciliation, he'd failed to mention he was dating one of the victims' aunts.

The waiter approached. He placed two coupes on the low table. "Leigh O'Donnell?" His expression opened. "Wow, I haven't seen you since high school. How have you been?"

I vaguely remembered the man's face. He had dark hair and light eyes. His belly sagged in the middle and his chin disappeared into his neck. He tucked his tray under his arm and told me about his life, his kids, his wife—another person we went to high school with—and how he only worked nights so he could watch his kids during the day. He started to continue. Janice cut him off.

"Steve," she said, her voice sharp.

"Right." Steve looked sheepish. "I should get to my other tables. Good seeing you, Leigh. Hey, welcome back."

As Steve disappeared behind the bar, Janice sipped her drink. She laughed the way you do when you get a flat tire. "I was always so jealous," she said. "How easy it was for you here."

As she focused on something in the distance, I watched her, unbelieving. All the years I'd spent here had been as an outsider. Then my father had died quickly and my mother had died slowly, and I'd been alone in a house with too many people. I wouldn't have used the word *easy*. It was curious to me that she would. I said, "Why was it hard for you?"

Janice swirled the lemon peel around in her glass. "Everyone had preconceptions about me. That my mom was easy. Just like her mother. That my dad was a drunk. Just like his father. That I'd be like both of them. Just stupid family drama. But you learn to live up to people's expectations. It's easier than proving them wrong."

She looked away from me. She bit her lip.

She said, "I guess you've figured out this isn't a social call."

"It had crossed my mind." I took a sip of my drink. She took a gulp of hers. She wrung her hands. I waited. I knew that why-ever we were here, whatever she wanted to say to me, it was more for her benefit than it was for mine. Yet I didn't rule out that she might tell me something useful.

I folded my hands. She said, "Every time someone requests a

record from the records room, I have to log it. Normally, the chief reads through the logs about once a month. But since you've been back"—her eyes flashed wide—"he's been asking to see them every day."

She took another swallow. I waited for her to continue.

"When you were just looking into the deaths of the guys from the Sticks, that was one thing. But then you asked for the files of Maude Hummel and Estella Wagner. After that, you wanted to know about the houses targeted in the meth raids."

She ran a hand over her short hair. She let her fingers rest on her mouth. She looked at a crumpled cocktail napkin on the floor. Her eyes were out of focus.

"Becker, I mean, he's kind of a dick about stuff anyway, especially when it comes to people he can't control. But now he thinks you've gotten carried away. Those were his words, *carried away.*"

Janice cut her gaze to me. I knew that look. She was watching for my reaction.

"Becker said I'm not allowed to give you more records. He's revoked your access. For good."

I took a moment to let this sink in. Yet I found I wasn't surprised. Maybe because of what Bear had told me about Becker stealing from the people in the Sticks. Maybe because of what Dr. Aliche had said about Becker requesting my medical records to see if I was fit to serve. Maybe because I didn't like him, and still, after everything, I trusted my instincts more than I trusted anything else. I said, "What doesn't he want me to find out?"

"I just . . ." Janice's cheeks were red now. Her lips pressed together and released. She was sweating. Her voice was low. "I can't lose my job."

"You can get another job."

"I don't want to be charged with obstruction."

"So don't obstruct anything."

"You don't understand."

"What don't I understand?"

Janice bit her lip. She looked out into the crowd. It was mostly people in their twenties and thirties. A handful were older. They were seated on tufted sofas and leather chairs with scrollwork arms. They sat in clusters, or in pairs, but never alone. The seats where Bear and his girlfriend had been sitting were empty.

"You know I went to the U of M, right?" Janice said.

She said it like there was only one U of M in the whole world. But I knew what she meant. The University of Michigan.

"I'd gotten into their School of Information. I was getting my PhD, studying with the great Margaret Hedstrom, if you can believe it. I mean, her paper on understanding electronic incunabula—that's what we call . . . oh, never mind. It revolutionized the field.

"I was going to be a real archivist. In Paris. Or New York. Willa and I were going to travel the world together. I was even thinking of asking her to marry me. I'd been looking at rings. But then everything changed."

The wall behind Janice was papered in dark paisley. It looked like a purple sea struck with moonlight. In it, Janice was drowning.

"At first, I thought I was just working too hard," Janice said, wiping sweat from her brow. "I would stumble and lose my balance at least once a day. I told everybody I was just getting clumsy in my dotage. It was funny."

Janice's gaze bounced around me.

"People kept saying I needed to get more sleep, but as it was, I was sleeping all the time. I thought I was fighting something. The flu? I don't know. Mono? Then I got into a car accident. It was like vaulting over a cliff. I knew I'd lost control."

Janice swallowed a mouthful of cocktail. I saw now what I hadn't before, the signs of inebriation. In her unfocused gaze. The slump of her neck. The sloppy shape of her mouth. Whatever she had to say to me, she'd gotten herself good and drunk to do it.

She said, "I couldn't see where my lane ended and the next one began. Then I got the diagnosis." She drew in her breath. "Multiple sclerosis."

I registered anew the curve of Janice's back. It wasn't from stooping over books. It was scoliosis. Probably associated with MS. Now it was my turn to look away.

"Because my case is so aggressive," Janice said, "soon I'm not going to be able to live independently. I'll lose control of my body one muscle group at a time."

I didn't want to talk about illness. I said, "So you came back home."

She searched the twinkling lights. Her eyes shimmered. "I didn't want to. God, I'd worked so hard to leave. Do you think this was what I'd planned? Willa and I were going to go to Amsterdam in the summer. But she took another woman on our vacation. I couldn't believe it. It was so easy for her to move on."

As Janice spoke, something hard pressed against my chest,

like a buckle cinching tight. I thought of Eric, his new apartment, his new *friend,* his new life. It'd been so easy for him. Yet I couldn't even make a move with Mason.

Janice said, "I tried to date other people, but I felt like I had to lay it all out on the table. I wasn't going to get hurt like that again. I needed the person I was dating to know that if we stayed together, they'd be signing up to be my caretaker. I needed them to know I'd die young and there was nothing anyone could do about it."

I drained my glass. So did Janice. Steve arrived with another round. The buzz of the liquor was kicking in now. My head, my limbs were floating but heavy. I needed to be sober enough to drive home. Yet I took another drink. I didn't want to stop.

"I told my dad everything," Janice said. "About the diagnosis. About Willa. He said to come home. He said the town would take care of me. Just like that. No questions asked. It was such a relief. Like you think you're in free fall and then you realize all along there's been this net."

She focused on my face. Again that flat-tire laugh. "What am I saying? You know what I mean. The town did the same thing for you."

I started to say it wasn't the same for me at all. But suddenly, I wasn't so sure. Was the reason Becker took me in because Ronan had asked him to? Or simply because I'd once lived here, too?

"The thing is"—Janice rubbed the knob of her shoulder—"I'm not cheap. I'm not talking about what they pay me. That's abysmal. Especially given my degrees. It's my health insurance bills.

"Because I went without insurance before the diagnosis,

when I enrolled again, I got classified as part of a high-risk group. The premiums are in the thousands of dollars every month. I have a GoFundMe page to help with some of the costs of the more experimental treatments. But my bills are just another thing we can't afford."

In the background, the music had changed. It went from doleful and brooding to a heavier bass, faster. The configurations of people in the bar had also changed shape. Bodies were closer together. Groups were bigger. Boundaries were less rigid. "Janice," I said. "What are you trying to say?"

Janice's gaze was unwavering. "Copper Falls is broke."

As she said this, my mind was already conjuring images to contradict her. The pristine grounds at the Historical Society. The impeccable Queen Annes on every street. The wraparound porches. The never-peeling paint. The ivy-strewn library. The gazebo and its marigolds.

"You can't tell, right?" she said. "That's the beauty of it. People feel like they have to keep up appearances. If the infrastructure starts to decline, nobody's going to want to live here. If people don't want to live here, then everything our ancestors spent generations working toward vanishes. Just like that."

She looked at her hands. Gathered her courage. Then raised her eyes to mine.

"The truth is, if we didn't get an infusion of cash, people would've had to start selling. They'd have had no choice. Developers have been circling the town area for ages. They want to put in condos. Chain stores. Maybe even a McDonald's."

Janice shook her head.

"If that happens, there's no community anymore. There's no

the town will take care of you. It becomes every man for himself. That's the thing that scares everyone. This town, it's all we have."

It would have been easy to make fun of Janice. Yet, I was surprised at how immediately I felt the loss. Even though I'd never really loved this place, even though there'd always been something a little too perfect about it, I also didn't want it to become what the rest of the Midwest had, for decades, been transforming into: a collection of box stores and parking lots, of drive-thrus and twenty-four-hour pharmacies, a place where people could only ever be workers or shoppers, but never anyone with power. I said, "So Copper Falls went into debt."

She nodded. "Our debts weren't huge, but we couldn't get out of them."

At last, the pieces were beginning to click into place. The money Bear said the police had stolen. Why they needed it. "To get out of debt, Copper Falls stole from the people in the Sticks."

"It's not like it sounds."

"Then tell me," I said. Janice, by now, was slowing down on her drink, which probably meant she wouldn't be coherent for much longer. I thought of what Janice said about her dad being a drunk, about living up to expectations. "Tell me so I understand."

"The Hummels stole money from the town," Janice said, her speech a little slurred. "Years ago. I don't know the details. But then, seven or eight months ago, these guys from the Sticks started hanging around Maude. Doing her lawn work or whatever."

I nodded. William's dad had told me as much.

"Next thing you know, she gave them a big chunk of that money. Something like fifty grand. Each."

I stopped nodding. That, William's dad hadn't told me.

"It wasn't even hers to give." Janice threw up a hand. She almost swatted the lamp behind her. She didn't notice. She said, "That money belonged to the town. Everybody knew that. They just didn't know there was any money left. So Chief Becker went to these guys—"

"Duncan Schott, Neil Mayer, and William Houser?"

"He asked them to do the right thing, to give the money back to the town. We were the ones who really needed it. But the people in the Sticks, they don't have our sense of solidarity, you know? What do you expect? Community means nothing to them. I mean, just look at where they live."

She sighed loudly.

"So the chief did what he thought was right."

I couldn't believe I was saying this. I couldn't believe it was true. "They seized the maple syrup production. And while they were at it, they swept Neil's, William's, and Duncan's houses and took all the cash Maude had given them."

Janice looked up at the lights. She swayed. "The chief said we had to make the truth so outlandish no one would think it could be a lie," Janice said. "The people in town were more willing to believe the people in the Sticks were dealing drugs than that they'd created a legitimate business."

I said, "Shortly after the CFPD stole from, among others, William Houser, Neil Mayer, and Duncan Schott, they ended up dead. Is that correct?"

Janice looked away. Nodded.

A flutter came from under my ribs. Here it was. The thing I had been missing. At last, I had a motive in the deaths of Neil, Duncan, and William. In the end, it'd had nothing to do with the caves. They'd been killed because they knew the town had stolen money. Someone was afraid they wouldn't keep quiet about it.

I still didn't understand why the person who'd killed them thought it more likely that William, Neil, and Duncan would talk than anyone else in the Sticks would. Maybe because, unlike the others, they hadn't been making maple syrup. There was absolutely no basis for raiding their homes. Maybe for some other reason.

I was sitting taller now. My heart was beating faster.

Janice said, "That's why they took out life insurance policies."

I blinked. It was like waking from a dream. "Life insurance policies?"

Janice fumbled in her bag. She dropped a ChapStick on the floor. I didn't reach to pick it up. At last, she pulled out a sheaf of papers. She handed them to me with a sloppy flourish. There were three packets of stapled-together printer paper.

For just a moment, Janice looked completely sober.

I started to read.

Each packet was the same, just with a different name and address in its preamble. They were from the Assured Trust Life Insurance Company. They were in the names of William Houser, Duncan Schott, and Neil Mayer. They were dated six months ago.

"Right after the raids, each of the men took out a hundred-thousand-dollar life insurance policy," Janice said. "William named the beneficiary as his father. Duncan named his girlfriend. Neil named his little sister, who had just been accepted to music school and was about to be saddled with debt."

I peeled through the pages. I searched for the suicide clause, which stated that a policy wouldn't pay out if someone committed suicide a certain amount of time after the policy was signed.

Where was it? How long was that period?

But even as I paged through the documents, I knew how long the period was. How long it had to be.

"I shouldn't have even seen these," Janice said. "But Neil mailed them to Becker at the police station. I guess he wanted Becker to feel guilty for what he'd made them all do. I mean, if Becker hadn't stolen that money, they'd have been okay. They'd each have had what they needed to get by and wouldn't have had to kill themselves to get it."

I was still scanning paragraphs. The words were blurring together.

"Then Becker just gave me these to file with everything else. I mean, you'd think he'd feel incriminated. But that's just so like him. He wants all of the information so he can control it."

The pages stuck together as I tried to flip through them.

"So you see," Janice said. "This is why Becker doesn't want you to know what really happened. The town's not in any legal trouble. Not for their deaths. And it's not like anyone can prove the raids weren't legitimate. But if people knew, I mean, about how broke we are, it would change everything. They'd want to leave. Get out while they can. Copper Falls only survives because of the story we tell about it. This threatens that story."

That's when I found it. The suicide clause, which invalidated the policy if the policyholder took his own life within six months of the policy being signed. It expired the day before William, Duncan, and Neil died.

"How did you get these?" I snapped.

Janice looked alarmed. "I just told you. Neil mailed them to Chief Becker at the police station to make him feel guilty."

Understanding dug into me like a knife. My voice was hollow. "Let me see the envelope. Where's the envelope?"

Janice pulled it out from her bag. She handed it to me. It was as if she'd dropped a handful of change into my palm.

It had the name of Chief Becker, addressed to the CFPD. I flipped it over.

The paper on the back was completely mangled. Just the way Ronan opened envelopes.

Rip and ride.

28

Saturday, November 11

IT WAS JUST AFTER MIDNIGHT WHEN RONAN STEPPED OUT OF his minivan at the abandoned lot of the Copper Falls Sawmill. He came toward me. All wide eyes. All concern. He said, "I came as soon as you called."

I was still wearing my clothes from the bar. My wool coat flapped open. I held the insurance policies in my hand like a baton. I walked past Ronan. I spoke over my shoulder. "Come with me." I didn't look at him. I took us deeper into the darkness.

Anyone else might have demanded an explanation. Though the moon was bright, all around us there were patches as black as pitch. Only, Ronan didn't demand anything. He just followed me. Like I'd followed him to Copper Falls.

We walked around to the back of the raised monitor outbuilding. Damp leaves covered the dirt lot. Wide eaves craned over stacks of lumber, piles of wood chips, towers of debarked logs. A logging truck was parked off to the side. Its bed was packed with felled trees. Since the sawmill closed, no one had even unloaded them. The wind howled.

"I was thinking," I said, my tone clipped, brutal, "about that time you fell from the dormer window. Do you remember?"

Ronan's pace slowed. He didn't speak.

"I was ten. You were eight. You kept trying to climb out the window. I kept trying to stop you. Finally, I got tired of trying to protect you. I said if you wanted to do something stupid that was up to you."

Cedar trees forested the land off to our side. Pine cones clustered under spindly trunks. The scent of pine mixed with the scent of sawdust until I couldn't smell anything else. I could only feel the effort of pushing against nature. Of nature taking over again. Of loss.

"So you climbed out the window. You slipped on a loose roof tile. You fell. The bone was sticking out of your arm. You couldn't believe how blue it was. When you'd been x-rayed and your bone had been set and your cast had been put on, do you remember what you said? About why you did it?"

"That isn't—"

I gripped his wrist. I made him face me. His expression was sheepish, plaintive. Understanding worked its way across his features. He knew he was on trial. I knew he had no defense. "What did you say?"

Ronan expelled a breath. "I said I wanted to punish you."

"Punish me *why*?"

He swallowed. "For not paying attention to me."

I still had the insurance policies rolled up in my hand. I threw them at him. They fluttered to the ground like severed wings. He looked down at the pages. He didn't pick them up. He didn't need to. He already knew what they said because he'd opened the goddamned mail. I said, "I thought we were past that point in our relationship. Yet here we are."

"Leigh, I—"

"How could you hide these from me?"

"I didn't hide them from you." Ronan stepped away from the bent pages. "I just didn't tell you about them."

"They're life insurance policies, Ronan. From the men who died. The suicide clauses expired the day before they drowned."

"Those policies don't prove they died by suicide. You said yourself, the deaths looked suspicious."

My ears, my neck were burning. "Their nails had been trimmed. They'd gotten their hair cut. They'd shaved their faces. Killers don't do that. You don't manicure a body just to throw it in the water." I thought of what Dr. Aliche had said about the suicide victim who'd shaved her pubic hair. "People only do that when they're preparing their bodies for sacrifice. Because they sacrificed themselves, Ronan, to save the people they loved."

"But the fish. In Duncan's body. It was a cavefish, so—"

I strode toward the original sawmill, the one that'd been used when Copper Falls had first been settled. Stone, two stories. Tiny windows. A waterwheel. Beautiful under different circumstances.

"Here, Ronan. There are caves here, too. At the sawmill. Where all three of the men worked until the town laid them off last year. They could have filled their pockets with stones and died here for all we know. They could have chosen this place to send a message about how little the people in the Sticks matter to the people in town. Just like the insurance policies they mailed to the police station sent a message to Becker. But it doesn't matter where they died. Not anymore. They weren't murdered."

"Then why didn't the bodies have any bruises on them? Huh?"

The moon made Ronan's skin look sick. His expression was always so elastic, so ready to smile. But not now. Not here.

"Look at all those rocks!" he shouted. "The bodies should be covered with bruises from traveling through the caves and then over the falls."

I vibrated all over. "They left life insurance policies, Ronan. They were in desperate need of money. They died the day after their suicide clauses expired. They were cleaned like sacrifices. A judge hears all of that? Case dismissed. It'd never even make it to trial."

Ronan scrubbed his hands through his hair. The sound of the wind made the space into a vacuum. He stopped pacing. He stood still enough to meet my stare. He said, "Look, I know you're mad at me."

"Mad at you? What are we? Twelve?" I came toward him. "The whole time, you knew what had happened. You kept it from me."

His voice was high-pitched, ridiculous. "Mason thinks there's something here."

"If you had questions," I said, "we could've talked them through. Over the phone. There was no reason for me to come back."

His voice made a guttural sound. "Yes, there was. There was a reason, Leigh."

"What, Ronan?"

He struggled for the right words. "I thought if you came back, if you saw for yourself how good this could be for you, then—"

"Then what? I'd stay here forever? Simone and I would move in with the uncles in the house where our parents died? That you'd pick me up every day so we could drive to work?"

His mouth worked before he spoke. "Is that so crazy?"

"Ronan, listen to me. I can't be that for you. I can't be the person you want."

"You don't have to be any of it, Leigh. You don't have to be anything. Just be here. Just be present."

I stepped closer. I was ready to lay into him. To land the final blow. But I stopped. There was something wrong with his face. It wasn't petulant. It wasn't indignant. Ronan's eyes were welled with tears. His cheeks were painted wet. It was a face I immediately recognized.

I'd worn it myself.

Ronan's voice was a whimper. "Cathy and I are getting a divorce."

The sides of his mouth pinched as he held his jaw closed. His voice broke.

"I know I should have told you about the insurance policies. I should have told you everything. I just needed to see you. I just needed you. Here."

Ronan tensed his jaw again. He swallowed. He bit his lip and then released it.

Softly he said, "I knew if it was just for me, you wouldn't come."

That's when my brother began to cry.

I felt his sobs under my skin.

29

IT WAS SATURDAY MORNING. RONAN WAS SUPPOSED TO MOVE out of his house before Cathy and the kids got back from their camping trip that afternoon. The uncles and I did what was instinctual to us, what's instinctual to every Midwesterner with family in need of moving. We helped.

Bear sat up front in the cargo van, pretending (I hoped) to teach Simone how to drive. Eamon went through Ronan's things. He packed up anything breakable, carefully layering newspaper and bubble wrap so nothing would clang together. Frankie and I threw clothes and shoes and DVDs into boxes and loaded them into the van.

Ronan was in the kitchen saying *Not that* or *Yes, that's mine* in response to Eamon's voice. Frankie was struggling with the packing tape in the hallway, letting the chainsaw rip of it reverberate through the house. It was just me in Ronan's bedroom, trying to push away thoughts of Eric, who, six months ago, had done this exact same thing.

I was digging in the closet to pack up Ronan's clothes. He had so many T-shirts from when he was in high school—Hoobastank, Interpol, even a Creed shirt I gave him so much shit about. He'd kept so much from that time in his life. From that same period, I'd kept nothing.

I pulled down a Red Wing box from the top of the closet. A flutter of photographs spilled out onto the carpet. I'd never been sentimental. Yet now, I picked through the photos.

There was one when Ronan's boys were young. Both of them piled on top of his lap as he made a funny face.

Another one had only Jerrod, their oldest, who was tiny and swallowed up by Ronan's hands.

In another, Cathy was wearing a white spaghetti-strap gown. Thin eyebrows. Puffed bangs. Her flat-ironed hair was pulled back in a half ponytail. I realized, belatedly, this was from their wedding.

In the next photo, there was Ronan, with a wide-as-your-face smile. A tux with tails. Frankie, in a polka-dot bow tie and white leather shoes. Eamon had his eyes closed to the flash of the camera. Bear's mouth was set in a hard line, which usually meant he was enjoying himself. They were all there. Yet I'd missed the whole thing.

This was before Simone. Before Eric even. Ronan had gotten married when I was in that eighteen-month period after I'd passed the detective's exam but before I got the title. The Friday before Ronan's wedding, a case had come up, a big one. A finance man with high-level connections and low-level enemies had been found shot in his penthouse, execution style. His family threatened to sue the NYPD if we screwed it up. Top brass had made a point of telling my partner and me this was our priority. For the next forty-eight hours, nothing else on our docket mattered.

I could have passed the case to someone else. I should have. But I was afraid of losing my status. I was afraid of not getting promoted. I was afraid of going back to the place that would threaten the walls of the compartments I'd barely been able to uphold.

"Leigh!" It was Bear. His hand cuffed over the doorframe of the master bedroom. "Will you watch your daughter while I give Frankie a hand with the boxes? He thinks this is Jenga."

"Tetris," Frankie yelled. "You mean Tetris!"

Bear gritted his teeth. "No, I mean Jenga!"

I remembered Ronan's *If it was just for me, you wouldn't come.* I slipped the wedding photo into my pocket. I went to find Simone.

Ronan moved into his old bedroom, a floor below mine. Overnight, the house was filled with him.

The box of Golden Grahams he always ate for breakfast sat on the kitchen counter, open. The medicinal smell of his dandruff shampoo wafted down the wide hallway upstairs. His fantasy books laid dog-eared on the sofa next to the bulge of his socks, which he always took off by hooking his big toe around the ankle loop of the opposite foot. They came out of the laundry in a ball, the insides still wet.

I was sitting with Simone on the floor of our room, putting

together a puffy jigsaw in the shape of a farmyard. Below us, the floorboards groaned as Ronan moved his furniture around. I'd thought it would make me crazy, Ronan's old scents. His old sounds. His old presence in this house. Instead, I found myself humming songs I thought I'd forgotten. With him here, I didn't have to remind myself to eat.

As Simone mashed together pieces that didn't fit, my mind cast back to the stolen money and the insurance policies and how easily they explained everything. Why the bodies had been manicured. Why all three men had died at the exact same spot on the exact same night. Why Becker had made it difficult for me to look into the case. Why Neil's roommates and Duncan's girlfriend hadn't wanted to talk to the police. I still didn't understand why the men had no postmortem bruising, but oftentimes cases worked like that. In the end, it was like Dr. Aliche had said: The simplest explanation was the one most likely to be right.

Now that the case was over, I should have been booking our flight back to New York. I should have packed our bags and arranged for Ronan to drive us to the airport in Detroit. Yet I hadn't begun doing any of that. I wasn't ready to analyze why.

Simone got frustrated that a piece wasn't fitting. She threw it down. "I want to call Daddy."

I handed her my cell phone and watched how, with an ease that still unnerved me, she found the button to FaceTime and swiped it to call.

"Can I have my headphones?"

We had special headphones just for her. They were big and

cushioned and fit her tiny head. I handed them to her just as Eric answered the call. "Hey, baby." His voice burned a hole inside my chest.

"What's that stuff?" Simone asked. I stood to leave them alone. "Are you doing therapy?"

I stopped. Eric was in therapy? He'd seen a therapist a long time ago, after he'd stopped working undercover. But I hadn't known him to go to therapy since. Simone glanced up at me. I turned away.

I closed the bedroom door behind me. Yet I held my back against it. I listened as Simone told Eric about losing Arnie and how she was trying to be strong. I listened as she showed him the pictures she'd drawn, the ones that were still hanging on the walls, the ones where our family was whole.

I couldn't hear Eric. So I had to imagine his replies: sweet things you say to your child when all you want to do is be with them. I hated that I was missing out on seeing my husband be sweet to our child.

Simone said something I couldn't hear. Then: "I don't know. It was scary."

A pause. He must have asked, *What was scary?* Was she talking about losing Arnie?

"I woke up. Mommy was gone. I looked everywhere."

Silence. I turned my ear to face the door, as if this would do anything.

"Uh-huh," Simone said. "The other night, too."

Another pause. Longer this time.

"No, they were here. Uncle Frankie made popcorn."

I closed my eyes. It was like standing in front of an oncoming train. I couldn't move.

She said, "I was watching TV. She smelled funny."

What program was on? Eric would say, trying to gauge the time I'd come back.

What did she smell like? Trying to determine where I'd been.

What was she wearing? Trying to find out whether I'd had sex.

I knew it'd only be a matter of minutes before he'd pull my phone records from our joint account. He'd have access to all incoming and outgoing calls. He'd have names, numbers, times, durations. Everything he needed to make a case for why I'd been unfaithful. For why I'd broken my promise to him. For why I'd dealt him the last straw.

I held the doorknob as if there were still time to intervene. I imagined barging in there, snatching away the phone.

But I knew what would happen next.

The argument. Simone crying. Me explaining that people could fight and still love each other. Me struggling to believe it was true.

I'd have it out with Eric, but he still wouldn't believe me. He had no reason to. Not when he wanted out. Not when he was already stepping out. Eric didn't believe in second chances. Especially not for this. Especially not now.

I stood at the door. It was like standing before a pane of shattered glass and looking down at all those fragments and realizing you don't have it in you to try to make the pieces fit. It was feeling the shards dig into your skin and knowing they'll always be there, biting into you, for the rest of your life.

30

IT WAS NINE THIRTY AT NIGHT. EAMON WAS IN THE LIBRARY. Bear and Frankie were off, as usual, at the lot. Simone was asleep. Ronan was sitting in front of the television in the family room. The blue light made his face glow.

I sat on the chair off to the side of him. A familiar music swelled. Rod Serling's voice came on with the usual bit about a *dimension as vast as space and as timeless as infinity.* About the place *between the pit of man's fears and the summit of his knowledge.*

It was an episode we'd seen before, in this room together, with our parents. It was about an aging starlet who spends her days watching movies of herself while her hapless manager, Danny, tries to make her acknowledge that the outside world exists.

The starlet is wearing a dress made of lace and tulle. A gauzy scarf is like a gauntlet in her hand. Danny reminds her it's 1959. She can't live in the past forever.

"As of this moment," she croons, "right now, Danny, these are the 1930s again, with all the charm and romance. All the gaiety. That was a carefree world, Danny. And I'm going to make it that way again."

I turned away from the television. "I hate this show."

Ronan shrugged. "I've seen this episode so many times, I can't even tell if I like it, or if I just like the memory of it. When life imitates art, you know? That used to be funny."

I stood. I stepped toward the front door. "Will you listen for Simone if she wakes up?"

"Where are you going?"

I slipped on my coat. "For a drive."

Ronan nodded. He stayed looking at the screen. I opened the door.

Behind me, Danny was pleading with the starlet. "Don't you understand?" he was saying. "You've built a graveyard here. You keep wishing for things that are dead."

I closed the door behind me. I shut out the sound.

Mason answered the door in sweatpants and a crewneck that read GOLD'S GYM. His hair was mussed like he'd been sleeping and his eyes were crinkled, happy.

"What happened?" I said. "J.Crew didn't shell out for leisurewear?"

Mason shielded his face. "Don't look at me. Here, let me get you good and drunk so you'll think I'm beautiful." Mason pressed his hand to the small of my back.

I pretended his touch did not burn against me.

In the kitchen, Mason mixed our drinks. He came back into the living room holding two coupes of amber liquid, dotted with cherries. "Manhattans," he said. "For irony's sake."

I sat on the rug and so did he. Mason pulled down a pile of blankets and laid them out for us. He opened the windows.

"I'm glad you got home okay," he said. "The other night. I tried calling. You didn't answer. We almost didn't make it out. I don't know what happened. Rocks were falling everywhere. I went back to look later. The crawl space was completely closed off."

I should have been grateful that he'd gotten me to safety. I'd put him in a dangerous situation, I'd risked his life, and yet he hadn't left me. But disappointment swelled inside me. I couldn't go back into the caves again. Estella wasn't going to tell me how to find the other entrance. I'd blown my only chance. I said, "Did you know about the insurance policies? For Neil, William, and Duncan?"

Mason hesitated. Behind his eyes, a calculation. At last, he nodded. "I heard a rumor about them. I managed to get ahold of a copy." His eyes stayed locked on mine.

"And?"

He took a deep breath. Held it. "Turns out," he said, "the company they bought the policies from was a fake. They were scammed." Mason sighed. "They went through all of that— they martyred themselves—and still their families aren't going to get any money. It's the very definition of tragedy."

I bristled. "So you knew their deaths weren't homicides? The whole time?"

Again, that calculation. He cleared his throat. "I came here to write a follow-up to my earlier piece about Copper Falls. I wanted to tell the story of small-town America through the lens of one town in the throes of death, whose members are killing themselves because they can't imagine a different future. That was always my angle."

I sipped my Manhattan. It wasn't hard to see how Mason would write this story. For Duncan, Neil, and William, their hopelessness was economic. For the three high school boys, the decision to kill themselves came upon them when they were meant to leave the nest.

It was all the same impulse, Mason would argue: a fear of a future they couldn't conceive of, the desire not to try. It all stemmed from this town's dangerous insularity that made people feel they had no choice.

I crossed my ankles. I leaned back on my arm.

"Why didn't you tell me what you knew?"

"I offered to share notes. You turned *me* down, remember?"

I flashed to the aged-out starlet. To Eric and shattered glass. To Simone. To Ronan. To New York. To Copper Falls. *Good and drunk,* Mason had said. I took a long swallow. That didn't sound so bad. I said, "When do you go back to L.A.?"

"Actually," Mason said, "things aren't exactly working out for me there."

His words came out slow, like islands.

"It's not an easy place to be freelance. It's expensive as hell. Rent, food. I love it. But I also know its faults. I hate to say it—I mean, I swore I'd never be one of *those* people—but it's become just another place to me. I don't love it like I did in the beginning."

His body was bent toward mine. He pinched the cherry from his glass.

"I came here for this story," he said. "But now I'm thinking I might not leave."

He pressed the cherry between his teeth until it bled. Just a flick of the eyes. A kick of the tongue. Yet it felt like free falling. I looked away from him. I said, "But the town doesn't want you back. Your mom—"

"It will take a while. Sure. But this new piece I'm working on will ingratiate me to the community. Whereas the other piece I did was a dirge, this one will be a paean. I'm going to highlight the town's quaintness. I'll pitch it as the last stand of an old kingdom. It's dying, yes, but it was once extraordinary. Maybe, I will imply, it will be extraordinary again."

"You really think that will work?"

Mason placed his glass on the rug. "I don't see why not. The people here are proud. Flattery—especially in print—goes a long way with them. Besides, there's always the off chance the piece will get money flowing here again. Tourists. Photojournalists. Hell, I don't know. I just might be the savior they've been waiting for."

"But your mother—"

"What about her?"

"She shut you out."

"Yes."

"How can you forgive her?"

Mason lifted a brow then. He gave me a long, scrutinizing look. "Are we still talking about *my* mother?"

I pulled away from him. I tipped the glass into my mouth. I was a slower drinker than he was. I regretted this.

Mason pitched his body closer to mine. Another small shift. He said, "You used to talk about this kind of thing all the time. With me. I didn't know it'd become a secret."

I shrugged. *Yeah well, things change.*

He shot me a look. *No, they don't.* "You know, it surprised me," he said at last. He leaned back on the rug. I pictured him naked. "When I'd heard you'd made detective."

"Oh?" Then I decidedly *did not* picture him naked.

"It's not that I didn't think you were smart enough. God, you're the smartest person I've ever met."

I made my voice flippant, unlike me. "Mason Vogel," I said, "are you trying to get in my pants?"

"Most people sense things with their intellect because that's the only lens they've got. But you've got all these other ways of seeing. There's something, I don't know, something very animal about it. It's hot."

I set down my drink. "Okay, now I know you're trying to get in my pants."

"You know I am." He looked deeper into my eyes. "But that's not why I'm saying this. That animal intelligence, it makes you rare. For detectives at least."

I adjusted the blanket over me. I was getting cold. Or hot. They felt like the same thing. I said, "You'd think that'd be an asset."

"When I was in Phoenix, I covered the crime beat. Did I tell you? All the detectives there projected this image of being driven purely by logic. Sherlock Holmes wannabes—the whole lot of them.

"That image, of the purely rational detective, it's a lie obviously. But a useful one, you know? People like a detective who is a rock. They like a detective who isn't swayed by feeling or sentimentality or by the kind of instincts that make them seem like a loose cannon."

Mason leaned forward again. He was so close to me now that I could have counted his eyelashes. The veins of his forearm bulged.

"But you," he said, speaking softly, "you've always had these big emotions, this deep gut. This strong intuition. It must be hard."

I tried not to look at his crotch. "What must be hard?"

Mason's gaze was searing. "Getting on at work. It must be hard to cover up the wild in you in order to be taken seriously."

Something about the note of understanding in his voice made something shift in me. "Actually," I said, "I'm not with the NYPD anymore."

Mason didn't look away.

"I was suspended. Indefinitely."

Mason didn't speak. He didn't move. He was, after all, a journalist. He knew when to talk and when to listen. On some level, I understood I was doing what he wanted. Trusting him. Yet I couldn't hold these words in my chest anymore. They were too heavy. I was too tired. I'd lost too much.

"I don't know what happened," I said, struggling to know how to say it. "One minute, I was this decorated detective with a better-than-decent solve rate, and the next . . ."

I lifted the glass to my lips. I drained it. Like medicine. Like hemlock. Still, Mason didn't speak.

"We caught this case," I said. "A kid at a bodega. Shot in the head. Security camera at the pet store next door spotted the suspect fleeing. Black man. Late thirties. Hoodie. It wasn't much to go on, but he had a tattoo on his neck we'd enlarged. We called tattoo parlors. We got a match. We had our guy."

The hinge of my jaw squeezed tighter. I rolled my tongue around inside my mouth. I was aware how my cadences had changed now as I told this story, how the emotion, the sounds, the smells of my experience were absent. Mason was right. I was hiding that part of myself. Even now.

I said, "We went to question him. But when he saw us, he bolted. Out an alley. Through a street blocked off by construction. It was luck that I caught up with him. I'm fast, but I can't outrun a man. Then I did what I'd been trained to do. I kicked out his knees. I knocked him to the ground."

Heat filled my cheeks. My eyes. My chest.

"I'd never done that before," I said. "Not since the academy. I never enter a scene unless it's secure. I point my service weapon, sure, but I don't fire it. Homicide, we're the brains. Beat cops, they're the brawn. I'm not supposed to be the brawn."

Mason's voice was soft. "So what happened?"

The wagon wheel lights blurred as I watched them. I released the words I'd been holding on to as if they were a venom I might still extract. "I let the guy go. We had him on video. The same tattoo. The same face. I let him go."

"Why?"

I watched the lights until they hurt my eyes. I didn't know.

"When my partner, Detective Lewis, tried to go after the suspect, I drew my weapon. I pointed it at him. People had their phones out. They were recording me. They were recording a detective pointing her weapon at another detective, but I didn't back down."

I shook my head at the memory, at the idiocy.

I said, "Officers caught up with the suspect a few hours later. They caught him anyway. Of course they did. Nothing I did even mattered."

Mason was thoughtful. He was sitting up straight now, away from me. "Did you know the suspect?"

"No."

"Did this Detective Lewis say anything that caused you to turn on him?"

I thought back to his words. Something like *We need to get this cancer off the streets.* Something like *What the hell is wrong with you?* I looked down at my hands.

Mason focused at a place in the distance. At last he nodded, met my eyes. He said, "I'm no psychologist. But it sounds like you sabotaged your career on purpose."

"Why would I do that?"

Mason shrugged. "Maybe, in that moment, you realized your hands are dirty, too. You solve murders, sure. But you also hurt people. You put them in prison. Especially Black people. A higher proportion of Black men are in prison than any other demographic, which I'm sure you know. It sounds like you finally confronted your role in the system that does that."

"If it weren't for the police," I said, "the gangs would've taken over. Whatever flaws we have, we're better than that."

"Just because you're better than the alternative," Mason said, "doesn't mean you're the good guys. Sometimes thinking of someone as a good guy makes you unable to see their flaws."

Mason inhaled a breath of cool air. Considered.

"The man you knocked down, he was in the same demographic as your husband, right?"

My lips clamped shut. I forced slowness into my breath. I'd never told Mason who my husband was. It'd have been easy for him to find that out. But it still hurt to hear him confirm that he'd known all along. He'd probably even seen the videos of me pointing my gun at my partner. Yet he'd had me tell him this story anyway.

Anger slipped in and out of me. I didn't want Mason trying to analyze me. Yet I also wanted to know this thing about myself. I wanted to know whether he was right. Was the reason I'd pulled my gun on my partner because he'd threatened a man who'd reminded me of Eric? Did he remind me of Eric?

The sad thing was, I couldn't even remember what the man I'd knocked down looked like. All I remembered was having an instinct, deep in my chest, that told me to let him go. It was the same instinct that had told me William, Neil, and Duncan had been murdered. Both times my instincts had been wrong.

"What did Captain Walker say?" Mason asked. He was treading carefully now. He knew he'd shown his hand, but he also couldn't walk this back. "I'm sure he had an opinion."

"I put him in an impossible position. He was left with no choice."

"You mean, your husband was the one who issued the suspension?"

This part was not public knowledge. I gazed into my empty glass. I did not confirm. I definitely did not deny.

"And he severed all ties with you?"

I bit back something sour. "To align himself with me was to fail to support Blue Lives."

"He doesn't believe that, does he?"

"It's political. You get a job like his, it's all political. Especially for Eric. There are some people who wonder how a Black man even takes that job. There are others who wonder whether a Black man can do what needs being done. Even his friends are his enemies."

What I didn't say was that sometimes I worried that's why he fell for me. Because I was an outsider. I thought of a conversation I'd once overheard, two Black women at Eric's cousin's wedding. The bride was white. One of them clicked her tongue. The other said, *His skinfolk's not kinfolk, you know?* They hadn't meant Eric. But had they meant Eric?

I flashed to my husband. To his voice in my ear. To his body wrapped around my body. To that warm-blanket feeling that could overwhelm me. To the musk and wool scent of him and how it could convince me we were immortal.

No, we weren't like that. What we'd had together was real. That's why we'd found a way to be together. Despite everything. That's why he'd vowed to protect me. So long as I was worthy of it.

I swallowed something sharp.

That was the caveat. I needed to be worthy.

I said, "Eric doesn't believe in second chances."

Mason's voice was gentle, prying. "Not even for you?"

"Especially not for me."

"And now?"

I felt his words up my back, over my shoulders, along my hairline. I felt their impact like blows all over my body. It was a fight I couldn't raise my fists for. I said, "He's with someone else now."

It was the first time I'd said those words out loud. They twisted my gut.

A second passed. A few more. Heartbeats at first dragging and then closer together.

At once, the distance between Mason and I wasn't a distance at all. Mason rested his hand on my hand.

His fingers laced between my fingers. His breath drifted over to me, mixed with whiskey, mixed with cherry, mixed with him.

His lips drew closer to mine. The heat of him touched my mouth.

I wanted to press into him. I wanted to sink into his body and close my eyes and believe this was my husband. That I was happy. That we were whole.

But he wasn't Eric. He never would be Eric.

I turned away. I slipped my hands out of his grasp. It was like pulling away from a hot stove, one I wanted to burn me.

I said, "I'm not ready." I didn't know whether I'd ever be ready.

Mason nodded. He leaned back against the blankets. He stared ahead for a long time. Outside, the wind whirled through the leaves of the bushes. It tapped against the windowpanes like a lover asking, *Is it time?*

When at last Mason spoke, his voice was raspy, like the aftermath of something we hadn't done but could have, if only I'd said yes.

"You wanted to know how to forgive your mother?"

"I didn't say that."

"You didn't have to."

I met his eyes. I was aware of how a wall I normally kept up wasn't in place.

"You rewrite history. You embody your mom's strength and her charisma. You keep the parts of her you loved and miss. But this time, you change the ending."

I felt unprotected, supple, more open than I'd thought. "How?" I said. I meant it. With every ounce of me, I meant it.

"Easy."

A pause like stepping off a plank.

"You stop being the sort of woman who dies because she's lost her husband."

I blinked too many times. I pressed my tongue to the top of my mouth. It was like applying pressure to a wound.

Eric and I in that glassed-in office.

Eric and I on that lake.

Simone growing in my belly. Eric smiling at me, so big, so gorgeously when he thought no one was looking.

His dimple winking out like a secret held in trust.

Eric on the sidewalk with me, always walking nearest to the road so any swerving car would hit him first.

Eric protecting me.

I said, "I don't know how to do that."

Mason's mouth cocked up in that half-smile I was beginning to like. "Sure you do. You're just being stubborn about it."

31

Sunday, November 12

RONAN AND THE UNCLES TOOK CARE OF SIMONE SO I COULD take Sunday to be by myself.

I hadn't spent any real time in the woods. Only, now I did. Now I started out on foot with a backpack and provisions. I let the animal in me set the course.

I arrived at a theater of trees surrounding a lake made holographic by the sun. I couldn't believe it, that I'd walked all this way only to arrive here. I couldn't believe this didn't hurt.

This was the lake where my mom had taught me to swim, where she'd taught me to enjoy the fish nibbling at my toes and the sinewy webs of algae that could make light spots dark. This was where she'd taught me to listen with my nose: to the dirt, to the trees, to the scents the wind carried like missives, binding you to something bigger than yourself.

I stood at the edge of the isthmus. I saw my reflection in the clear blue water. I took a deep belly breath. I dove.

The water's pulse beat through me. Bubbles spilled around me, wrapping me, keeping me safe. I opened, became gentle. Weightless.

I closed my eyes, and I could smell her. The perfume she wore everywhere. I imagined her cells swimming around me. I imagined her here, beside me, not as a ghost but as a guide. It didn't hurt.

By the time I walked back to the house, it was nighttime. The crickets hummed their white-noise calm, lulling the forest to sleep. My hair was wet, as were my socks. I was dressed in dirt-speckled jeans and a warm flannel. I smelled of lake and forest. My fingernails were mooned with silt. Yet, I wasn't in a hurry to clean myself up.

When I opened the door, the scents overwhelmed me: roast chicken, mashed potatoes, butter beans, red wine. I'd only taken a few steps into the foyer when Ronan emerged from the kitchen. He had on a tuxedo apron. Simone, standing beside him, wore an apron shaped like a dinosaur. It must have been one of his kids'.

"The mistress has at last arrived," Ronan said. He tapped Simone on her nose with a wooden spoon. She erupted with giggles.

I bent down to hug her. She yanked on my hand. "Mommy, come see. Come see!"

The dining room glowed amber. My mother's good china glistened from the lace-covered table. The crystal stemware brimmed with wine. Lidded platters hissed with steam. Someone had even gotten out the gold flatware, which I hadn't seen since the Christmas before my mother had died. I was surprised at the lightness in my chest when I saw it. I was surprised my body did not insist on retreat.

The uncles were arranged in a tableau around the sideboard. They'd dressed for the occasion, each wearing a collared shirt. Frankie's sleeves were too short for his arms. Bear's sleeves were too tight. Eamon wore his tweed jacket, the one with patches over its elbows. Between them sat a bottle of Jameson. They each cradled a lead-cut glass. I wasn't dressed for dinner. Yet I didn't even think about this.

Instead, I thought of that final Christmas together, after Dad had died, when Mom's skin was papery thin and spidered with veins. We were, all of us, here together in this room. The uncles were standing just like that. My mother was at their center. She'd looked so frail. Yet her voice had been all fire, all vim, so similar to who she'd once been: *You all going to just stand there, or is somebody going to pour me a drink?*

Before I could think, before I could consider, her words emerged from my mouth like a possession, like being in that lake had made her spirit accessible to me. I said them as if she were me.

Just like that, an energy in the room, long dormant, came to life. Eamon poured. Simone scrambled back to the kitchen with Ronan. Frankie beamed his moon-faced smile. Bear met my eye. There was a twinkle in his gaze, something I hadn't seen since I'd been back. "How's that G-Wagen working out for you?" he said. He spoke out the side of his mouth.

"It needs an oil change," I said, "but I'm thinking I'll trade it in for a Saab."

Bear's belly strained the buttons of his shirt. Eamon handed me the drink. I never drank whiskey straight. Only, now I couldn't remember why. Frankie slapped Bear on the back. He towered over us like a flagpole, reclaiming this island as ours. He said, "I know that Bear here looks like he's got deep pockets, but he can't afford that. He gives out too much for free."

Bear scratched his beard. "I can't afford it because somebody keeps making mistakes." He slapped Frankie's chest with the back of his paw. "Go on, tell them what you did. Tell them."

Frankie's face bloomed. "Naw, they don't want to hear about none of that."

Eamon fastened the button of his jacket. He said, "I'm always eager for a tale. History is nothing but stories."

My mother's voice filled my mouth. With it, a power I hadn't expected: "Just tell it, Uncle Frank."

For a moment, the uncles were silent. I looked among them, at their half-mast eyes, at their mouths curling up at their edges. I was like a foal who'd just taken her first steps.

So this is what it is to refuse my pain.

"Well, there I was," Frankie said, "I'd only just barely finished my first cup of coffee . . ."

He wound up, the way he always did, making his eyes wide and shifting between the balls of his feet like he was in the ring. I had trouble following the story, something about pouring gasoline in a place gasoline shouldn't go. A pop and an explosion that *burned the eyebrows off his damned face,* according to Bear, even though Frankie's eyebrows were clearly intact.

Frankie was animated by his own energy. Bear peppered in stern asides. Eamon, who had thus far remained quiet, came in with a rejoinder so unexpected that a burst of laughter emerged from us, like we'd opened a door to a party we'd long ago sealed off. Bear's throaty laugh mixed with Frankie's high-pitched one. Even Eamon chuckled to himself. The only one missing was my mom.

I felt her absence. Yet I didn't pull back.

Ronan emerged from the kitchen. His hands were on his hips. He held a spatula like a teacher's paddle. Simone stood beside him. "When you're done with whatever it is you're doing," he said, "dinner is ready." But he didn't sound angry. Not even a little.

The four of us drained our glasses and left them on the sideboard. Eamon, Frankie, Bear, and Ronan took their usual spots around the table. Simone sat in mine. Dad's place wasn't set. I took the only seat left. It was the seat of my mother.

I pressed into the heavy, wooden chair. I spread my hands down the armrests that had been her armrests. I felt another shift in the room, a settling.

Frankie slapped his palms on the table. "Well fuck me sideways and buy me a pony. All of us finally together? I think this calls for someone to say grace!"

Bear groaned.

Eamon fluttered his eyelids.

"As I'm the most, well, not religious per se but, you know, spiritual," Frankie said, "that task falls squarely on my capable shoulders. Come on, slap those palms together. Don't act like you don't know how this works."

Simone giggled. The rest of us held back smiles as we made a circle with our hands. I held Ronan with one hand and Simone with the other. I felt the warmth of each of them.

Frankie closed his eyes. He made his voice low and solemn. "In the name of the Father, the Son, and the Holy Ghost." He took a deep breath. "Whoever eats the fastest gets the most. Amen!"

Simone laughed. Eamon's smile was crooked but real. Bear chuckled into his chest. Ronan held up his wineglass, and it was as if he'd grown wings. As if all of us had. "To family," he said.

Then in unison, like we'd practiced, like we'd never forgotten, "*Sláinte.*"

Even Simone knew to knock back her glass of juice.

I knew the tender spots on the stairs. As I climbed, I avoided them instinctually. I eased open the door to my bedroom, ready to redo Simone's twists and tuck her in. But she wasn't there.

I checked the bathrooms, then the library. I looked in the closets, in case she was playing a game. I went down to the second floor, about to knock on Ronan's door to check if he'd seen her. But as I held the butt of my hand up to the flat of the door, I saw it. At the end of the hallway, the door to my parents' room was cracked open. From inside shone a faint yellow light.

The runner muffled the sounds of my steps as I made my way toward it. I hadn't been able to go near it since I'd come back. But something had shifted in me. It was okay now. I'd be okay. I pushed open the door.

In the center of the room stood a wide canopy bed, dressed over with gauzy fabric. Tasseled rope knotted around each bedpost.

Painted on the far wall was an enormous armadillo, colored

over with red and gold. There, in the bed, under the tufted bed-spread, was my daughter. She was nestled under the covers. There were stuffed animals everywhere. All of them were armadillos.

I kissed her forehead.

She opened her eyes. She said, "I fell asleep."

"I can see that."

"They said it's for me."

"Who said that?"

"Everybody. Uncle Eamon. Uncle Bear. Uncle Frankie. Uncle Ronan, too. It took all day."

I ran a hand over the top of her head. "It's beautiful." I touched the scarf that was tied around her hair. I inspected her twists. "Who did this?"

"Uncle Ronan did a YouTube. Mommy, can I sleep here?"

There was something about the way the moonlight hit her eyes then that made me see in her my mother. It hit me with a force I hadn't expected, like I'd touched my finger to an outlet. Simone's eyes were brown and my mom's had been green, but theirs were the same. They were connected. This place had connected them.

I pressed my forehead against Simone's. Our noses were touching. My eyes were hot.

I said good night. I tucked the quilt over her shoulders.

On my way out, I didn't close the door all the way, just in case Simone got scared and wanted to come find me in the night. But I knew she wouldn't.

This house was no longer haunted by its ghosts.

32

Monday, November 13

IT WAS FIVE TO NINE IN THE MORNING. RONAN WAS SHOUTING for me to hurry.

I was still standing in front of the cheval mirror in my room. I was still holding the wedding photo from Ronan's closet. I stared at his grinning face and gathered my courage. I turned away from the mirror. I climbed down the stairs.

The air was dewy and the trees were in partial shadow. Ronan was leaning against the hood of the cruiser. When he saw me, he lifted up. "Holy. Shit."

I stood tall in a navy Class B uniform. I felt awkward in the heavy utility belt, uneven with the radio on my shoulder. I said, "How do I look?"

"Like a beat cop." Ronan's expression stretched to concern. He stepped toward me. He examined one eye and then the other. He said, "Are you sure you want to do this?"

I heard my mother's voice in my head, that same matter-of-factness that refused to admit discomfort. I said, "Am I sure I want to do what? Dress like my brother?" I stepped around to the passenger side of the cruiser. "Not really. But you were wearing it first, so I won't make you change."

Ronan spoke from over the dome of the cruiser. "I know it's not the same. For you. Homicide and beat cops. They're not the same."

I felt the pull of a ship whose anchor sinks. The recognition that, no matter how it adjusts its sails, it will never move from this spot. "They're the same," I said. "They always have been."

Ronan asked, "Does this mean you're staying?"

I hesitated. There'd have to be lawyers involved. Talks about custody. It would mean Simone would grow up as the only Black kid in a town washed over with white. It would be so complicated. So simple. I opened the door. "Come on," I said. "Becker will blow his top if we're late."

We checked in at the station before heading out on our rounds. Ronan sat behind the wheel as we drove deep into the Sticks. I looked out the window as if our surroundings were something that might change the closer I examined them. But the tawny fields and brown-gray forests were the same as they'd ever been. They were the same as they'd always be.

We came upon Ted Ferguson's house. Ronan and I waited for him to come out. When he did emerge, we searched around him for anything suspicious, as if there was anything to find.

We drove up to the houses of Daniel Greene, of Edmund Garner, of Antonia Beck. We waved hello and treated them like criminals. Because they were. Even if they'd never done anything wrong, they were criminals because that's what we'd named them. It was all so wrong. But then, maybe most things I'd done as a cop had been wrong. Here, at least, I could be with my brother. There for him in a way I'd failed to be for so long.

Ronan and I pulled up to Maude Hummel's house last. We climbed the cracked front steps. We stepped through her house, shouting for her to come out. But this time, we found only emptiness and debris. We hinged open the back door. We searched the line of the trees. She wasn't there.

Ronan stepped in beside me on the back lawn. He spit gum into a wrapper and replaced it with a fresh piece. "Well," he said, "she must have gone out."

"She leaves the house?" I stepped onto a manhole cover. It seemed like a strange place for it. Then again, Janice had said Maude's father dug sewers. Sure enough, *M. K. Hummel* was inscribed on its lid.

"Sure she does," Ronan said. He turned around.

I followed him back to the front of the house.

"She drives around in that rickety Cadillac of hers. Lots of times I'll find her. I'll roll down the window. We'll chat. She's usually confused, so I end up escorting her home."

"Confused how?" I asked. The one time I'd met her, Maude had seemed sharp, quick to anger. What she hadn't seemed was senile.

"Oh, you know." Ronan pinched a cobweb off his pant leg and flicked it onto the floor. He opened the front door. "She'll tell me she's headed home, but she's going the wrong way."

Behind me, the door wheezed shut.

"It's not a big deal. I always make sure she gets back." He shrugged. "We'll probably see her when we do traffic stops."

As the day progressed, as house checks became traffic stops, became paperwork, Ronan and I cycled through a banter that reminded me of cheesy sitcoms, the kind involving families that stay together, where everybody ends up happy at the end.

Ronan would oscillate between earnest and injured by some perceived slight. I would oscillate between impersonating my mother and missing my husband.

At five o'clock, Chief Becker emerged from his office for long enough to squeeze Ronan's shoulder, for long enough to grace me with a "Good work today." I forced myself to smile. When I did, something behind Becker's eyes relaxed.

Janice approached Becker as he was reaching for his coat. "Hey, that reporter called again today." She handed him a thin slip of paper.

Becker made a show of balling it up and dropping it into a wastebasket. "Some people," he said, "never know when to give up."

When Becker was gone, the room shifted. Two officers stood from their desks and unbuttoned their collars. One looked to be about eighteen with biceps the size of my thighs.

The other one was short and round, like a meatball.

"I'd say that's my cue for a drink," the round one said. He turned to face me and Ronan. "You in?"

"Hell yeah," Ronan said.

Janice shut down her computer. "Tell me about it. It's been that kind of week."

"It's Monday," said Biceps.

Meatball elbowed him. "Just think how much she'll need by Friday. Remember her last week? By the end of the night, she was so blitzed she was hitting on Miss Carol."

Ronan said, "The preschool teacher?"

They laughed like a studio audience.

The four of them put on their coats. As the station door opened, the outside air blew in, clammy now, easing into winter.

I knew they expected me to come with them, but I also knew what would happen if I did. The buying of rounds. The easy ribbing. The inside jokes. The mundane moments spun into stories that would go on for ages until somebody—probably Janice—cut them off. At last we'd stumble to our homes and eat dinner standing up.

Ronan was the last one to the door. When he came upon the threshold, he looked over his shoulder. "You're coming, right?"

"Next time," I said.

Ronan nodded like he didn't believe me.

The house wasn't usually this quiet. But Ronan still hadn't come back from the bar. Eamon was giving a talk at the Historical Society, and Bear and Frankie were at the shop, doing god knows what.

I peeked in on Simone as she slept. I watched her chest rise and fall under the heavy quilt. I thought of the way she'd looked last night when I'd tucked her in. I thought of all the memories she'd missed out on because I'd been too afraid to return. All at once, I wanted to find a photo of my mother.

The closet in my room produced nothing of use, not even in the shoebox that held my defunct Tamagotchi and football-shaped letters, written in colorful gel pens.

There was only one other place I knew to look.

I hadn't gone in the study since I'd been back. In part, because my parents had loved it so much. They'd both been big readers, my mom preferring Dean Koontz to romance novels, my dad loving poetry. Yet they'd both wax on about the heft of physical books, their pleasure at the feel of them. They preferred hardcovers to paperbacks, leather-bound editions to those with dust jackets. They believed deckle-edged paper was pretentious and they both had definite opinions on typography. As I stepped over the threshold and onto the patterned rug, I remembered all of this.

As with the rest of the house, the uncles hadn't changed much about this room. Unstained bookshelves still lined its edges, made from the sort of wood you imagine coming from the same tree. The shelves still held all my parents' old volumes, arranged so the spines were flush with the shelves. Someone had even dusted them.

There were still two armchairs set off to one side, with a table in between where Mom would put her spritzers and Dad would put his tea.

I opened the file cabinet first, finger-stepping through the various manila envelopes, labeled with my mother's neat hand. There was a file for each year Ronan and I had been in school.

At last, I came upon the folder marked *Kathleen O'Donnell*. I slipped it out. I sat on the rug and braced myself. I flipped it open.

There was her high school diploma, printed on thick paper. Her certificate of marriage with its scrollwork border. As I turned to the next document, I hoped for a newspaper clipping, an engagement announcement, something that I could show to Simone.

Instead, I found records from the Cleveland Clinic.

Instead, I broke open.

33

Tuesday, November 14

THE NEXT MORNING, EVERYTHING WAS CLOAKED IN GRAY.
Fog wrapped around the trees. It curled over the cobblestones.
Even the birdhouses were shrouded in it. As Ronan and I rolled
down the long drive leading away from the house toward our
rounds, Ronan kept giving me looks.

"A penny for your thoughts?" he said at last. We passed under a veil of trees. He added, "Okay, a quarter?"

I closed my eyes. I opened them. But the haze was still there.
I reached for words I didn't yet have, for a history I still, despite
all the evidence, didn't quite believe. I said, "Did you know
Mom died from skin cancer?"

We were at the edge of the drive now, at the place where
Mom used to hop out to fish inside the mailbox. Ronan stopped
the cruiser. He shifted his body to look at me. His eyebrows sat
low on his face. "I don't understand what you're asking me."

But I had my answer. It was in the way his eyes glassed over, in the slow slant of his shoulders. I swallowed. I peered out the window.

"You don't remember?" he said. His voice was quiet, concerned.

I tried to shake my head, but the movement was small, like a shiver.

He said, "How did you think she died?"

I cleared my throat. "From grief." Now that I was saying it out loud, it seemed ridiculous. Yet I'd always believed it was true, for as long as I could remember. Dad had had a heart attack, and Mom stopped eating. She stopped sleeping. She stopped going outside. She was exhausted all the time. I thought it was because she was sad. "Cancer," I said. The word still cored me. "How could I not have known?"

Ronan looked down at his hands. "Probably because in the beginning, she lied to us about it."

I examined my brother's face.

"She'd been sick for years, but the cancer had been in remission for so long that she thought she didn't have to tell us. Then when Dad died, the stress of it was just too much. The cancer came back. Her body couldn't recover. It was a long time before she admitted to us what was happening. She didn't even tell us about her chemo. Until then, we did think she was just grieving."

Ronan drew his teeth over his lips.

"Mom only told us about the cancer a few weeks before she died."

I tried and failed to swallow. Ronan looked away.

He took his foot off the brake and turned onto Sugar Ridge Road, driving deeper into the fog. It rolled over the car now. It lingered over the windshield. The air vents were still blowing cold.

After a few heavy minutes, Ronan said, "In my psychology classes, there's this whole thing about repression. We actually need to repress difficult memories to survive. Like, if you remembered every time you hit your head as a kid trying to walk, you'd never walk anywhere."

"But not knowing how my mother died?" My voice was shallow, brittle. "That's not normal."

"I don't know that there is such a thing as normal. There's just how each of us deals."

I wanted to ask what all this meant. I wanted to ask how I could believe anything I thought was true if my memory could lie to me like this. Instead, I said, "You never told me why you're taking those psychology courses."

We were on the part of Sugar Ridge made of brick now. I searched the sky for sunlight.

"It started with these weird dreams," Ronan said. "The same image kept coming to me over and over again. I just felt like my body was trying to tell myself something my brain didn't get."

I thought of my own dream about the snake. "Did you figure it out?"

Ronan adjusted his hands on the wheel. He drew in breath. "Yes."

His cheeks and neck flushed. His lips thinned.

"Leigh, I'm gay."

Ronan slowed for the turn. The clicks of his signal measured out the time. Ten, eleven, twelve seconds. His chest went up and down. He turned the wheel. The pulse in his neck was throbbing.

I knew he was waiting for me to say something. A part of me didn't believe him. Another part of me didn't believe he would make this up. "Oh," I said at last.

He swallowed. "And while we're at it, you should probably know that I'm seeing someone."

"Okay." I couldn't believe how inarticulate I could be. Yet no part of me had seen this coming. I said, "Is he someone I know?"

Ronan bit his lip. Swallowed. "I thought you knew, actually. You seemed to pick up on there being something not quite workplace appropriate about our relationship."

"No." The word was a cough. I was actually shaking my head.

"Yeah," Ronan said. He kept his eyes fixed on the road.

My mouth hung open. I had to hear him say it. "You're dating Chief Becker?"

We stopped for the stop sign. The car didn't move. "I mean . . ." He swallowed again. "I figured if you could sleep your way to the top, why not me?"

There was a pause, pregnant and halting. Both of us held our breaths.

All at once, laughter burst from my lips. Ronan laughed, too. He put his foot on the gas. We were moving again.

It was a long while before either one of us spoke. I was still adjusting the cogs in my brain to fix on what this meant.

This explained why Ronan was getting divorced. This explained why he'd wanted me back. He wanted to tell me. He didn't know how.

I said, "But why Becker? He's such a prick."

"A prick who gave you a job."

"At least now I understand why." It'd never made sense to me, why Becker would let me come here, let me turn over rocks that might implicate him in a crime. He hadn't done it as a favor to his subordinate. It was an indulgence for his boyfriend.

The trees had become skinnier now. The grass was thinner. We were entering the Sticks. I said, "You do know they never found any meth in those raids, right? Becker stole from these people?"

"Yeah," Ronan said. "Bear told me last night, when I came back from the bar."

"And you still want to date him?"

Ronan motored air through his lips. "Probably not. But then, I've known that for a while. He was just there, you know? When I was figuring all this out."

Ronan slid his hand down the wheel. He cut his eyes to me.

"I guess we both know what it's like to be with someone who's bad for us."

"Eric was never bad for me." I cracked open the window. "We were always better together. He always defended me."

"Until he didn't."

"Until he couldn't."

"Do you still love him?"

"Do you still love Cathy?"

A train sounded in the distance. Neither one of us spoke as the roar of it receded and then faded into silence.

At last I said, "Does Cathy know? About you?"

Ronan nodded. "The whole coming out thing didn't go so well. She thinks I used her to have children."

251

He ran his teeth over his lips.

"I tried to tell her that I didn't know. It's just that sometimes our brains do funny things."

I met his eyes.

"They blind us from things we aren't ready to accept."

By the time we climbed the creaky front steps of Maude Hummel's house, the fog had long ago lifted. The sun was bright red. From the door, Ronan called to Maude. She didn't answer. We stepped inside.

We stalked past the terra-cotta rubble, past the closets with empty hangers, past the porcelain knickknacks on the walls. Only, this time I found myself lingering.

The figurines were characters from stories. Some of them I knew, like Snow White. Others I didn't, like a fisherman lying beside a skeleton. All of them were broken.

I stood at the threshold of the study. It was a room I'd only glanced at before. The rug was crumpled in a corner. The brittle-paged books were spread-eagle on the ground. I picked one up at random. It had a red cover. Its title was inscribed in gold: *Mythologies and Stories: A Searcher's Guide*.

I picked up another, this one leather-bound and smelling of ash. *The Falsehoods of the Western Canon.*

Another read: *Mythos as a Guide to the Psyche.*

They all seemed so academic, so theoretical. It made me wonder whether I'd underestimated Maude, whether I'd done to her what people often do with the elderly, treating her like she was beneath me because her insights weren't ones I could grasp.

As I paged through the *Mythos* book, my phone buzzed in my pocket. I saw the number. I swiped the screen. "Dr. Aliche?"

"Don't sound so surprised to hear from me." Dr. Aliche spoke with his usual animation. "You did give me a jar of your urine. While it's not exactly a ring on the finger, it did bind me in a promise. Of a sort."

"If you called to gloat"—I started walking toward the front of the house—"I'm not—"

"Why, I'd think you'd be the one gloating."

I pushed open the front door. I stood on the wraparound porch. I touched my hand to the chipped paint of the banister. Its cold spread up my arm.

"I'm calling with good news," Dr. Aliche said. "You were drugged."

A cough lodged in my throat. The cold settled.

"I had my suspicions for a few possible candidates," he said. "But in fact the real culprit is even juicier than I could have imagined."

My breath was captive in my chest.

"It was ethylene, Detective."

I searched my brain for any mention of that drug before. I came up blank.

"It's produced when you use sulfuric acid to heat ethanol. But it can also be found naturally." The phone scuffed as he switched it to the other ear. "In geological chasms."

Behind me, Ronan stepped through the door. I walked away from him, around the porch.

"When I called this in to the reference lab, I was poking fun at you a bit, if you must know," Dr. Aliche said. "I said how you were underground when you believed you'd hallucinated a snake. I teased there must have been a hallucinogenic in your perfume because you reported it smelling sweet. I hung up and that was that. But it got me thinking. I started googling. Are you still there?"

"I'm here." My voice sounded far off, hopeful.

"I played around with the search terms. Finally, Miss Google sent me links about the Oracles at Delphi. Scholars now believe that a sweet-smelling drug was emitted from the rocks to cause the Oracles to access their *visions*. That drug was believed to be ethylene.

"I called back the reference lab and—no doubt utilizing your trademark out-of-the-box thinking—had them test for it." In the background, a finger drumroll. "Detective, we had a match!"

By now, I had walked the entire circumference of the porch. My fingers, my toes, my chest filled with blood. If ethylene had caused me to lose consciousness, there was a chance that ethylene had caused Duncan, Neil, and William to lose consciousness, too. I started down the stairs. I said, "I need you to readminister tox screens for—"

"I already did."

"And?"

"All three of your victims consumed ethylene in the hours before they died."

My mind was racing. "How common is ethylene?" I said. "Could it have been present in different parts of the caves?"

"Detective." Someplace far behind me, water rushed over rocks. "There's a reason there weren't oracles all over the world.

Ethylene is *exceedingly* rare. I doubt very much there are multiple areas in the caves where the drug is present."

A stone skipped across my chest.

"I'd say you've stumbled upon their exact place of death, as well as the cause. Overconsumption of ethylene would lead to a loss of consciousness that, if near rushing water, would prove fatal. They wouldn't have had to go over the falls to drown."

I hung up. I stood on the porch staring, not seeing. Duncan, Neil, and William hadn't drowned because they'd swallowed too much water going over the falls. They'd drowned because they'd been knocked unconscious—poisoned. So either they'd intentionally entered a place they knew would poison them, or they hadn't killed themselves after all. But if they had died by choice, why that way? It seemed too convoluted to be plausible.

Ronan arrived beside me. "What's going on?"

I'd been so sure Duncan, Neil, and William had killed themselves because they'd taken out those insurance policies that expired the day before they died. If they hadn't actually taken out policies, it'd change everything. I turned to Ronan. "Keys."

Ronan looked confused. After a beat he fished his keys out of his pocket. He handed them to me. I jogged to the cruiser. I popped open the trunk.

There they were, the case files, right where I'd left them. I shuffled through them. I pulled out the background check done on each of the victims. William and Duncan had never opened a bank account. They didn't trust banks. But Neil had. I found the number. I dialed.

"Leigh, you're freaking me out," Ronan said. "What's going on?"

I held up a finger. I spoke to a manager. I gave her my badge number. I asked for all the incoming and outgoing transactions for Neil's account. She verified my identity and apologized for the wait. She was emailing them to me now.

I pulled the records up on my phone. I scanned the list. There weren't many transactions, so it was easy to parse. I turned to Ronan. "Neil's account shows no outgoing payments to Assured Trust Life Insurance."

Ronan's brow furrowed. He scratched his neck.

I said, "If these guys really bought life insurance policies, they'd have had to pay premiums. Right? That's how it works. So where is the record of them ever having paid premiums?"

Ronan took a beat to process this. At last he said, "What are you thinking?"

"We thought Neil mailed the insurance policies to the Copper Falls Police Department as a giant fuck you to Becker so that Becker would feel guilty about what he'd made them do. But what if Neil didn't? What if someone else mailed them?"

Ronan searched my eyes. "I want to understand you."

I expelled my breath. "If Neil, William, and Duncan never paid any premiums, then that means they didn't take out any policies. Even if the company they bought the policies from was a fake one, everyone knows you don't get life insurance for free. They'd have to have paid something to someone."

Ronan nodded. "Okay."

I took a step closer to him. "But if they didn't pay any premiums, then they didn't mail the insurance policies to the CFPD. Why go through all the trouble of drafting fake insurance policies to send to the police when they could've just as easily sent suicide notes? It doesn't make sense. Someone else drafted the fake policies and mailed them to the police department."

In the distance, the wind shifted, sending a shiver through me. Ronan scrubbed his hand through his hair. "But why would someone do that?"

I took a moment to think about this. I found that the answer was obvious. "Becker stole these guys' money, right? So he wouldn't want to investigate their deaths anyway. He wouldn't want people poking around, finding out that he'd used the department to orchestrate this massive theft. Still, he is chief of police. He might have felt a duty to investigate their deaths. Unless—"

"Unless he had definitive proof they killed themselves."

"These policies gave him that proof. They ensured no one would look into the circumstances surrounding Duncan's, Neil's, and William's deaths."

Warmth spread down my arms, across my chest. I felt lighter, taller, sure of myself for the first time in days.

"The only reason someone would want to stop that investigation is if they weren't suicides after all and they weren't accidents."

34

RONAN AND I PULLED INTO THE PARKING LOT OF THE COPPER Falls police station, alongside two other police cruisers and Chief Becker's Ford pickup. Pretty soon, the other officers would be coming in from their traffic stops, ready for paperwork. I turned to Ronan. "You can handle today's reports, right?" I didn't wait for an answer.

I stepped across the parking lot and unlocked the G-Wagen. I'd asked Bear to drop it off there after changing the oil.

As I climbed into the driver's side and started the car, Ronan appeared in the passenger's seat.

"What are you doing?"

"Helping my sister with the investigation of a case."

"There could be nothing here."

"But what if there is?"

"I don't need help."

"I know you don't." Ronan reached over the seat and gripped hold of my hand. "But what if you accepted it anyway?"

It was something about his hand on mine that did it, something about feeling I'd been so wrong in trusting my gut and then finding out I might still be right. I felt it now, the final cracking. The compartment where I'd kept Ronan, where I'd kept my parents. It collapsed under that weight.

I expected searing pain and gushing tears. I expected a flood, a fire. I expected it to hurt like it always did when I let down my guard and remembered my vulnerabilities. Yet instead, warmth bloomed inside me. I gripped Ronan's hand. I swallowed something solid. I took a deep breath.

Just like that, I told him everything I'd been holding back.

I told him about my trips to the caves and about the snake I'd hallucinated when I'd come close to reaching the shrine.

I told him how the entrance to the cave was closed off now. There was no going back.

I told him how Dr. Aliche had called to say I'd been drugged, that William, Duncan, and Neil had been drugged, too. It'd knocked them unconscious—just like it'd knocked me unconscious. When they'd died, I believed they'd been in the caves trying to reach the shrine. That would explain how they drowned without plunging over the falls, which would corroborate what Maude had told us about them being dead before they went over the waterfall. Depending on where they drowned underground, that might also explain why they had no postmortem bruising or broken bones. And it would explain the ethylene in their blood.

I told him how Estella had said she'd been to the shrine to the Hunter, how she knew another way to reach it. That's the route Neil, William, and Duncan must have taken.

When I was done, Ronan was silent for a long time. At last he gave a nod. "So," he said, "we need to find that other route to the shrine. There might be evidence of whoever sent them there, or whatever they were hoping to find."

"These guys might not have been murdered at all," I said. "We still don't know that they were.".

"What does your womanly intuition say?"

"Instincts. Can we just say instincts?" I shook my head. "They've been so off."

There was a glint in Ronan's eyes. He looked so much like our father. He said, "Or maybe there's something your body is trying to tell you that your brain doesn't yet understand."

We traveled through the apple orchard, bursting with color, then onto the dirt road that led to Estella's cottage. The sun was making its long climb toward the horizon. Red saturated everything. Ronan gaped out the open window. "Wow," he said. "I didn't even know this place existed."

"No one really knows about it," I said. "Or about Estella. Janice said the people in town just pretend she doesn't exist." I recalled how Dr. Wagner had said that secrets between people tighten bonds, and how angry he'd looked when I asked about her. I said, "I don't think Estella used to be a secret, but I think she's a secret now."

"Is she really that unhinged?"

I thought of her mystical musings. I thought of how someone had set fire to her brothers' cabin, burning them alive. I thought of how, apart from Maude, she was the only one who knew how to find the shrine. At last I said, "I don't know."

As I pulled along the last stretch of lane, the G-Wagen kicked up dirt like sparks. Birdsong chattered over the rustling leaves. Water whooshed in the distance. I parked in front of Estella Wagner's house.

As we got out of the car, Ronan said, "Maude and Estella really are opposites, aren't they?" He craned his neck to get a better look at the place.

"Because this house isn't falling apart?"

"Yeah," he said. "And because I can't imagine Mrs. Hummel keeping animals alive."

Ronan's gaze stretched out over the paddock in the distance. The fencing was made of thick, knobby wood, painted white.

At first, I thought the paddock was empty. But as I traced its periphery I saw that, there, at the corner closest to us, stood a white goat with a thick beard. It was biting into a mound of grass, not paying attention to us. Off beyond it stood a gable-roofed chicken coop. It shocked me that, before, I hadn't seen any of this.

We were at the front door now. Ronan thwacked the iron knocker.

A beat.

He tried again. Harder. The fixtures shook like manacles.

Ronan pulled the wrought-iron handle. It gave.

It didn't surprise me that Estella's door was unlocked—most people's doors around here were—but it did surprise me that Ronan opened the door all the way. It surprised me that he stepped inside Estella's house.

I put my hand on his arm.

"What?" Ronan said. "She's not here."

I started to tell him Estella Wagner wasn't like Maude Hummel. While they might be twins, Estella was not infirm. She was not open to intruders. She would report us for illegally searching her house.

Yet I also wanted to know if she really was as crazy as the town believed.

I took my hand off Ronan's arm. He went ahead of me. I pushed on the door until the heavy latch thwacked into place, sealing us inside.

The cottage felt different now with Estella not in it. The floorboards creaked. The rug had a layer of dust to it. The windows rattled as they caught a blast of wind.

The smell was different, too. Gone were the scents of apples and cinnamon, of yeasty bread, of chicory coffee. Instead, it smelled of meat scraps left to sit. It smelled of must.

"Oh god," Ronan said. His voice was muffled. "Oh. God." He was in the back room. Past the neat bookshelves and the lace curtains. Past a wall of porcelain figurines and through two sets of round-topped doors. I arrived at Ronan's side.

He'd opened a panel of the wall. I didn't ask how he knew it was there. It was obvious. There was a pool of red liquid seeping out from its edge. The smell of it hit the back of my throat. Blood.

The meat-scrap smell grew more intense the closer I got. I knew now what it was. The stench was unmistakable. This was a dead body.

My heart thrummed against my chest at the thought of

seeing Estella Wagner murdered. I was aware of every surface I'd touched, every place my feet had stepped. If this really was her body in this closet, if she'd been dismembered or stabbed, if her wrists had been slit, I needed to remember all of it.

"Step back," I said to Ronan. "Don't touch anything." I un-clipped my Colt.

As I approached, Ronan continued to hold up his Maglite. A cone of light stretched out before us.

I held my gun in front of me.

I turned my gaze toward the room hidden in the wall.

"Fuck."

"Yeah," Ronan said. He held his fist to his mouth.

My relief at not finding Estella dead was short lived. In its place arrived a different feeling. It reminded me of elevators that descended too quickly, of the part of roller coasters I never liked.

Under the low ceiling of the closet, scrubbed bones hung like wind chimes. Blood splatters climbed up the walls and dripped. On the floor gleamed an arsenal of knives. These were not kitchen knives, not the kind for buttering bread and slicing ap-ple cake. These were hunting knives, the kind it takes real mus-cle to heft.

There were other things, too—balls of matted fur, nests of mangled feathers, sharp shears the size of hedge cutters—but my eyes blurred all of it. Instead, I focused in on the centerpiece of the macabre display.

There, hanging from the ceiling, upside down and lifeless, was a goat that might once have been white. Its throat had been slit. Its blood dripped into a silver bowl, overfilled and spilling.

Ronan turned from the door. "I guess I can see why people wanted to keep her a secret."

I holstered my weapon. Ronan handed me his Maglite. As I held it up, my eyes caught on a circle of bones. They were tied together with entrails so they formed a web. In it, someone had sewn knuckles and jagged teeth. The teeth were human.

35

IT WAS STILL DARK OUT BY THE TIME NEIL MAYER'S ROOM-
mates came chugging down the gravel in their beat-up Pontiac Sunfire with the low hum of folk music scratching out
from the speakers. The car slowed as it approached.

Mel was driving. Ronnie held up her phone's flashlight to
point inside the G-Wagen. It shone from me to the empty seat
beside me. It was six A.M. and Ronan was still sleeping. I thought
it'd be better if only I came.

"Isn't this a nice upgrade," said Mel. She wasn't wearing a
flannel anymore, but navy scrubs, like the kind staff wear at nail
salons. Ronnie was wearing the same thing, though hers were
too big for her frame.

I held up my hand to shield the light. Ronnie lowered her
phone. I said, "I need to go through Neil's things."

"Not gonna happen," shot Mel. "You need a warrant for that shit."

"We don't have a problem with you personally," Ronnie said.

"But we're not about to let you plant anything on us," said Mel. "You're still a cop."

I got out of the vehicle then. I waited for Mel and Ronnie to get out, too. Standing across from me, I was reminded just how small they were. They had the narrow hips of girls whose bodies haven't spread into their adult shapes. There were bags under their eyes. For the first time, it occurred to me to wonder whether this was just because they worked all the time or for some other reason. Maybe Neil had been like a brother to them, too. I said, "We got some news about Neil yesterday."

Mel said, "It can't be worse than him being dead."

Ronnie shot her a look.

I said, "He was drugged."

The lines on Mel's forehead relaxed. Ronnie's mouth fell open. I waited.

Ronnie held out her hand to Mel, who handed her the keys. They opened the door and let me inside.

Neil's room was spare and messy in the way of someone who was always on the road. A twin air mattress, half deflated, sat on the floor along with plastic shelving blocks, which were stuffed with magazines and sheet music, a mug full of pens, various ephemera: a carved wooden owl, a toy submarine, a Rubik's Cube. As Mel and Ronnie stood in the doorway, I searched through Neil's papers.

"What exactly are you looking for?" Ronnie asked.

"Where would Neil keep something that was important to him? Something he wanted to make sure he didn't lose?"

Ronnie walked across the room and opened a closet. She leaned over and pulled out a black instrument case. Of course. Everything that mattered to him would have been with his trumpet.

I laid the trumpet case on the ground and undid the clips with two loud snaps. The case was hard, lined with velvet. I felt around the top edge and pulled.

My fingers touched upon it before I could see it. Flat and thick. An accordion folder.

I withdrew it and Ronnie and Mel clasped hands.

On its face were scrawled the words *important stuff* in careful handwriting. I lifted out Neil's birth certificate, his Social Security card, a yellow immunization card, the manufacturer's warranty for his trumpet. No receipts paid out to a life insurance company.

I flipped over an envelope to find two out-of-town phone numbers written there.

This surprised me. We'd never recovered any of the victims' phones from the plunge pool, but their call records had shown only local calls.

The first number had a Toledo area code. It had a name beside it, Sasha Daniels. I knew her as the local ABC news anchor. She'd been doing the news since I'd lived here.

The other didn't have a name beside it, but it had a Los Angeles area code. I could have traced it easily, but I didn't need to. I remembered every digit from when Mason had written it on the inside of my hand.

I stuffed the papers back into the folder. "I'm taking this with me," I said.

I pushed out the door.

As I drove to Mason's, I dialed the number for Sasha Daniels, the anchor at ABC. "Detective Leigh O'Donnell," I said. "Out of Copper Falls. I'm calling about Neil Mayer. I believe you had been in touch?"

"Finally," she said. In the background, she was thanking someone. I heard the jangle of a door and then the faint zoom of traffic. I thought she'd give me a hard time about the hour, but she didn't seem to care. She said, "I've been trying you for weeks."

I remembered Janice handing Becker a phone message from *that reporter*. I remembered him crumpling it up: *Some people never know when to give up.* I switched the phone to the other ear. "What is it you've been trying to say?"

She gave one of those empty-belly sighs like, *Where do I start?* Finally, she said, "Neil and his friends were supposed to be on my program. You know, the six o'clock news? It was going to be a big story. They were coming on to talk about this massive theft happening in Copper Falls."

I nodded. I could've pinched myself. The haircuts. The trimmed nails. The shaved faces. The explanation was so much simpler than I'd made it out to be. They weren't preparing themselves to be sacrifices. They were preparing themselves to go on TV.

"Neil told me they uncovered looting of indigenous artifacts in Copper Falls."

"Artifacts?" This was the first I was hearing about indigenous artifacts.

"I don't know much more than that," she said. "They said it was tied up with the town, but that's all they'd say."

I heard the beep of a key fob and then the creak of a car door.

"So that night, I had the whole crew there for a taping. I mean, this was going to be a really big deal. People care about that stuff these days, you know? Even my boss made a special trip. He's been saying that Copper Falls is shady for years. Nowhere can be that perfect. But Neil and his friends, they never showed."

I slowed for a turn. "Did you try to reach them?"

"Neil and I had always been in contact through this app. Signal? I guess you've probably heard of it. He was paranoid.

"Anyway, I tried to message him that way, but he never responded. I thought he just got scared or something, but the next day, he ended up on our program anyway."

I knew what was coming next. Still I let her say it.

"That's the day that he and his friends were found dead."

36

I KNOCKED ON THE CARRIAGE HOUSE DOOR WITH THE
vehemence of someone not trying to be polite. I yelled Mason's
name.

I pressed my face against the lattice window. I cupped my
hands around my eyes. Mason had withheld the fact that he was
in contact with the victims before they died, which meant he
hadn't come here to investigate their deaths, not in the way he'd
tried to make me believe. I would find him. I would hunt him
down. I would learn the truth.

"He's not here," came a voice from behind me.

I turned to find a figure on the stone path. "Mrs. Vogel?" I
made my tone professional. "Leigh O'Donnell."

Mason's mother wasn't wearing lipstick, as she had been in
her picture in *Rolling Stone*. Instead of a tiny-waisted dress with
a Peter Pan collar, she was wearing a heavy knitted sweater and
cotton pants. She was heavier than when last I'd seen her but
also more sure of herself.

"Do you know where I can find Mason? It's urgent."

She clicked her tongue. "My son goes to the gym every morning. Drives all the way to Toledo. Of course, I can't get him to step foot inside the Curves we have on Front Street. He's usually gone for a good three or four hours, with the trip there and back."

I was still holding the accordion file from Neil's trailer. "When does he usually get back?"

"Around eight or so." She pursed her lips. "I told him it's not good to be obsessive about his body, but he's never cared much for what I think. He used to listen to his father, but now I'm lucky if he lets me make him breakfast."

I scrutinized her face. "I thought Mason wasn't allowed back in the house?"

Lines stretched across Mrs. Vogel's forehead, down the sides of her mouth. Confusion.

Mason had told me there was a rift between him and his mother. I'd had no reason not to believe him.

"That's news to me," she said. "He's taken over my whole sewing room and converted it into a war room dealing with those poor young men's deaths. I don't go in there. I wouldn't even get my quilting hoop. It's just too gruesome."

My mouth fell open. I couldn't shut it. Mason had lied to me. About this, too. For a moment, I couldn't understand why. Then I did understand, and rage tore through me.

Mason had wanted me to feel connected to him, for us to be orphans together, so I would open up to him. It was a classic con. And it'd worked.

"Actually," I said, plastering a smile on my face, "would you mind if I asked you a few questions? There are some things I think we should talk about."

Mrs. Vogel pursed her lips again. She sucked them in with her teeth. At last she said, "I don't suppose you want some eggs?"

It was eight o'clock in the morning when I spotted Mason Vogel walking across the parking lot of the grocery store at the center of town. I spun the wheel to park in the lot and slammed the door.

"You lied to me," I said.

Mason had a tote bag slung over his shoulder. At my words, he stopped.

"You said you were here covering the suicides," I said, "but you lied."

Mason smiled in that coquettish way of his. It was a smile that didn't take me seriously. He sidled toward me. "I don't know where you got your information, Wildcat."

"Don't call me that."

"I can assure you I didn't—"

"I talked to your mother."

Mason stopped midway across the parking lot, right on the yellow line.

"She confirmed that you got here the day *before* Duncan, William, and Neil died. She even printed off your flight confirmation for me. Now I'll just bet if I recover Neil's phone, it will show messages between the two of you on an encrypted app."

Mason's expression faltered.

"You lied to a homicide detective about an ongoing murder investigation. What am I supposed to think?"

"Come on," Mason said. He started toward a Jeep Wrangler, because of course that's what he'd rented for northern Ohio in the middle of autumn. "I've got ice cream in here. We can talk back at the carriage house. I'll tell you everything. I swear. You'll see. It's nothing like that."

"We're talking right here."

"You can't stop me."

"Wanna bet?" Then, because I was feeling hurt, I said, "Aren't you the one who kept wanting me to handcuff you?" I was wearing my suit. I touched the cuffs clipped to my belt. "Here's your chance."

A toddler and his mom were holding hands coming out of the library. Mason headed in their direction. He climbed the white steps of the gazebo and took a seat on the center bench. I climbed the steps and stood in the archway just as he dug his arm into his tote.

I unclipped my sidearm.

"Seriously?" He looked up at me, injured. He withdrew a pint of ice cream. "I don't suppose you have a spoon?"

"Why don't you start by telling me why you lied?"

He sighed. "You're really making a very big deal of this."

"No, me making a big deal of this would be me placing you under arrest. This is me being nice. Why did you lie to me about why you were here?"

Mason dragged his tongue over his teeth. "A Montague and a Capulet, remember? I told you that right from the start."

"That doesn't explain anything."

"I couldn't have you scoop my story."

"I'm a detective," I said, "not a rival."

"You *are* a rival if you make an arrest before my story comes out. Who's going to want to read about something the AP has already covered?"

"That's sick, Mason."

"That's life, Leigh."

I pinned him with my gaze. "That's also accessory."

Mason groaned. He popped the lid off the ice cream. He looked sullen. "You really don't have a spoon?"

"Why would I have a spoon?"

"Aren't you a mom?"

"Aren't you a grown man?"

Mason pulled a jar of chili paste from his bag. He unscrewed the lid. He used it as a spoon, running it along the surface of the ice cream to peel back a layer of Chunky Monkey. After he'd swallowed, he said, "I was in L.A. when Neil Mayer messaged me on Signal."

I pulled my notebook out from my jacket pocket. I clicked open my pen. "When?"

"Two days before they died. I was the only journalist he knew. And, in his words, I'd already *fucked over the town once*. He figured I'd be down to do it again. He had dirt on Copper Falls he wanted to expose."

"What kind of dirt?"

Mason dipped the lid into the ice cream again. "I told him not to talk to reporters. I said what we needed to do was to develop this big investigative piece and really let it grow from there. I tried to convince him a magazine feature would carry more weight than talking to some hack at the local ABC station. He said he'd think about it, which of course meant *fuck off*. So, I took the next flight out here to try to change his mind. The next day he was found dead."

I still didn't know if I believed him. He'd lied to me so many times. "What exactly did Neil say he was going to tell the reporter?"

Mason swallowed another lidful of ice cream. He squeezed his eyes shut. "Hang on. Brain freeze."

"Take your time," I said, when what I meant was *Fuck you very much.*

At last, Mason recovered. "The town has money, right? Those of us who've lived here all of our lives just accept it. You know, the way living in New York, you probably accepted that there were skyscrapers and museums and homeless people. It's just in the fabric of things.

"You drive around here, in town, and you look at some of these houses. They're huge. They have chandeliers in their dining rooms and bone china for the guests. But if you think about it, it doesn't make sense. Where does everyone get their money?"

He held up the lid and gestured with it.

"Growing up, we all thought the money was coming from the mills. We had a gristmill and a papermill. But they're long gone. Last year, they finally closed down the sawmill. Yet, folks around here—not folks in the Sticks, mind you, but the people in town—still had money. How?"

Janice had said the town had raided the Sticks to pay their

debts. Yet, there was only so much money the Sticks would have. Not enough to run a town, certainly. Not enough for bone china.

"After Duncan, Neil, and William got robbed, which I know you know about, they discovered some more interesting facts. According to this source they had, some old lady in the Sticks—"

"Maude Hummel?"

"They never gave me a name. But according to her, for many years, the town made money by selling indigenous people's artifacts to private collectors."

Sasha Daniels had said the men were going to be on her program to talk about the looting of indigenous artifacts. This is what she'd meant.

I asked, "How much money are we talking about?"

"You wouldn't believe me if I told you."

"How much?"

"From what I understand? Millions. It was enough to sustain this whole bootstraps facade."

The longer I thought about it, the more it made sense. Estella had married Dr. Wagner's brother. That would have given her access to privileged information about the history of the town. She must have told Maude.

Maude must have told Neil, William, and Duncan about the sale of the indigenous artifacts. They'd have realized that the civil asset forfeitures were only the latest iteration of the town's thieving.

Mason said, "Unfortunately, when the selling of artifacts became illegal the town went into debt."

I rolled my tongue over my teeth. "So they started robbing people."

"When Neil's, William's, and Duncan's families got robbed so that Copper Falls could pay the piper, it was the last straw. They threatened everybody. The police station. The Historical Society. They called every business in town. They said if they didn't get back their money, they were going to drag the town through the mud and expose the looting."

"But why did it matter?" I said. "It'd hurt reputations, but that's it. No one was going to jail for any of this." I caught a glint in Mason's eyes. "Or were they?"

"That's the thing," Mason said, drawing each word out like a trail of bread crumbs he knew I'd follow. "Neil seemed to think the looting wasn't only historical. Someone was still selling artifacts. Maybe more than one person. He wouldn't say who."

I looked out over the town: at the grocery store, the library, the antiques shop, the gardens, the toddler and his mom, who were now sharing an apple on a bench. Ronan had lied. Janice had lied. Mason had lied. Everybody had lied to me. From day one.

Mason took another bite. "I saw Neil that night. The news taping was the next day. He looked good, cleaned up. He said they had to be very careful about their appearances or else people would think they looked too poor to be credible. They washed up in the plunge pool the next morning. I've been here ever since, trying to figure out what happened."

I held my notebook aloft. "That's it? That's everything? You're sure?"

Mason looked down at the empty pint. "Would I have eaten an entire tub of ice cream if I was holding anything back? Fuck, it's not even my cheat day."

I turned. "Don't leave town. I may want to talk to you again."

I was halfway down the gazebo steps when I looked back at him. I didn't want to say this next part. I did anyway. "All that stuff you said about being in love with me, was it even true?"

Mason's expression was not mocking. His face was open, guileless. "Yes."

"Then why—"

"Because I love my job more than anything." His gaze was penetrating. "Isn't it the same for you?"

37

IT WAS A CALL I DIDN'T WANT TO MAKE. I WASN'T READY TO hear Eric's voice. I wasn't ready to be on terms with him that were not as married people but as the legally separated. I knew the papers were coming any day now, the way I knew it was going to rain by the scent of the air, the way I knew the night was coming by the hum of crickets. We had avoided a legal separation because of what it implied would follow. But we were so far past that point now.

I'd just parked the G-Wagen in the driveway of my house. I was far enough back so that no one inside would see or hear me. It was stupid to be nervous. This was just Eric. Even if we weren't together, that didn't make him a stranger. Or an enemy.

As I made the call, my finger slipped. Instead of a voice call, that familiar FaceTime ring came up. The word CONNECTING shone on the screen.

I could have swiped to end the call. It would've been so easy to hang up before I saw him. But instead, I sucked in my breath. I waited.

A flash. That musical note. Then there he was. My husband. "Hey, baby, I—" Then Eric saw it was me.

It hurt to see his smile unstitch like that. It hurt to see that cold harden his skin. His eyes had turned to stone. Those stones could turn to weapons. I needed to get through to him before he used them.

Eric was sitting up in bed. He said, "Listen. Now's not a good time for—"

"I need to ask you a favor," I said. "It's urgent."

A woman called to him from another room. Her voice was older than I'd expected, buttery and warm. The throaty scratch of it made me think of sex. "Honey, do you want me to—"

Eric put the phone on mute. He turned the camera away as he replied to her. His room was different than the last time I'd seen it. Still tidy. But there was a metal rack near the bed. I wondered if she'd bought it for him, this woman who'd called him *honey*.

Eric steadied the phone. He unmuted himself. I swallowed back something tasteless. Quickly, I said, "I believe some individuals here are in violation of the federal Archaeological Resources Protection Act." I tried to make my voice emotionless. "Possibly the Native American Graves Protection and Repatriation Act as well. I believe the same individuals who are illegally selling indigenous artifacts are also involved in a triple homicide. When you have time . . ."

At this, my voice faltered. Eric was busy, clearly. There was sex to be had. Brunch in bed. There was his life and there was mine, and these were two spheres that no longer connected.

I said, "Please call Mack." Mack was Eric's friend at the FBI. They'd worked undercover together years ago. "Ask him if he's heard anything. The person—or people—who are selling indigenous artifacts are likely doing it out of Toledo or Cleveland. Maybe Detroit. My C.I. tells me the sales are being made to private collectors, not museums."

I expected Eric to get angry, for him to ask where Simone was while I was continuing my investigation. Instead, he nodded, slow and deliberate. His eyes were sleepy, though it was almost noon. "Yeah," he said. "I can do that."

"Eric?"

I didn't know why I was asking this. It was his day off. We weren't together. It wasn't my business.

I said, "Are you okay?"

He didn't hesitate. "I'm fine."

"I just get the feeling that something's . . ." Only, I couldn't finish that sentence.

Eric slow blinked. He smiled weakly. He was similar to my husband, but thinner, ashier. Something about the look of him chilled my skin. He said, "I'll let you know what Mack says." Then Eric hung up.

I stared at the screen, at where his face had been. My phone's wallpaper shone back at me: Eric, bright and happy. Simone, on his shoulders. Me, smiling at the camera.

I closed my eyes. I pressed the phone against my chest.

38

IT WAS A LITTLE AFTER SIX O'CLOCK AT NIGHT. I COULD TASTE the solve in my mouth as if it were cooking on the stove. Yet, as I stared at my handwritten notes, as I considered the people who could be selling artifacts to private collectors, who were afraid of what Neil, Duncan, and William would tell the media, all I could see was Eric's face. All I could hear was the taunt of Mason's voice, *Isn't it the same for you?*

All at once, it felt stuffy. Hard to breathe. I needed air.

I kicked my legs out over the ledge of my bedroom window. I stepped over the rough roof tiles. I pulled myself over the banister of the widow's walk and stood. I'd been back for almost two weeks. Yet this was the first time I'd come out here.

I ran the palms of my hands along the top of the banister. I slowed my breathing. The horizon was deep orange now, like the flash of houselights before curtain call. All I could see were veins of water and molting trees. All I could feel was the ache of my husband right in front of me, yet impossibly out of reach.

Even if I solved this case and made national headlines, even if, by some miracle, I eventually returned to my old job at the NYPD, Eric wasn't going to take me back. This case—the deaths of Duncan, Neil, and William—they had nothing to do with him. Yet, as I stood there, looking out, I couldn't shake the feeling that it had everything to do with Eric. With us. With how I'd failed him.

Mason had asked me whether the reason I'd let that suspect in New York go was because he'd reminded me of my husband. I hadn't known the answer then. But I knew it now.

No. The man I'd knocked to the ground hadn't reminded me of Eric. He'd been as invisible to me as all the other souls I'd testified against in court, who'd always be defined as the worst thing they'd ever done. How I'd acted hadn't had anything to do with that man or with my partner. It'd had everything to do with me.

Mason had said I wasn't one of the good guys. Eric had called me reckless. Both of them were right. I'd played out my internal dramas on other people because the institution I'd pledged my life to had told me it was within my rights. I'd knocked a man down, I'd let him go, I'd pointed my gun at my partner—all the while, something subconscious was at the wheel.

Yet after all of that, I still didn't understand why.

My gaze fixed on the waterfall, surging in the distance. My mind fixed on the caves beneath them.

I knew what I needed to do.

I climbed back over the banister. I swung around to kick my feet inside the dormer window. I rooted in my closet and came back outside with my old telescope. My fingers found the right adjustments. My hands pulled the arm at the base with just the right force to swivel it.

With the telescope, I searched the area surrounding the waterfall for another fissure like the one I'd entered the caves through. If I could find an alternative entrance to the Hunter, I wouldn't need Estella Wagner. I searched and I searched. Yet all I could see was the moonglow of limestones and the tall grasses surrounding them. All I could make out was the rush of water that looked like blown glass.

A breeze swept across the widow's walk. I adjusted the lens. Through the red dot viewfinder, Estella's tiny cottage was fuzzy, as if from a dream. A movement caught the edge of my lens. I adjusted the aperture. It was Estella.

She was wearing a duster-length coat and work boots, the rubber kind, splattered with mud. She was carrying a fan-shaped basket.

I dialed Ronan. "She's there. At her house." He didn't have to ask who.

"I'm on my way," Ronan said.

I hung up. We'd bring her in. We'd make her tell us how to find the other entrance to the caves. We'd make her tell us what she knew about the stolen artifacts. Yet something told me it wouldn't be quite that easy.

As Ronan closed in on her, I kept watch.

Estella's basket was resting in the crook of her elbow. It was filled with roses. With her quick, short steps, she walked to the garden at the edge of the clearing. She leaned over a tomato trellis. She placed the basket down and got on her knees. She picked up a shovel that must have been waiting there. She dug it into the ground.

I adjusted the aperture. I cranked the arm of the telescope to keep it from shivering with the wind. I could almost make out what she was doing.

From behind me, "Hi!"

I snapped around. There was Simone, holding Bear's hand. I dropped the telescope's arm. "How did you get up here?"

Then I saw. The trapdoor that had always been stuck was now open. A ladder reached down into the closet below. Bear must have helped Simone find it. I was furious. "What were you thinking? She's afraid of heights."

We both looked at Simone, who hesitated. Slowly, she removed Bear's hand from hers. She peered down over the railing. She touched the telescope. "Mommy," she said. "Make it so I can see?"

I couldn't believe it. How many times had she been afraid of high places? Now, here she was, acting like being up here was nothing at all. Here she was, knowing what a telescope was.

I looked at Bear. Had he done this?

Bear shrugged. He climbed down the ladder back into the house.

I turned and helped Simone adjust the settings.

Simone put her eye to the lens. "Mommy, I can see so far!" After a moment, she added, "It's not so scary, you know."

"What's not so scary?"

"Here."

I couldn't tell whether she meant being on the rooftop or

being in Copper Falls. If she meant being away from her father or being without her armadillo. Maybe she simply meant that none of this was scary right at this moment but that it could be again soon.

"But you know," she added, "I'm not staying here forever."

Her words lodged in my throat. Of course she didn't want to stay in Copper Falls. She wanted to go back to New York, back to her father and friends. It'd only been a fantasy, keeping her here, keeping her inside this bubble.

She said, "When we're done here, I want to travel."

"Travel?"

Simone looked up from the telescope. She had a circle around her eye from the eyepiece, like a pirate's patch. "Uncle Eamon got out his big book. He showed me where the armadillos live. They have such big trees there!"

I squinted. I said, "He showed you the Amazon?"

"He kept turning the pages of his maps." Simone's eyes were filled with delight. "Mommy, there are so many places!"

I brought Simone to my chest, squeezed her tight. How had she grown so much in just two weeks?

But of course she was right. There wasn't just here and New York. Our choices for the future weren't just between versions of our old lives. There were indeed so many places.

From inside, Bear bellowed, "Y'all done with your Hallmark moment? I got things to do."

Bear crawled up the ladder. His head poked out. I hugged Simone tighter. I told her to go with Bear and get ready for bed. As she joined him on the ladder, Bear held out a scrap of paper.

He said, "You were asking for this."

I unfolded it. It was the name and phone number of Eddie Cain. The man whose house this used to be. I scrutinized my uncle. "How did you get this?"

"Your mom gave it to me. Years ago. In case we found anything valuable at the house we should pass on to him." Bear's eyes had a gleam to them. "Funny, right? That she chose me as the most ethical one, out of all her options. She always was the smart one in the family."

At that, Bear helped Simone climb down the ladder. I folded the slip of paper and put it in my pocket. I would call Eddie in a minute. Now I returned my attention to the telescope. I refocused.

Ronan was standing in Estella's yard. He was scratching his head and searching around him.

But there was no sign of Estella.

39

Thursday, November 16

THE NEXT MORNING, I DROVE THE HOUR AND A HALF TO
meet Eddie Cain at a community center in Detroit.

When I arrived, I checked in with the receptionist. Her swivel
chair sprung up as she stood. "Grab yourself a coffee. Let me go
find him."

The rec room was big and open. Daylight filtered in through
the vertical blinds, shining on the flat, blue carpet. Plastic tables
stood at uneven intervals, all of them filled with people.

At one, two Black men in collared shirts and tennis shoes sat
at a square table playing dominoes.

At another, three older Black women in colorful dresses and
matching hats passed around paper plates while a fourth cut
into a loaf cake.

At another, an East Asian woman in a peasant top and a
white man in a T-shirt huddled over a Scrabble board, both of

them playfully glancing at the hourglass timer while a South Asian man in corduroy worried over his tiles.

I found the industrial coffee maker in the kitchenette and a packet of Lipton. I used the spout to release hot water and dunked in a wedge of lemon. When I turned to face the rec room, I saw him: Eddie Cain.

I couldn't say how I knew it was him. Maybe it was his blue eyes or his sandy hair or the particular shade of pink of his skin. Maybe it was because everyone in Copper Falls wore the same grab bag of features, like a clan who'd never commingled.

Eddie was delivering a plate of cookies to the men playing dominoes. He laughed with the older one. When he looked up, Eddie met my eyes. The laughter fell from his features. I got the impression that even if he'd agreed to see me, he wasn't exactly happy I'd come.

We found an empty card table in back. Eddie unfolded two metal chairs. He brought us out a plate of brownies, which neither of us touched.

"I don't suppose you remember me," Eddie said. His voice was phlegmy, like someone who smoked too much, or talked too much, maybe both. "Naw, you wouldn't. You were so young when I met you. Must have been four or five. I came to deliver the deed for the house. You all lived out on Euclid Avenue? A duplex if my memory's not playing tricks on me."

It took a second for me to understand what felt off. I said, "You didn't have the deed with you when you lost the house?"

"I just had the keys with me. I laid them down in the pot like I was some big man, though. But I wasn't so big if I lost it all, huh?" Eddie's eyes focused on something beyond me. "Hey, 'scuse me a minute, would you?"

He stood and I glanced behind me. Eddie had rushed to hold a ladder so a white woman in pleated trousers could climb up it. She was pulling a plastic tub from a shelf.

"Sorry about that," he said once he was back. "That thing's not as sturdy as it looks. What were we saying? Right. You had some questions for me about Copper Falls."

I searched his face. I knew he'd changed the subject. I just didn't know why. I said, "I'm investigating some potential homicides in town."

The skin on his forehead wrinkled.

"You hadn't heard?"

"I don't keep in touch with anyone there. My parents died years ago. I had one brother, but he's gone now, too."

"Why did you leave?"

"I don't see what that's got to do with any murders."

"I can't reveal the specifics of an ongoing case."

A flash in Eddie's eyes. "Now, let's get one thing straight." He leaned on his elbows and dropped his voice lower. "I'm talking to you out of the goodness of my heart, Detective. That doesn't mean you get to pry into my private life."

The words came before I knew what I was saying. "Every gift comes at a price."

Eddie drew back. "Excuse me?"

I cleared my throat. "My parents couldn't have afforded the life you gave us. Dad was a tradesman. Mom managed the house. We never could have lived in Copper Falls without your help. You gave us that life."

Eddie started to speak. I cut him off.

I said, "Don't tell me you just so happened to lose the house in a game of cards because I don't believe you. There were few things my dad cared about more than home. He wouldn't have held you to that deal unless you wanted to give it to him."

Eddie looked chastened.

"Every gift comes at a price," I said again. "My dad used to say that. Now I want to know. What was the price of ours?"

Eddie held my gaze.

Softer I said, "You owe me that."

Eddie drew his eyes away from mine. He searched the room, as if trying to find someone who needed him. At last, he folded his hands. But I knew they wouldn't stay like that. Eddie Cain was not someone who enjoyed being idle. The anger had fallen out of his voice. "I was sorry to hear about your parents. They were good people."

"So you do still talk to people in town?"

He shifted in his seat. "Over the last decade, a couple times, sure. I'm not completely cut off."

"You just didn't want to live there? People think of that place as paradise."

"Well, it's not like that for everybody," Eddie said. He was wearing a hooded sweatshirt. He stuffed his hands into its center pocket.

I thought back to Mason, to Janice, to everyone I knew who'd wanted out. "You mean it's not paradise for people who are different?"

Eddie was silent for a long time. I was worried that this was the most I'd get out of him. "My brother and I"—the words came out scratchy—"we had a hard time all throughout elementary and high school. Just kids being kids is what we were told.

But the bullying was relentless. I don't even know what made us so different, but they knew, even if we didn't. And the thing is, after we graduated? It didn't stop."

"How did your brother die?" I couldn't have said how I knew his death was connected, but one look at Eddie told me I was right.

"I was the one who found him." His eyes were rimmed in red. "When he didn't come home, I was his whole search party. Everyone else thought he was being dramatic. But I knew. He'd threatened to do it before. I'd tried to talk him out of it. I didn't make it in time."

"He killed himself?"

Eddie scrubbed a hand over his face, shunting the emotions there, failing. "He threw himself over the falls." A tear slipped down Eddie's cheek.

I said, "What did his body look like?"

Disgust warped Eddie's features. "What kind of a question is that?"

"A relevant one."

"He looked dead, okay? He had a gash above his eye the size of my fist. All his fingers were broken. His ribs—" Eddie lifted up his hood. He started to stand. "Look, I can't . . . I can't do this with you."

I put a hand on his arm.

His eyes were watery.

"I know your brother isn't the first one they've bullied." I needed Eddie to stay. "The police stole huge amounts of money from people in the Sticks. They took money from these three men who are dead now. They pushed Estella Wagner to the fringes of town. They—"

"Estella Wagner?" Something unexpected swept over Eddie's face. Like I'd reached across the table and cut him. "Maude Hummel's sister?"

"You know about her?" This surprised me. I thought most people had no idea she existed.

Eddie shook his head. "My mother was a few years above her in grade school. Estella married my mother's high school sweetheart."

"Carmichael Wagner."

Again, that look like I'd cut him.

"Mom used to say how beautiful she was."

"She's still beautiful."

"You mean Maude?"

"Estella."

Eddie kept staring. From underneath his hood he looked sinister, startled. The tears in his eyes had dried. He said, "Estella's been dead for longer than you've been alive."

"You're misremembering," I said. "I've met her."

"A lot of people in Copper Falls look alike. You might have thought—"

"I wouldn't—" But then, bit by bit, the pieces came together. How, when I'd first met Estella, she'd already known my name. How Janice had told me the sisters hated each other, so they were never in the same room.

Dr. Wagner's face had frozen when I'd asked about Estella. Ronan had asked why the town wanted to keep Estella a secret. I took a long sip of my tea. I'd forgotten to take the tea bag out. The water was deep brown. But if it was bitter, I couldn't tell.

I said, "How did she die? Estella."

Eddie sat. He pulled his hood back to rest on his shoulders. He said, "I only know what my mother told me. She only told me because I was dealing with a bad breakup. I haven't fact-checked any of it."

"Just tell me."

Eddie ran a hand over the top of his head. At last, he laid his palms flat. He was calmer now. For some reason, he was calmer. "According to my mom, Maude and Estella had been through a lot. When they were teenagers, they'd lost their parents. For a while, they were raised by their brothers.

"But their brothers were hard on the girls, overly protective. They wanted to control them. The brothers didn't want the girls to get married, especially not to Wagners, and so of course, this made the Wagners even more appealing.

"Carmichael Wagner, my mom said he was the cool one. Slicked-back hair. Loved danger. They'd been an item, he and my mom, and then, as my mom put it, Estella bloomed.

"Carmichael left my mother to be with her. Within a matter of months, he was engaged to Estella. Around the same time, Calvin, the nerdy brother, he fell in love with Maude."

"Calvin Wagner? From the Historical Society?" I couldn't believe it. Dr. Wagner, who was so proper, so poised, he'd once been in love with Maude Hummel?

Eddie nodded. "Then came the fire that killed Maude and Estella's brothers. Arson, some said, but that could be rumor. All I know is once their brothers died, Maude and Estella made plans to marry their sweethearts. They were just sixteen."

As much as I didn't want to believe it, the facts lined up with what I'd already learned about Estella's and Maude's lives.

"As a wedding present, Carmichael built Estella a cottage, the exact kind of place she'd always dreamed of having. They were set to move in right after Maude's wedding to Calvin, which was to happen a few months later. But then Estella died. Everything changed."

"What happened?"

Eddie blew air through his lips, shrugged. "Supposedly, Estella started disappearing. Into the caves. Eventually, she stopped coming topside at all."

I stilled.

Eddie said, "Maude would go down there and leave her food. Then she stopped doing even that. Estella had gotten lost or had stopped wanting to be found. No one ever saw her again.

"My mom tried to rekindle things with Carmichael, but he was heartbroken. He died just a few years after that. An infection that didn't heal properly. Mom said he'd lost the will to live."

"And Maude?"

"She never got over it, either. She never married Calvin. He never married anyone. She was the love of his life."

The room bustled around us. Cleared plates. Sips of coffee. A woman lifting a trash bag from its can. I was numb to all of it. I said, "Did they ever recover Estella's body?"

A pause then, like the moment between movements. Eddie's eyes were penetrating. But even before he told me, I already knew what he would say.

40

BY THE TIME I PULLED THROUGH THE APPLE ORCHARDS AND down the cobblestone path to Estella's cottage, the sun was resting low on the horizon, making the skyline glow. Normally, I liked the ease into night. Normally, I felt the darkness like a protective crust. Yet now the hairs on my neck stood on end. Something cold gripped me like I'd stepped on a grave.

It'd all come together on the drive back to Copper Falls. Maude had been impersonating her dead sister. She'd been playing me the whole time.

As Maude, she'd teased me about the men's deaths not being suicides, urging me to build my case. As Estella, she'd told me to stop my search, trying to scare me away. A part of her felt guilty and another part of her didn't want to get caught, which meant only one thing.

Maude had given the men tens of thousands of dollars. The CFPD had found half a million stashed in her house. I'd assumed she'd inherited that money from her parents' windfall, but no. She had to be the one selling the artifacts. She was the only one who knew the other entrance to the shrine. She was the only one who knew how to find the artifacts. It had to be her.

Neil, Duncan, and William must have realized this during one of their visits. She'd tried to buy them off—hence the huge gifts of money. After their money was stolen and they threatened to go to the media, Maude must have sent them along a route where she knew they'd be drugged and die—to avoid getting caught.

I still didn't know why Maude had done it, why she needed all that money. I didn't understand how she'd managed to forge life insurance policies when, from the looks of it, she didn't even have a computer. But as I pulled up to Estella's house and killed the engine, I was sure I could make her tell me. Interrogations, after all, were where I excelled.

I stepped down the drive, around to the front of the house. I rapped on the door with the iron knocker. I wanted to call a name, but I wasn't sure which one to use. "Maude?"

Nothing.

I unclipped the Colt from its holster. I kept the safety on as I stepped inside her house. Whereas before the house had smelled musty and dead, now the burn of sage touched the back of my nostrils. It mixed with something sweet. Cinnamon. Clove.

"Maude?" I called again. As I stepped through the hall, the stained-glass window streamed colors on the credenza. I eased my shoulder through the threshold of the tiny kitchen. By the farmhouse sink sat vegetables in a strainer. Beads of water clung to their skins.

I stepped through the dining room. I moved faster now, sure Maude must be close. I approached the table where we'd eaten apple cake. On it, lacy napkins and two plates. In between them sat a porcelain platter. In its center, an apple tart, half covered with a faded tea towel. I touched my fingers to the tart. Still warm.

I went through the cottage, room by room, closet by closet. Yet, every place I searched was empty of life.

I stepped through the rest of the house, into the tiny library with its hand-bound books, into the bedroom, where a wedding-ring quilt hugged a thick mattress.

I approached the hidden closet. I popped it open. I pointed my gun.

The floor inside was clean. It'd only been two days since I'd been here, but the blood, the bones, the feathers were gone.

I replaced my sidearm. I pushed open the front door. Out on the cobblestone drive, I spun in a circle. But everything was the same. The same gardens. The same lawn. No Maude.

It didn't make sense.

A memory hit me then, like a firecracker bursting. I looked up at the house—my house—higher up on the hill. I looked down over the garden. I spotted it, the pyramid trellis where I'd seen Maude last night with the shovel.

I stepped through her gardens, passing patches of cabbages and lettuce. I passed garden beds that were all dirt. I passed shriveled tomato vines clinging to their stakes.

At last I came upon the trellis. It was made of thin wood, stuck together by nails that were just beginning to rust. Ivy climbed up its sides. Just below the ivy sat the cover of a manhole with the letters *M. K. Hummel*. It was just like the one I'd seen at Maude's house. Only, this time, beside it sat a long metal rod with a hook on its end.

My breath caught in my chest.

It hadn't been a shovel I'd seen Maude using the previous night. It'd been this.

I remembered the crash I'd heard the day I'd met Maude. It must have been the manhole cover in her backyard. She must have been coming through it. She must have been coming home.

I stood, dumbstruck, understanding. Maude was always disappearing. Yet Ronan and I could never find out where she'd gone. Janice had told me: Her father dug sewers.

Dr. Wagner's brother had built this house for Estella. Estella must have chosen to live here, where the tunnel outside her sister's house ended. They were twins, after all. They must have wanted a way to be together even after Estella was wed.

I saw it now, each piece of it. This is how Maude moved between the two places, pretending to be two different people.

I reholstered my weapon and jogged back to the G-Wagen. I grabbed the backpack I'd used when I'd climbed into the caves. I tried to call Ronan, to tell him where I was. But out here, I got no bars.

In my head, Eric's voice was screaming, *Don't be thoughtless*.

In my blood, my instincts were pounding, *Don't stop now*.

I stood at the top of the manhole, at war with myself.

Both times I'd gone underground, I'd come out alive. I'd probably be fine. Besides, Maude had already slaughtered a goat. Who else might she kill once she realized I knew her secret?

On the other hand, I'd already screwed up our lives by being reckless once. Following a potential killer into a sewer would fit the bill of exactly the sort of person I didn't want to be.

Yet for all my vacillation, there was also this other thing. This thing that lived in the molten core of me. The thing my body knew that my brain couldn't understand. I needed to go.

I needed to go now.

I crouched in front of the manhole cover. I lifted the heavy rod.

The lid prized off. I moved the cover out of the way. I released my breath.

I shone my Maglite into the shaft. There was an iron ladder with rungs like handles. The rest was black.

The wind swept through my hair. Scents spilled over my face: of wildflowers, of grass, of topside life. Blood pulsed in my ears. My heartbeat slowed to a sleepy pace. My skin unknitted. My shoulders fell away. I spread open my lips.

I slipped the backpack over my shoulders.

I began my descent.

41

I'D NEVER BEEN IN A SEWER BEFORE. I'D EXPECTED SLOSHING water, a stench that was overwhelming. Yet, when my feet touched the bottom and I shone the flashlight all around me, I found I wasn't standing in a sewer at all. It was a cave. But it was unlike any cave I'd ever seen.

There were no stalagmites or stalactites jutting out like teeth. Rather, the cave was shallow and smooth. It spread out before me like a long fish. Shelves were carved in the stone walls. On them sat dozens of wares.

Hand-stitched dolls wore patchwork dresses. There were gemstones in the shapes of flowers. Vases blown from glass. Colorful beads hung from the ceiling like icicles. As I shone my flashlight up at them, their facets formed prisms on the walls. It made the whole cave colorful, shimmering.

"Maude," I called.

My own voice echoed back to me from deep in the darkness. As I followed it, I beamed the flashlight.

The mood, which before had been so cheerful, became dark. The beads hung from the ceiling still, but they no longer had facets that would make rainbows on the walls.

The yarn-headed dolls and fabric flowers were replaced by broken pottery, by porcelain dolls with cracked faces. By matted tufts of feathers and bones and fur. All of these were arranged on the shelves like treasures.

A cold breeze swept over my chest, my shoulders, like a wind that causes boats to tip. I wanted to turn back. To find a signal. To tell Ronan where I was. I stepped forward instead.

"Maude?" This time, it wasn't just my own voice I heard in reply.

What I heard wasn't a cave sound. Not water dripping. Not the flap of bats or the zip of insects. I heard an old woman. She was singing.

I stepped around the bend. I could just make out the glow of candlelight up ahead.

I took another step forward. My boot splashed up water. Just a puddle. But it was enough for me to register the change in orientation. The ground here was lower. I was going to a deeper level of the caves. Down.

The wall curved before me. I followed around its bend. The song grew louder. The tune was low and throaty. It was in a language I didn't understand. It used sounds I did not grasp and could not have re-created. Yet my body knew. It knew the feeling of it. This was a song of adoration. Of supplication. Of relinquishment.

Curiosity had supplanted the fear in me. I moved forward in

the way of salmon headed upstream. Feeling the danger. Unable to stop.

Up ahead, there was paint on the walls, black and rust colored. The pockets in the walls were no longer filled with broken things but with colorless pottery that looked very old. Some of it was cracked.

There were wooden masks with long noses and closed-eyed faces. A mortar and pestle made from pockmarked stone. Carved beads, stunning, unsymmetrical, ancient.

I touched my fingers to a carved figurine. I thought to the artifacts the town had been selling.

I unclipped my holster. I stepped in the only direction I could. Ahead.

As I made my way around the corner, the singing grew stronger. It was a single voice. Yet its echo bounced off the walls like a chorus. The perfume of roses filled my nose. I pointed my sidearm down as I walked, ready.

I stepped under an arch and through to the final stretch of tunnel. I spied around the edge. The room was round, intimate. Dripping candles nestled into spots along the walls. They were configured like constellations. The stone here was different, too. It wasn't the moon rock of limestone from the other caves. It glittered like granite.

Then there she was.

Maude knelt before a platform with her back to me. Her hair was covered by a scarf.

There, before her, lying on the platform, was a dead woman.

She was not as Dr. Ortiz had described her, a skeleton with

bones swollen and sparkling. Her legs were not hinged open at the hip so she could lie on her back with one arm reaching above her while the other reached below, balancing between worlds. She was not the sacrifice to the Hunter.

Instead, she was on her side as if sleeping. A mound of salt rested under her head. Salt was everywhere. She'd been preserved in it. Her skin was desiccated and stretched tight over her bones. Her teeth were gone. But her hair and clothes were intact. They tangled around her shrunken body.

Although her eyes were gone, I knew they'd once been iced blue. I knew this because I recognized the girl from her wedding photo. She was young. Probably around sixteen. This was the body of Estella Wagner.

Maude was praying at her sister's feet.

Spread all around Estella's corpse were roses. They were red and yellow, pink and white. Some had their stems kept long. Others were cut just below the bud. Petals carpeted the floor. The smell of them, which before had been pleasant, now was overwhelming.

There were photos spread around her sister's body. William Houser's high school graduation photo. A photo of Neil Mayer dangling a fishing pole off the side of a dinghy. Duncan Schott, with his arm around his girlfriend, in front of a fireplace. A monogrammed flashlight.

There was a photo of Rich, the swimmer who'd died at the falls, bare chested in a Speedo with a medal hanging around his neck. There was a Polaroid of Brett, the stoner, out of focus, his eyes glassy and red. Owen, the math geek, stood uncomfortably in a group photo, though the rest of the people had been cut out.

As I approached, Maude shushed her song.

I took another step closer.

Maude pressed the rose she was holding to her face. Not the part with the petals but the part with the thorns. It reminded me of that first visit with her. The one where she'd told me about her dead brothers.

"We warned you to stop searching." Her voice was like stone scraping stone. "We tried to stop you."

"Estella tried to stop me." The words were out before I realized my mistake.

Maude touched her hand to her sister's face. She ran her knotty fingers along her sister's jawbone.

I felt it in my spine.

"There are times when I lend her my body. It is her body, too, after all. We are exactly the same. But when she's inside of me, I'm still there, in the background. Those times, I am her witness." As Maude spoke, she stroked her sister's face.

I said, "Why do you have those photographs?"

"Estella is not like us. She isn't forced to choose between the stars and the earth. She lives in both places. When she is in the stars, she watches over them. She keeps them safe in death, as I failed to do in life."

I still had my sidearm out. Maude still had her back to me. I said, "How did you fail to keep them safe?"

Maude shook her head. "When the first ones came, it was by accident."

I lifted the phone from my pocket. Still no signal. Maude picked up another flower. I pressed RECORD. "You mean Owen,

Brett, and Rich. You mean the high school boys? How were their deaths an accident?"

The breath fell out of her. "They were sleeping in the woods. It's a tradition, the night before people leave. In the old days, the townspeople would dress up in costumes and scare them. They would say, under cover of darkness, what they were unwilling to say during the light.

"The three were set to leave the next morning, I was told. They'd been smoking. Drinking. Their eyes were red. They were so loud." Maude shuddered. "So very loud. We wouldn't have been outside. But Estella wanted to see the moon. She has so few wants, my sister. So few ways I can please her.

"Estella had been dancing under the light of the moon. The young men saw her. They thought she was a ghost or an enchantress or mad. She descended into her cave so she could rest. She needs so much rest. But they followed her."

Maude's voice rattled.

"They believed they were above consequences."

Maude pressed a flower to the foot of her sister's corpse. I had stepped to the side of her so I could see her face. Her eyes were cloudy, unfocused, like an old dog's. I couldn't understand why she was so calm. She had to know her life was over. She had to know that this confession would seal her fate.

"But the others," she said, "those were not an accident. We tried to help them. We gave them thousands. It wasn't enough. They came back for everything our parents left us. They had guns, uniforms. We gave them everything. They weren't satisfied. They kept needing more, more, more. They did not stop until we were empty."

There was so much about this story Maude had misunderstood. Clearly, she didn't know the police had stolen the money from Duncan, William, and Neil. She didn't know the police, when they'd come for the rest of her money, hadn't been associated with those men. Maude thought she'd given the men all her money only to have them want more of it. No wonder she'd killed them.

Maude tended to the shorn roses as if they were a garden, arranging, pruning. Now that she was talking, she didn't want to stop. She said, "That policewoman was always down here, snooping into this world without ever wanting to understand it. She told them how to find what was left of the pottery." She clucked her tongue. "Nothing was ever enough."

The policewoman? Understanding dawned on me in waves. "You mean Janice?"

Maude looked at me from the sides of her eyes. "We do live up to our names, don't we? It makes one wonder. About the power of names."

I checked that my phone was still recording. I spoke loudly to be sure the microphone caught it: "You're saying Janice Haas told Duncan Schott, Neil Mayer, and William Houser to come here to find artifacts to sell?"

But as soon as I said this, I knew it must be true. Janice had lied to me all along. I'd been like a ship she could steer at her will. All she'd had to do was decide which facts were relevant to the story she wanted me to believe. I didn't know why I'd trusted her so easily—because she was the authority on the town's history, or because I'd confused wokeness with being good.

"I saw her down here," Maude said. "Looking for pottery. I told them about it. A few nights before they died." Maude inhaled.

"They confronted her. They told her they knew what she was doing. They wanted to blackmail her, to put pressure on her to change Chief Becker's mind about something. I don't know. But Janice had another trick up her sleeve."

Maude drew in a ragged breath.

"She told them what we had here—our pottery—was worth more than all the money I'd given them, worth more money than they'd ever need. Especially if they kept going. If they made it to the shrine to the Hunter, they'd be able to steal enough to make millions."

I was still going over Maude's words in my head, trying to put the pieces together as fast as I could. "You're saying you told Neil, Duncan, and William that you saw Janice down here? That you saw her stealing artifacts?"

Maude scowled. "I didn't know they would join her. They seemed like such nice young men. Maybe they would have stayed nice young men if Janice hadn't told them how to find me."

I was still trying to keep up. But I had to keep her talking. "Why were there three each time? Did you plan it that way?"

Maude looked over her shoulder. "Don't you read stories?" Her face was soft. Her voice was softer. "Bad things always happen in threes."

My hands were weak from holding my gun. I worked to steady them. "How did you do it?" I said. "How did you kill them?"

The blankness over Maude's face dissipated. In its place, a look of concern, like a tutor when her student is reading from the wrong book. "Kill them?"

"Yes," I said. It was a struggle to keep my arms raised. "How did you kill them?"

"We didn't kill them, dear." Her eyes were so big then, so full of tragedy. I didn't understand it. "We tried to save them, just as we tried to save you."

I kept waiting for my adrenaline to kick in, the way it always did at the point of confession. But my knees were tired. My whole body was so tired.

Maude turned to her sister. "We offered sacrifices for them, just like we have sacrificed for you."

Cold swam through me. I followed Maude's gaze. That's when I saw it.

Nestled under a garland of roses. The dead goat. Its throat was slit open.

I couldn't focus my eyes. My limbs, my neck were heavy. Then it came to me. That sweet scent that, underneath the smell of roses, underneath the scents of copper and stone, I'd failed to detect.

Ethylene. The same drug that'd almost knocked me out when I'd searched for the Hunter the second time. It was coursing through my veins.

"How . . . ?" I didn't know what I was trying to ask, only that it was a matter of life and death. *My* life. *My* death.

Again, that look of tragedy. Only, this time I understood it. "We told you, dear. We've been coming down here all our lives. The Hunter's powers do not affect us anymore."

My mind was scabbed over, aching. Fog wrapped around my thoughts. Yet I knew what she meant. Maude had built up a tolerance to ethylene. It didn't incapacitate her the way it was now incapacitating me.

Maude stood. She came very near to me. She touched my

face, the same way she'd touched the face of the corpse of her sister. "We didn't want this to happen," she said. "We tried to warn you away. We tried to warn everyone. We reported every-thing to the police. They didn't do a thing. How could they? Man's justice can never hold a candle to the design of the stars."

I was on my knees. My gun wasn't in my hands. It was beside me. I tried to reach for it. I fell backward. When my head hit the rocks, I didn't feel the crash. I didn't feel anything. Maude stood over me. Tears fell from her eyes. I couldn't speak.

"The tide is coming in," Maude said. "I must go." In the glow of candlelight, I saw her then, both her selves, as clear as if there'd been two bodies standing above me instead of one: Estella, the doting mother whose love extended to everything she touched. Maude, the outcast who saw no reason to play nice. They were life and death. They were two sides of the same coin.

I pushed the words up my throat. It was a miracle any sound came out at all. "What's going to happen?"

Maude frowned. She didn't want to have to say this. She thought I already knew.

Maybe I should have. But my brain wasn't working.

Her voice was slow and sweet, like a morphine drip. "The same thing that happened to all the others. The Hunter will take you into her mouth. She will hold you between her jaws. She will spit you out."

Patches of black clouded my vision.

Wait, I tried to say. But my mouth didn't move.

Then Maude was gone.

I was alone with Estella and my own terrible consequences.

42

I TRIED TO MOVE MY BODY, BUT THE DRUG HAD ACTED TOO fast this time. I'd breathed in too much. The only thing I could do was roll my head to either side and try to make out what exactly Maude had meant.

I'd thought this part of the cave was round. Now I saw it was shaped like a cross.

Water seeped through one arm and flowed out the other. When the water came, it would sweep me away. I would ride into the second arm of the cave, where I was sure a deeper tunnel awaited, one so large, I wouldn't scrape the walls as I drowned. I didn't know how long I would stay in that deeper cave, drowning—minutes? Hours?—before the current would pitch me into the plunge pool. Just like all the others.

I pushed with every ounce of my strength, trying to stand. But it was like being caught under the weight of a mountain. Tears sprung from my eyes. I couldn't feel anything. Not the ridges of the stone. Not the air as it swept by me. Then I did feel something. Then I wished I hadn't.

Cold encased me. It plucked every hair on my skin. It washed my flesh away until my bones were stone and fossilized.

Then I was moving.

Then I was underwater.

Then the world went black.

Yet, it didn't stay black.

All at once, I was in my galley kitchen in our Union Square apartment. I was waiting for the coffee to finish brewing. The smell was everywhere.

It was Sunday. I knew this because Eric and Simone had gone out for pastries at that overpriced bakery. It was their tradition. They'd come back with chocolate babka and croissants the size of my hand. For hours after, the whole apartment would smell like butter and newsprint. As the coffee maker dripped and puttered, as I pulled out mugs from the shelves, someone knocked at our door.

I stepped down the hallway, across that braided rug from Eric's grandmother, past the little lamp on the credenza. I looked through the peephole. I opened the door.

It was the little boy from down the hall, the one with red hair and outrageous freckles. He was handing me a piece of mail.

"My mom said to give this to you. We got it by mistake."

I thanked him. I took the envelope in my hands. It had Eric's name on it.

As I shut the door, I started to toss the letter on the credenza with the rest of the mail. But as I went to place it down, I read a line. It was unintentional. Just a return address.

Memorial Sloan Kettering Cancer Center.

My heart was in my throat.

I ripped the letter open. The envelope floated to the floor. I read *Stage 4* and those words slit me open.

I couldn't move.

Then I couldn't stay still.

I grabbed the envelope from beside my bare feet. I tore up everything. I stood over the toilet as I watched it gulp and swallow it all in a sickening whirl.

I scrubbed the tile in the bathroom until my hands were raw. I scrubbed every place I'd held that letter.

When Eric and Simone burst in with a big paper bag made greasy by croissants, I was still cleaning.

Eric scanned my face. "What's gotten into you?"

I told him I'd just gotten the bug to clean.

We had dinner that night in Central Park, on our pastel blanket, the one we always used. Simone ran. Eric chased her. At last, both of them were tired.

Simone was catching popcorn in her mouth. I leaned against Eric. He wrapped his arms around me like a shield. His sun-warmed skin made mine sweaty. The sky behind us was cream and mist and terrifying. Eric kissed the top of my head like he did sometimes in his sleep. He said, "You're being awfully quiet."

I swallowed. "I'm just thinking about sex."

He squeezed me tighter. His mouth brushed my ear. "Then what are we still doing here?"

When Simone had finally fallen asleep, Eric followed me into our bedroom. He shut the door behind him. I undid his belt.

I eased him onto the bed, so gently. I slipped off his pants. I got on my knees in front of him and his eyebrows made a rainbow. His lips parted when he smiled. I felt the heat of it in my hips.

I took him in my mouth. He touched his thumbs to my cheekbones. I wrapped my hands around his thighs. I flicked my eyes up at him as his rolled back in his head. I kept going until he reached down for my mouth.

He was shucking the clothes off me. I was peeling them off him. We were naked and pressed together. We were breathing each other's breath. He picked me up and climbed on top of me. I ran my fingers over his biceps, across his back. A tear escaped from between my lids.

Eric pressed his face between my legs. I pulled him up. "No?" he said.

I hooked my ankles around him. I flipped him onto his back.

I rode him, hard. I sunk my chest into his face like I wanted him to eat my heart and take my strength. His nails raked my back. My hands held tight. He bit my ear. My body opened. Relief.

I eased off him. I wiped my tears. They were down my neck, on my hands, everywhere.

His voice was concerned. "What's all that?"

I disappeared into the bathroom. I locked the door.

Under the rush of the shower, I did what I'd always done when things got hard. I did what I'd had to do when the uncertainty was just too fucking much. I built a compartment inside my brain. I sealed off Eric's cancer, too far back to reach.

The next morning, I got myself suspended from the NYPD.

The next week, Eric moved out of the house.

43

THE MEMORY FADED INTO THE PRESENT. WATER SWELLED around me. The cold laid siege to my blood.

I opened my eyes. It burned like fire. But I could see now. Inexplicably, I could see. The things I'd done that had led me here. The truths I'd failed to grasp. Even if it was too late. Even if I would soon be dead. At least now I knew why I'd pointed my weapon at my partner. It'd been the most efficient way of sabotaging my life, of never having to confront a truth I couldn't endure.

I started to close my eyes. My arms, my hands were numb. I was glad for it, glad to at last feel nothing. I was so tired. So done with being wounded and still trying to fight. That's all I did anymore. Fight. Fight. Fight. And it never meant anything.

My arms were heavy, and my chest was cold. I'd run out of air and run out of something else I couldn't describe except to say that I was dying and I knew it. I knew it like I knew when a storm was coming, like I knew when something was wrong with my child.

I sank into the cold darkness, and I waited to die.

Before my eyes could close, I caught a flicker.

I flinched.

I squeezed shut my eyes. I opened them. It was still there.

This was a hallucination. This wasn't real the same way that, moments ago, I hadn't had my legs wrapped around my husband. Yet there it was. Right above me.

This time, I didn't see a red-bellied snake, like the one that had saved me in the caves with Mason. There, above me, was a hand.

It had wide, flat fingernails and a beauty spot along the thumb. The skin was dark brown on one side and pink on the other. Over the palm stretched lines I'd memorized like a map I'd know anywhere, like a map of home.

I was deep underwater, too far down for anyone to reach. Yet there was Eric's hand.

Even though it was impossible, even though my body was too tired, I reached out my hand to meet his. My small fingertips almost brushed his blunt ones. That *almost* burned in me like fire.

One thought pulsed down my legs, up the length of my throat.

I need to hold that hand.

All at once, Eric's hand slipped into the darkness, out of sight. But I could still feel it. I could still feel the pulse on Eric's wrist like a second heartbeat. I had to get to him.

I was nearly dead now. My movements meant nothing. Yet I

pushed with every reserve of my strength. I pushed my dead body up and through the deep, dark water even though it was impossible. Even though it didn't make sense.

I scraped and I scraped and I scraped at the shell of me until I found the last fumes of whatever life I still possessed.

I touched upon it, that rock. I kicked my feet. I made myself parallel to it. By some miracle, I could.

A guttural scream spilled out of me. A siren. A keen. I pulled myself onto the ridge.

I barked out mouthfuls of water. My mouth searched for his. I couldn't see anything. I couldn't feel anything. Eric wasn't here. He'd never been here. Still I called his name.

Water rushed around my feet, across my fingers, down my chest. I called *Eric, Eric, Eric.* My voice was hoarse from it. I did not stop.

This time I would not stop.

Minutes passed, maybe hours. The moon wheeled down close to the horizon. The sun was preparing to take its place.

"Stay right there," someone was saying. The sound was far away. Ronan. "Don't move. Whatever you do, don't move."

I couldn't see anything. My chest burned. Ice crystals crusted my lashes, my lips.

Tears spilled down my cheeks.

He wasn't there.

Eric hadn't come to save me.

44

THE FBI FIELD OFFICE WAS AS GENERIC AS ANY OTHER
government building, with utilitarian carpet and a drop-tile ceiling. The perimeter offices had windows, while the rest of the
space was lit by uncharitable fluorescent lights.

It'd been seven hours since Ronan had fished me out of the
water, and I was still dizzy and rough on my feet. But the Feds
had picked up Janice. I didn't have time to waste. I had Ronan
drive me in the cruiser while, in the passenger's seat, I curled
away from him with my hands on my stomach. I was too tired
to even try to hide how nauseated, how weak I felt.

Over the course of the morning, Ronan had filled me in on
what had happened while I'd been out. Eric had called Mack, as
he'd promised. Mack had learned there was already an open
federal investigation against Janice for her role in the illegal sale
of indigenous artifacts. In fact, the Feds been preparing their

move for months. My investigation had accelerated their time-line. In a few hours, Janice would be processed in federal lockup while she awaited her bail hearing. If I wanted to talk to her, now was my only chance.

As a receptionist led Ronan and I down the hall, Mack strode up to greet us. "Leigh, good to see you. You look like hell." Mack thanked the receptionist. Shook my hand. "I heard you had quite the ride."

My voice was scratchy and felt like shit. "Just another Thursday, sir."

Mack laughed, big and messy. He looked meatier in his suit, like the sort of man with a low tolerance for disagreement and an outrageous temper. When we'd first met, I'd immediately disliked him. He'd reminded me of wife beaters, of entitled pricks. It'd only been because of Eric I'd given him a chance. I was glad I had.

"This is my brother, Ronan," I said. "He's been helping with the case."

"I hope you know what a rock star your sister is," Mack said, shaking Ronan's hand.

Ronan nodded. His smile was wan. His skin was pale. It'd been hard on him, finding me, almost not finding me. As Mack turned to guide us away, I squeezed Ronan's hand.

We followed Mack down the long hallway and into a massive office with a heap of papers piled at the end of the desk. There were framed photographs on the shelves—all facing down—and an old-fashioned birdcage with a red-breasted parrot standing on a perch. It seemed like a security risk, having a parrot. Maybe it was just a subtle reminder that here, secrets shared were not kept.

Ronan excused himself to go to the bathroom—from the

look of him, maybe to throw up. I sat on the clunky chair in front of the desk. Mack sat in the swivel chair and grimaced. "The guy who works in this office weighs like a hundred pounds." Mack pulled the lever to adjust the height. "I said to him, where's that corn-fed brawn I've heard so much about? Guy tells me he doesn't like eating. We placed our lunch order? The fucker ordered soup."

I glanced over my shoulder. "What's with the parrot?"

"Oh that? I think it's mute." To the parrot he said, "Say, *Eat the damn cheeseburger. Eat the damn—*" He shook his head. "See?"

"You didn't have to come up here." I touched my fingers to my throat. It still hurt to talk. "I know this isn't your case."

Mack slapped his palms on the table. "I wanted to give Eric a shout. It's been years. Besides, I'm so fucking sick of Dallas. The potholes, Leigh. They're unreal. I'm not kidding you when I say *everything* is bigger in Texas."

"Eric's not staying." I swallowed. My throat felt like sandpaper dipped in acid. "He's picking up Simone and then flying her back to New York."

"Same day?"

Instead of answering, I looked out the window. It was one of those unseasonably warm autumn days, with blue skies and clouds like cotton. Eric would have had an easy flight. He'd have picked up his rental by now and be well on his way to Copper Falls. According to the email he'd sent me, he'd collect Simone from the house, shower and change at the B and B. Then he'd catch his return flight. He'd be headed out just as soon as he'd come.

Mack leaned back in his chair. It gave him the look of a college dean, of a football coach, of the type of man who, in certain circles, has undeserved power. He said, "You know, some people never understood the two of you."

"Sir?"

"You're so different. You're like oil and water some days, and others, like fire and gasoline. It never made sense to people."

I felt flushed, woozy. "I don't think that's—"

Mack's chair sprang forward as he leaned in to me. His woodsy cologne burned my throat. "Look, I don't know how to say this, so I'm just gonna say it."

I drew in breath.

"He needs you, Leigh."

Still, I did not breathe.

"Something's going on with him. Now, he won't talk about it. You know how he is. He'll go to the grave still acting like there's not a weak muscle on his body. I blame his father for all that machismo bullshit. My own father did a number on me." He looked down at his hands.

Unexpectedly, Mack's eyes flicked up, and they were blazing. It always surprised me, the speed at which men could force sadness into the shape of something angry. It made me jealous, uncomfortable.

"But, Leigh." Mack's voice was devastating. "You are still his wife. You hear me? You're his wife."

Mack held my gaze.

"Don't fuck this up."

The air between us stretched tight. I couldn't look away from Mack, but I also couldn't tell him the truth: that even if Eric did find a way to forgive me, he still might die. That even if I pulled off the impossible and got him back, it would still mean risking everything. I opened my mouth to try to explain this, but just then, Ronan slipped through the open door.

He was wiping his hands on his Class B like they were wet paintbrushes. His face had regained a little of its color. "Sorry," he said, still standing. He looked unsure whether he was supposed to sit. "There was some reusable towel situation and it was . . . complicated."

I dug deep to give steel to my voice. To Mack I said, "When are you filing the complaint against Janice?"

Mack sighed. He made a show of looking at his watch. It was this big, expensive thing that wanted you to know it was big and expensive. "We're meeting with the judge in two hours."

After Mack filed the complaint, Janice would be arrested. She'd go through processing. She'd lawyer up. She wouldn't talk to me. I stood. I held the chair to steady myself. "Then I guess I should get to it."

"Don't fuck this up," Mack said.

"She won't," Ronan said. "She's aces at interrogations. You said it yourself. A rock star."

Mack shook his head. He held my eyes. Lower, he said, "Don't fuck this up."

Two metal chairs sat around a matching table, which was bolted to the floor. One chair was empty and on the other, Janice sat with her arms crossed over her chest. She saw me at the door and stood. "Thank god you're here," she said. She went to hug me, but I stepped back.

There were cameras on the walls on every side of us. She shifted her gaze across each of them. At last she took a seat. She folded her hands on her lap. She spoke through gritted teeth. "So this is an interrogation?"

I sat in the chair opposite her. I Mirandized her. At each syllable, a new muscle in her face wove tight. I ended with the usual "With these rights in mind, do you wish to speak to me?"

Her voice was level. "With those rights in mind, why would I wish to speak to you?"

I resisted the urge to rub my throat. I wanted a glass of water. But I never brought anything into interrogation rooms. Men could get away with shuffling through notes, with water dribbling down their chins. Their suspects didn't grab their case files, rip up their notes, get sweaty fingers over everything. "Because in a little less than two hours," I said, "a magistrate judge is going to approve a complaint to have you arrested on federal charges. Once that happens you will officially be in federal lockup and I can't help you."

That morning, I'd made some calls. It wasn't hard to get people to talk about Janice's medical case. It wasn't hard to find out what she was planning to do. Across from me, under the buzz of fluorescent lights, Janice's body clenched.

I said, "You're supposed to start chemo in a couple of weeks, right? After, they'll take the stem cells you've been harvesting and put them back in your body to help you grow a new immune system. It might cure you. But while you're in federal lockup awaiting trial, all of that's put on ice. That's time you don't have."

Janice crossed her arms. She was silent for a long moment. At last she said, "I'm not an idiot." But her voice faltered.

"No," I said, "you're not." I rested my hands on the tops of my thighs. I came at her square. "That's why you'd have found a way to get what you needed without breaking the law." This was a lie, obviously, but also a challenge. "So take me through it. Show me you were in the right."

There was a mesh wastebasket bolted to the wall. Janice stared at it. At last, she crossed her legs, facing me obliquely. Her voice had lost some of its defensiveness. It tried at earnestness now. She said, "I'd been working to organize all the files in the records room for something like six months, when I found the bills of sale.

"They were hidden in a box that said it was tax documents from the 1970s. They contained everything about how the town had made its money. Where the artifacts had been found. How old they were. How much they sold for. Who they'd sold to."

"That had made it easy to tell Mitchell and Frederickson how to find more," I said. Frederickson and Mitchell were the officers I'd called Biceps and Meatball. They'd been the muscle behind Janice's operation. She'd been the brains.

Janice anticipated my route. She said, "I had no idea what they'd do with the information."

"Nor what they'd do with the certificates of authenticity you drafted for them?"

Her face was guileless, contrived. "I assumed they were going to turn them over to federal agents. As anyone would."

It was with some effort I didn't glance at the cameras to emphasize her lie. Surely the observation room was going batshit. Instead, I nodded. "Yet after you told Mitchell and Frederickson where to find the artifacts, they gave you large amounts of money." According to the FBI records, the men had made a series of anonymous donations to Janice's GoFundMe page shortly after each sale.

Janice made a show of putting two and two together. "Wow, really?" She planted both feet on the floor. She sat up tall in her chair. "I had no idea they'd given me any money, not until you told me just now. So many donations to my page were anonymous. I couldn't have known."

I doubted a jury would believe Janice's story, especially when there was so clearly a paper trail between the money from the illegal sales of the artifacts and the money Janice received for her treatments. But maybe that didn't matter.

If I didn't nail her for Murder One, it was possible she'd never go in front of a jury at all. If she was smart, she'd try to turn state's evidence. Mitchell and Frederickson would take the fall for the illegal sales, and she'd become an informant. That is, unless I could charge her.

I looked at her sympathetically. "It sounds like you did nothing wrong."

The skin around Janice's eyes relaxed. The tension in her body eased.

I said, "You just shared information that was available to anybody, had they known where to look."

She nodded. She was trying not to smile.

I said, "Since I have you, though, I wonder if you could help me with a puzzle." I crossed my legs like hers had been. I folded my hands over my knee. Her shoulders stayed square to the table. "Yesterday, I had a long talk with Maude Hummel."

Janice didn't blink.

"It turns out, Maude was the last person to see William, Duncan, and Neil alive. She was the last person to see those high school boys alive, too. The ones from seven years ago. What do you make of that?"

Somewhere in the distance, the heater kicked on. The hum of it filled the silence.

I let my arm rest on the cold, metal tabletop. I lowered my voice. "You're in a unique position. You've read every file in that records room. You told me yourself, you deal in secrets. You probably have an idea what happened. You could really help us."

Janice's chair groaned as she leaned back. She kicked out her legs, crossing them in front of her. She picked an invisible speck off her flannel. "If you want to know the truth," she said finally, "I'm not surprised."

I released the smallest of exhales. She'd taken the bait. It was a simple solution, to let another person take the fall. It was such an easy role for her to inhabit, that of the one who knows everything.

Janice said, "After those three high school boys died, Maude actually came to the police station. Supposedly, she was headed down into the cave by Estella's house. When the boys followed her down there, they drowned. It was all very mysterious. Maude couldn't tell us why they drowned and she didn't."

"But they were three able-bodied men," I said. "She's just an old woman."

"I'm no detective," Janice said, "but she probably drugged them."

I adjusted my posture so Janice and I were like that night at the bar, that night when Janice was just an old classmate with information I needed. I said, "We actually found evidence the three high school boys died in the exact same place that William, Neil, and Duncan died."

"No kidding?"

"That surprises you?"

"Like everyone, I thought they'd died on the falls."

"Because they were found in the plunge pool? Like the three high school boys were? But you just said you knew they died in the caves. So why didn't you think the new set of deaths had happened there as well?"

There was the smallest twitch across Janice's forehead. I felt it in my gut. Janice was incapable of playing dumb when it meant being thought of as stupid. She should have said the thought hadn't occurred to her. Instead, she said, "I mean, I thought they *could* have died at the falls. *Or* they could have died in the caves. Both were possibilities."

"Right. And if you believed Maude had drugged the other guys before, you must have thought it was possible she'd drugged Duncan, William, and Neil?"

"Anything is possible."

"So, yes?"

The heater hummed, but Janice didn't speak. She had to know, as I did, that the wind in our conversation had shifted. Now was the time to take my shot.

"Maude saw you," I said.

Behind Janice's eyes, the faintest flash of panic, like she'd stepped on cracked ice.

"In the caves. Scouting for artifacts to sell. When the artifacts went missing, Maude connected you to the whole thing. She told Duncan, Neil, and William that you were stealing from the town just as generations had before you. Maude didn't think there was anything they could do about it. But actually, there was something they could do."

Janice was standing now. She was rubbing her hip as if the problem was that she just needed to stretch, but her fingers shook.

"Even if they couldn't nab the CFPD for the civil asset forfeitures," I said, "even if they couldn't do anything about how Copper Falls had gotten rich to begin with, they could talk to the press about what you were doing, about what Copper Falls had always done. It might put pressure on the CFPD to release their money. It might put pressure on Copper Falls to be better than its past."

The wall behind Janice blurred, so I could only see her, could only focus on this one thing. Janice rubbed harder. She was in pain. I was buzzing.

I said, "You found out that the three men were going to talk to the local ABC station, to tell them what you had been doing. Maybe they even told you as a courtesy, thinking you'd pressure Chief Becker to return their money. But you didn't do that. Instead, you used what you knew about how the high schoolers had died to ensure the same thing happened to William Houser, Duncan Schott, and Neil Mayer."

Janice was hunched as she rubbed her hip, too hard. She

wasn't looking at me but at the floor. That's when I caught it. The whiff in the air that would not keep her secret.

I smelled Janice's sweat.

I felt taller, powerful. My throat ached. I didn't care. "You told William, Duncan, and Neil that there was another way for them to get their money back. The town would never return the money they'd confiscated. The only way they'd get the money they needed was if they stole artifacts, just like you'd been doing for years. They trusted you."

Just like I'd trusted her, even though I'd had every reason not to.

"But instead of telling them to enter the caves through the entrance you, Mitchell, and Frederickson had been using, you told them to go in near Estella's house, where you knew they'd die."

Conviction rang through me like a bell. Janice had killed those men. Even if she hadn't held them underwater as they drowned, she might as well have. She'd sent them into the caves with the sole intention that they not come out alive. She did it to cover up her multiple felonies. It was a clear case of Murder One.

"I don't know what you're talking about," Janice said. Her face was cast in stone. Yet the smell of her sweat was everywhere.

"Maude Hummel says differently."

"Do you really think she's a credible witness?"

"She doesn't need to be credible. Not if Mitchell and Frederickson corroborate her story."

Janice stepped toward me. Her movements were jerky, desperate. "They won't corroborate shit. They don't know shit."

"Really? They told the FBI otherwise. They said you coerced them into doing it. You used them to get what you wanted. We've seized your work computer, Janice. It's only a matter of time before we find the fake insurance policies you sent to Becker to ensure he'd never investigate the men's deaths."

"Everyone has access to that computer," Janice spat. "It's not even password protected. Those can't be assumed to have come from me."

I had Janice right where I wanted her. Her words were coming quickly. She'd all but admitted to having fake insurance policies on her computer. She was making mistakes. Soon she'd make the mistake that showed she'd sent those men to their deaths and then tried to make everyone think they were suicides.

Now was the time to hammer her with questions, to insult her. This was where I excelled. At being instinctual. Emotional. Relentless.

Yet, as I raised my eyes to meet hers, a movement behind her caused me to break focus. My eyes found the broad-faced clock just as the minute hand pushed the hour hand another notch. My stomach dipped and I knew: Eric had just arrived in Copper Falls.

I watched Eric pull up to the house in his rented car. I watched him gather Simone. I watched them leave for the airport and step onto their plane. Without me.

I looked back at Janice. She was red faced now, fuming. I tried to muster it: that conviction that being here and eliciting a confession was the most important thing I could do, that putting

Janice away was the key to getting my life back. But my instincts were failing me.

Pain shot across my forehead. I closed my eyes.

That's when I saw it.

Eric's hand.

That's when I saw me, reaching to grasp those fingers. Surviving.

I didn't think. I didn't consider. I just stood.

Janice's eyebrows knit together. She looked confused, unsettled.

I banged my fist against the steel door. Not two hard knocks to signal I wanted out. But over and over again, like a drum of war, like a plea for help, like I was dying.

The door opened. Concern deepened Mack's features. "What's wrong? Are you okay?"

My voice was low, aching. "I can't fuck this up."

He searched my eyes. He nodded, slowly at first, then quickly.

I felt sick, overwhelmed, not at all ready for what was about to go down. I said, "I have to go."

45

I DIDN'T EVEN WAIT FOR RONAN TO DRIVE ME. INSTEAD, I jogged to the cruiser. I ran lights and sirens all the way back to Copper Falls.

The rush of pavement beneath the wheels made bile rise up my throat. I shouldn't have been driving that fast. But I didn't have time to go slowly. I only had a short window to get Eric to stay. Already, I might have missed him.

I pulled up to the B and B. The innkeeper came out of the big Victorian house. She looked unsettled. I'd left the lights running. I turned them off. "Eric Walker," I said. My words slurred.

She pointed me to the second floor.

My head ached. My limbs seized. I was moving too fast. I climbed the spiral staircase to the second floor. I lost my footing. I kept going.

At last, I found the door without a tasseled key ring hanging from its knob: the only room occupied. I stumbled to it. I went to knock on it. But as soon as I lifted my hand to the door, it swung open.

There he was. My husband. All at once, my lungs were filled with him. His musk and wool, and that chemical scent he'd had when I'd last seen him. Only, now I knew what it was. Only, now I hated myself for pretending I didn't.

Eric's body was smaller than I remembered it. His skin was ashy. His eyes were tired. Yet the sight of him hummed my veins as if they were strings he could thrum.

Relief shone in Eric's eyes. For just a second. Then it was gone. A star, falling.

I gripped the doorframe to keep from swaying. Anger tightened Eric's features. Behind him, Simone was on the bed, asleep.

"Aren't you supposed to be at an interrogation?"

"Mack's handling it. Or maybe Ronan. I don't know."

Eric's voice was hard. "Wait, who drove you?"

I started to answer. He cut me off.

"Jesus, Leigh, you could have gotten yourself killed. You could have gotten someone else killed. You're so reckless. If you came all this way because you think I'll just—"

"I made a god out of you."

Whatever Eric had planned to say, it died in his mouth.

My voice sounded terrible. I pushed through the pain. "That's what it was for me, falling in love with you. I made you superhuman. You would always protect me. You would never die."

Eric went to close the door. I fell in front of it. I had one foot in the hallway, the other in his room. We locked eyes.

I said, "You needed me. I knew it. I let go of your hand."

"Leigh, you have to leave. I can't—"

"I know about the cancer."

At this, Eric's face froze. His cherrywood eyes locked us together. I felt the pulse of his heart under his shirt like it was in my body. It'd always been in my body. Just like my heart had always been in his.

Simone had asked if all the equipment in his apartment was for his therapy. She'd meant chemotherapy, even if she didn't know that's what it was.

The woman in his apartment had called him *honey*. She was the nurse administering his treatment.

His thin body. His ashy skin. The letter I'd ripped into a thousand tiny pieces. I'd locked it in a compartment inside my head. Yet it hadn't changed the truth.

I said, "I know it's bad."

Eric glanced behind him. Simone was still asleep. He paused. He swallowed. Minutes passed. We stood frozen in time. At last, Eric stepped into the hallway. He pressed the door closed behind him. It didn't make a sound.

There was a bay window and a bench in front of it. We sat on the floral, ruffled pillows, with the sunset colors of Copper Falls blurring behind us. Eric was leaning forward, his chin on his fingertips.

"Who told you?" His voice was rough, like he hated me.

"I saw an envelope."

"When?" he asked.

"The day before you suspended me."

I could see him putting together the pieces. The frantic cleaning. The day at the park when I'd barely spoken. The sex. The tears. I saw the flash behind his eyes the moment Eric realized I'd fucked over our lives because I couldn't bear to live with the reality, with *his* reality, from which he couldn't escape.

His face cycled through emotions as he understood the extent of my betrayal, that I would rather believe he had a lover than that a nurse was coming to administer his chemo. That I would destroy our life together just so I didn't have to deal with his death.

I'd told myself a story about our lives that wasn't true so I could live with myself. So I could start the process of living without him.

"Sometimes." He didn't look at me but at the ground. "I feel like we live on different planets. You get to have your reckless-ness and your impulsivity. And I'm on the planet where I do everything right, and still, I am dying."

Eric shook his head. I breathed in the familiar musk and wool scent of him. I was present.

"When you pulled your gun on Detective Lewis, I hated you. I felt, here's another thing you're going to get away with. Here's another mess that I, as your captain, have to set right. Mean-while, I am still on the planet where I am dying."

Eric swallowed, but nothing moved down his throat.

"You could afford to sink deeper and deeper into your de-spair. You could afford to have your existential dilemma about who you are without your badge and sidearm, about whether you're emotionally unstable or had a moment of weakness, about what you're meant for. All the while, I am on the planet where I am dying."

"Eric, I'm sorry."

He glared at me. His face contorted like he meant to spit. "You always say that, and it never means a thing to me."

I slid off the bench. I knelt in front of my husband. I was woozy. I was scared. I pried open his hands. His skin was hot. I said, "Eric, I'm sorry."

"What do I need your *sorry* for?" He tried to slide out of my grip. I wouldn't let him. "Is your *sorry* going to take away this cancer?"

I held on to his hands.

"Is your *sorry* going to deal with all the racist assholes I have to manage day in and day out, whom you conveniently get to avoid in your homicide bubble? Dead bodies, that's all you mess with. Well, the rest of us have to deal with all the gray and it is taxing. Let me tell you."

I held on to his hands.

His eyes were red. "You're reckless, Leigh. You're thoughtless. You always think you get a second chance. I'm not going to give it to you."

I held on to his hands.

A line broke out across his face, right between his eyebrows. His voice was hard but cracking. Like a stone that cannot bend and so must become two pieces of itself, forever divided. He said, "You keep saying you want your job back. I can't give it to you. You pull your weapon on a civilian? *Maybe* I can do something for you. But pull it on a cop? No way. You know that. You know you can never work as a New York City police detective again."

I held on to his hands.

He said, "Do you understand me? If you want to be a cop, you can stay in this place and you can be a cop. But you're never going to get a shield in New York. You can never be my wife and be police. You've made that impossible."

"I know." I held on to his hands. He blinked and blinked and blinked. The sheen didn't leave his eyes. I held him harder.

"Do you think I want Simone to grow up without a father?"

I raised up to my knees. My head was in line with Eric's head now. I pressed our foreheads together.

His voice was a whisper. "Do you think that doesn't gut me? To think I could be gone from her life and never get to see her grow up?"

I kissed him softly.

"God dammit, Leigh. Will you just—"

I kissed him harder. I closed my eyes and moved my mouth against his mouth, his taste mixing with my taste to create a signature he had to remember.

I kissed him, and I prayed he would feel what I would never be able to say and have him believe. I prayed he would restore his trust in me not because I would never break it, but because I would never leave him. I prayed he would let me love him as divine and as mortal, and that in doing so we could find a way to mend each other's cracks.

We were better together than we were apart. I prayed he would remember this.

I pressed so much feeling into that kiss. Yet Eric's mouth stayed hard. It did not yield.

That's when I knew it. I knew, deep in my bones, this would

be it. There would be no tearful reconciliation. He would not give me a second chance. Eric had done what he always said he would. He'd made up his mind. There was no going back.

A tear slid down my cheek.

I hated myself. I hated that I was crying now when he was dying.

Then a second tear hit. It landed on my forehead.

I opened my eyes. I lifted off him. That's when I realized, the tears weren't mine. Eric's eyes were red at their rims. His cheeks were streaked. His mouth had fallen open. He was crying.

I pressed my lips against his lips for the third time. Maude had said bad things happen in threes, but maybe miracles came in threes, too. I held him with my mouth. I prayed for a miracle.

Eric's mouth moved.

Just a twitch.

Then it was more than a twitch.

Then it was a key finding its slot.

Then it was an engine turning over.

Eric's mouth pressed against my mouth. The rush was like a crash. He drew his hands to the sides of my face. His long fingers brushed my eyelashes. He kissed me, long and deep and filling. I kissed him and blood rushed to my chest, my face, to everywhere he touched me.

We were on the floor then, both of us on our knees.

I felt the pain I'd caused and the pain I hadn't caused. I felt the ache in him meet the ache in me. I felt old and also electric.

I sank into my husband, to the parts that might be dying and the parts that never would.

I did not fight.

Acknowledgments

As a literary agent, it is my job to make sure that any contributions I make to a work stay invisible, so that the author's voice shines. Such is the life of many publishing professionals. For every book that's published, there are dozens of people working behind the scenes, making corrections and suggestions and asking questions that transform a work. It is with great pleasure that I reveal some of mine.

Katie Zaborsky: You were the first person to lay eyes on *The Hunter* and the one whose keen editorial vision helped me focus in on what was new and interesting in the work and pull back on what had already been done. This all started with you.

Taina Coleman: Your support and friendship these past however many years have changed me as a writer and as a person. Your brilliance in our every conversation about this book, and about art and life in general, has been transformational. Yours is one of the defining friendships of my life.

Acknowledgments

The Inklings—Melissa Gorzelancyk, Colleen Riordan, and Genevieve Artel—where would this story have been without you? We show up for each other every week. We analyze and critique each other's work. We put in the hours. We rest when we need to. We made this happen.

Heather Jackson: From that first time we talked on the phone all those years ago, to our meet-cute moment when you offered to represent *The Hunter* even though I told you we couldn't work together because of our relationship, you've been not only a friend but also a fairy godmother. You take your magic with you everywhere you go.

Danielle Dieterich: I am in awe of you. From your ingenious editorial insights to your behind-the-scenes hustle, to your availability whenever I want to hop on the phone and talk something through, you are the real deal. I feel like I won the editor lottery, and I'm so grateful you fell in love with this book, and with Leigh.

Sally Kim and Ivan Held: Thank you for believing in this book and for trusting that it would fit in with the rest of Putnam's extraordinary list. Alexis Welby and Ashley McClay, thank you for all of your efforts to help *The Hunter* find its audience. Tom Dussel, thank you for selling this book across the world. I love that we both share a connection to northwest Ohio. Madeline Hopkins and Brittany Bergman, thank you for helping me remember where Leigh parked her car and for questioning how much red meat a Midwesterner really can consume. (The answer: quite a lot.) Rob Sternitzky and Nicole Celli, thank you for keeping every character on every page from shaking their head and for reminding me how math works.

Thank you to the outstanding design team: Nancy Resnick, who created the perfect interior layout, and Anthony Ramondo and Tal Goretsky for a cover I could never have envisioned and yet is absolutely perfect for this book.

Thank you to my parents, Julie and Mike, and to my brother and sister, Mike and Shannon, for always believing that I could do anything. You have no idea what a difference your confidence has made in my life.

Connie, Lisa, Walt, Adriana, Gregory, Phoenix, and Devin, thank you for your constant love and encouragement. David, Susan, Gary, Sarah, Rica, Joy, Rachel, and Anagha, thank you for always reminding me why stories matter. Lindsay Jackman and Emma Kaster, thank you for assisting behind the scenes. Lara Jones, Molly Malone, Laurel Rakas, Brita Lundberg, Tiff Liao, Mary Cait North, Mary Dauphinee, and Abbye Caplan, thank you for being my hype crew and my dear, dear friends.

Finally, thank you to my husband, David, and to our kiddo. You make everything possible.